I0708947

THE HAMBLEDOWN DREAM

a novel

DEAN MAYES

ireadiwrite
publishing

2010

ireadiwrite Publishing Edition

This ireadiwrite Publishing edition is published by arrangement with Dean Mayes, contact at banistersmind@internode.on.net

ireadiwrite Publishing - www.ireadiwrite.com
First edition published by ireadiwrite Publishing

The Hambledown Dream
ISBN 978-1-926760-33-9

Published in Canada with international distribution.

Cover Design: Michelle Halket
Cover Photograph: Melissa Alexander

Acknowledgements

My thanks goes to my editor Judith Kavanagh whose skill and amazing eye made the manuscript something really special. Judith taught me that people do not always stare away into space. To Allison Margharitis for finding those little things that helped make the book that much better. To Jarrett Williams who helped me out with describing music in the written word and for honing the description of the wonderful sound of the guitar. I would also like to thank my friend Linda Peers who freely admitted to bawling her eyes out when she read my very first draft. It was the nicest compliment I could have hoped for. To Mel Alexander, my 'sis' who captured the cover image so beautifully and gave life to a motif I had visualized for so long. Finally I would like to thank Emily, Xavier and Lucy for giving me the drive and the single mindedness to push on -
to always push on.

*The Hambledown Dream is dedicated to the memory of
journalist Matt Price,
a man who was my hero (1961 - 2007).*

DM

"Walking on a dream,
How can I explain?,
Talking to myself,
Will I see again?"

N. Littlemore, J. Sloan, L. Steele

THE HAMBLEDOWN DREAM

Chapter 1

How could it have come to this?

He had the world at his feet. He had a life that was the envy of all those around him. He was handsome and athletic, he was warm and funny. He had a loving and proud family. He had many friends. He was young and seemingly indestructible. With his university degree, he had a bright future to look forward to and could put his name to just about any architectural firm he wanted. It was said that he had wanted to draw buildings since he was six years old.

For this was his great love.

Denny Banister loved complex problems, raw ideas that could be assessed and developed and turned into a real thing: a building, a tower, a house, a home.

He was in love with a beautiful woman - a woman who was his kindred spirit. He secretly held a desire to ask Sonya Llewellyn to marry him once they had graduated. Well, it wasn't so much a secret between Denny and Sonya than something they wanted to wait for, once their respective degrees were out of the way and they could celebrate with their families. They had fallen in love through the guitar. He played for her, the most beautiful pieces - classical pieces, lyrical pieces, soulful pieces.

For the guitar was Denny's passion.

He played for her songs of love, of traveling, of life, of living. Denny had exquisite fingers, which were able to dance across the guitar as though they were floating on air. But more than that, he was able to evoke the most vivid musical imagery. He poured himself into a piece of music. Sonya had once joked that Denny had cast a spell on her, for his music was the most enchanting she had ever heard. It had hypnotized her.

Their conversation was intimate. It was synchronous. They had similar values, beliefs and viewpoints, yet each of these differed just enough so that they challenged one another. Sonya was studying law, so Denny knew very early in their relationship that in order to be a good lawyer, Sonya had better be able to deliver a damned good argument. Denny and Sonya's debates were the stuff of legend amongst their friends, that it was these that fired their imagination and gave a strength to their relationship. They were constantly challenging each other because they believed in each other.

For Sonya was Denny's life.

Together they dreamed of traveling. Of visiting obscure galleries in Europe. Of making love in a villa on the shores of Lake Como in Italy. Of skinny-dipping in the Mediterranean Sea near Valetta in Malta. Of growing old together in the house that had once been Sonya's grandfather's on a hillside overlooking a quiet stretch of tranquil Australian coastline.

Now it was all about to be lost.

Denny lay in the bed, a shadow of what he had once been. The life - that vibrancy that had so drawn others in - was fast disappearing from his sunken eyes. His face, once strong and proud, was skeletal; his skin was bruised and pasty. His beautiful light brown hair was almost gone; a few faded tufts were all that remained. Those fingers, which had once danced across the guitar with such beauty and grace, which had translated onto the page complex algorithms and intricate equations, which had held the fingers of Sonya's own hands. They were limp now, cold and barely useful. A warm feminine hand was entwined in them. He felt them, but he no longer had the strength to lift his own fingers.

It had taken mere months. It began as a few days of feeling unwell, with swollen glands in his neck. Denny had passed it off as the flu. Even though he had gotten better, the lump in his neck had refused to go away. Still he ignored it for a time, until it began to bother him. In what seemed like a matter of moments, it had become all too serious.

Lymphoma.

Under normal circumstances it was treatable, and the outlook for a cure was good. This, however, was a particularly aggressive cancer that had already metastasized before Denny even knew he had it. Lymph nodes, liver, one kidney, four ribs on the left side and most cruelly of all, his brain. He was doomed from the start. Treatment was a stalling intervention only, and not a very good one. All it really did was halt the spread of his dementia and rob him of his hair.

Denny was 25.

The room was nice. As far as hospice rooms went. There was a pretty rose garden through the single window. Denny had looked through there sometimes, but hadn't been able to venture out to appreciate them. Today, the sky was dark and brooding. A thunderstorm threatened.

A Simon Marty guitar stood on its stand in a corner of the room where Denny could see it. The handmade instrument had been a gift from his parents on his eighteenth birthday. For a while, just having it there was soothing. In his fractured mind, he could hear his favorite sonatas and fantasias and movements, and it helped him to block out the pain. Now the only thing that helped was the morphine that slowly dripped into his body from a pump via a needle in his arm. At the end of the bed lay his puppy Simon, a black-and-white crossbreed, curled up and fast asleep. Denny's nurse had allowed Simon to be here.

Sonya sat beside him; her head lay on the bed near his arm. He could smell her lustrous auburn hair, freshly washed. The scent was a combination of rosemary and mint - a shampoo she loved. He could hear her soft breathing, even and steady. He could feel the warmth of her skin, the touch of her fingers. Sonya had been there for days, or what had seemed like days. Denny was no longer sure of time anymore. All he was sure of was that she was still there. Occasionally she would stir, lift her head and gaze at him through those wondrous eyes. Though their world was falling apart around them, her face kept him anchored. She kept everyone anchored. Throughout their ordeal Sonya had never fallen apart. She tended to Denny's needs unfailingly. When others were losing control of their emotions, she was there for them too, with an arm around a shoulder, a hand in a hand, or a loving, comforting hug.

Now, in these final hours, they were all here. Denny's mother, father and younger sister, Sonya's mother and older brother. All sitting quietly, waiting.

Denny flinched reflexively, causing everyone else in the room to do the same. He grimaced and attempted to move himself, but was prevented from doing so. His abdomen was so distended from fluid collecting inside, it made simple movements impossible. The catheter that drained urine from his bladder caused him intense pain, and it had done so now.

Sonya squeezed his hand and slid hers up his right forearm, her gentle touch soothing him. Her fingers passed over a faded tattoo on the inside of his forearm - an inscription in a cursive font - *Ancora Imparo*.

How could it have come to this?

The single lucid thought punctured through his narcotic haze. The pain in his penis settled and he blinked, looking up at his family who were all gathered around his bed.

His mother and father, eyes reddened and tear-filled. His sister, normally vivacious, a perennial social butterfly, was stony-faced now, barely able to hold it together. Denny knew this must be ripping her apart. Sonya's mother, her brother - his best mate, similarly wooden with barely contained grief.

Sonya...

Denny turned his head slightly towards her. Sonya met his eyes with hers and held them. She stroked his brow gently and smiled warmly. Oh, how he wished to kiss those lips...

His breath caught in his throat suddenly, and his eyes rolled up towards the ceiling. The room began to spin, and Denny's heart thumped noisily in his ears. He was overwhelmed by a surge of panic and with a great effort he grasped Sonya's hand as firmly as he could. When he looked back, Sonya's face had swollen with tears and a single drop trickled down her porcelain cheek. In that moment Denny knew.

It was time.

In that last terrible moment, when all else was spinning out of control, as lightning crackled ominously outside the window, Denny gazed firmly and deeply into his beloved's eyes. When he spoke, his voice had never sounded stronger.

"This is not over..."

And with an abrupt finality the eyes fluttered closed, the body sank back, the life dissipated. Denny was dead. Simon the puppy let out a yelp, leapt from the bed and disappeared down the hall.

Sonya sat there stunned, the grip of his hand relaxed in hers. The warmth disappeared quickly. As the family gathered around her and held her collectively, Sonya's expression remained frozen. Tears welled in her eyes and they fell down over her cheek, but she did not cry. She could not bring herself to let go.

Everything seemed to stop. Time, space, air, life. And nothing would ever be the same again.

Chapter 2

How could it have come to this?

The gurney rolled like a freight train down a dimly lit corridor, shepherded along by a medical emergency team dressed in green scrubs.

A doctor with a salt-and-pepper beard and gold-rimmed glasses rode on top of the gurney, straddling a limp figure beneath him. He was shouting desperately at his colleagues as he pumped the chest of the young man who lay lifeless on the gurney. The young man's skin was a pasty white. His eyes were ringed by dark circles, mascara stains had bled and ran along the tops of his cheeks. His black clothing was dirty and damp. Everyone was damp. One mother of a storm was brewing outside, and the team had barely made it indoors before being thoroughly soaked. Stringy, greasy vomit-stained hair covered the young man's face and chest. There were blood spatters everywhere, but no one had determined yet, where the blood was coming from. Nor had anyone had a chance to work out who he was. At this point, all they knew was that he was about 25 years old, that he had been found unconscious at some sort of rave party in the north of the city and that drugs were involved.

Yet another dead shit drug addict.

An oxygen mask concealed his mouth and nose as a nurse, Selwyn, pumped a balloon attached to it, forcing air into his lungs.

Across from her, a second doctor, Kost struggled to secure a newly inserted intravenous cannula in the man's ragged arm to replace one that had failed in transit. A transparent bag of fluid hung from a pole, and as Kost checked a small chamber below it he saw, to his great relief, a steady drip, drip, drip inside it. The infusion was working.

The medical team fairly burst through a set of double doors and into a fully equipped trauma room. Lightning flashed through a window somewhere nearby. Already, additional staff were ready and waiting with emergency equipment set to go. The doctor astride the patient saw a young woman - a nurse named Ruddiger - approach with two familiar-looking paddles. He leapt from the gurney, nearly losing his glasses, as myriad hands went to work, applying lines to the young man's chest and abdomen. Another intravenous cannula was quickly stabbed into his opposite arm.

Satisfied the line was secure, a second flask of intravenous fluid was hastily commenced, the flow rate thrown wide open. Large pads were slapped down onto the man's chest, and for a moment all eyes in the room turned towards a monitor above the victim's head. An erratic green line squiggled its way across the screen accompanied by several other, different-colored lines that were equally chaotic.

Lifting his glasses so that they were perched just above his brow, the doctor grabbed the defibrillator paddles from Ruddiger beside him and shoved his dog tags - which identified him as Ellis - down the inside of his scrubs. Nodding to Selwyn, who was still manning the oxygen mask, then to Ruddiger beside him, Ellis adjusted his grip on the paddles and approached the victim on the gurney. Another crackle of lightning flashed nearby, seemingly closer this time.

Ruddiger turned a dial on the defibrillator and listened to a high-pitched whine emanating from within. Her eyes met Ellis' and she nodded. Everyone stepped back from the gurney on Ellis' command, and he positioned the paddles on the chest of the young victim before him. As he did so, a shrill alarm sounded from the monitor.

Flatline!

Though he had done this hundreds of times before, Ellis felt the same nausea ripple through him every time he shocked a patient. Forcing the sensation away, he thumbed the triggers on the pads, sending an electrical current streaming into the patient. The young man bucked sickeningly on the gurney, his muscles spasming and holding their tetany for a moment before he slumped back on the hard surface again. Everyone in the room looked back to the monitor.

Moments ticked by...

The green line remained stubbornly flat.

As if reading Ellis's thoughts, Ruddiger immediately dialed up a higher charge and nodded to him. Ellis pushed down on the paddles and pressed the triggers again. The victim bucked wildly on the gurney, this time lifting a full three or four inches into the air.

Electricity crackled through his darkened mind, briefly filling his consciousness with a blinding white light. The light dissipated and, for a moment, there was nothing. He was gripped by sudden panic. He tried desperately to move his arms and legs, but couldn't. Wherever he was now, he was totally and utterly trapped.

How could it have come to this?

Beams of light stabbed through the darkness, somewhere nearby, yet not close enough for him to grab their attention. Steady beams of a torchlight. Were they searching for him? He tried to scream, but he couldn't fill his lungs. No air! Panic again!

But it didn't last. The panic melted away and was replaced by an enveloping peace. The beams of light continued to work their way closer to him. He was floating now.

The green line on the monitor failed to budge. Ellis spat an expletive so loud his saliva stippled the patient. Ruddiger dialed up the defibrillator once more. It was all or nothing now. Ellis slapped the paddles down and discharged them immediately. Kost, beside him, shuddered.

Blinding white light again. Where was it coming from? He became aware of a taste in his mouth now. What was it? No, it wasn't a taste at all. It was a smell. He let it fill his nostrils.

A herb of some sort, perhaps? Yes, that's what it was. Something he couldn't quite put his finger on. His grandmother used it in her cooking. Goddamn, what was that!? An oven door opens. Roasted meat - lamb. She had sprinkled some herbs on it.

Why would I remember that?

The oppressive blackness parted slowly, replaced by shades of gray. There was movement and shadow, texture and something else. What was it? The texture was incredibly soft. Skin, perhaps? Soft skin. A cheekbone. The cheek of a woman. A familiar woman? He couldn't be sure. A tear trickled down, over the cheek and down.

"This is not over," a whispered voice echoed in the gloom.

Ellis and Selwyn barely leapt back in time as the patient suddenly vomited a thick stream of detritus and began thrashing wildly on the gurney.

"We got him!"

Selwyn tossed the mask assembly aside and grabbed a suction catheter as the victim was quickly rolled onto his side to prevent him from choking.

Ellis leaned in close, stifling his sense of smell against the odor of vomit, alcohol and blood coming from the kid.

"We've got you! We've got you! You're all right! You're safe!"

The young man coughed and spluttered and retched over and over while Selwyn suctioned the offensive detritus from his mouth. Kost came in with another mask and positioned it near to his mouth and nose. He tried to resist, but Ellis held him firmly.

"Just relax. Relax. Let the air wash over you."

Ellis expected the kid to continue thrashing, but strangely, a calm seemed to come over him and he let his body go limp.

"What's your name, son? I need to know your name."

My name? What's my name? I can't remember!

Through a phlegm-filled throat came a single utterance.

"An...Andy..."

Andy?

"Andy, my name is Dr. Ellis. You're in the hospital. You were brought here in an ambulance."

Ambulance? And what's with the weird accents?

"Can you hear me, Andy?"

Andy attempted to nod against the hand that was holding his head down. Ellis nodded to the other team members who were holding him. They relaxed their grip and stood back. Satisfied they had him under control, Ellis began issuing orders to all present. Bloods, chest film, CT, ECG, IV antibiotics, catheter.

Catheter? Oh Christ!

A hospital orderly entered through the double doors holding a small, clear plastic bag. One of the trauma room staff took it from him and casually inspected it. Wallet, keys, cell phone, a couple of guitar picks, a pack of cigarettes. Some foil-wrapped objects the size of a nickel. She gave the bag to Ellis, who rifled through it, plucking the foil objects out. He tossed the bag on a nearby bench and hastily unwrapped one of the foil objects. Inside was a white pill. He flicked it over with his finger and saw a small, vicious-looking skull imprinted in purple on its surface. He eyeballed Kost, beside him, and handed it over. They shared a knowing glance.

The kid was coming around, yet he remained calm and submitted to their care without protest. He was in a lot of trouble and he would surely know it, Ellis thought. These idiot kids were all the same. But, as Ellis checked his vitals then turned back, he felt a sudden chill. The young man's eyes were wide open and a strange expression had crossed over his face. He was very serene. His eyes were turned up towards the ceiling and fixed on a spot there, focused intensely. Hard and fast. Ellis shivered.

Chapter 3

The L train trundled noisily along the tracks through northern suburbs of the city. The Chicago skyline passed by the window to his right, the urban sprawl laid out before him, but he noticed none of it. He sat hunched, alone in the rear of the car, his head against the window, dozing, sleeping ... but not quite.

Four days had passed.

It had been four days, and no one had come to see Andy in the hospital. Not his father; nothing short of his son actually dying would have pulled him from his 18-wheeler and his long-haul runs. Not his friends; well, with maybe one or two exceptions they weren't so much friends as they were hangers-on, attracted more to his ability to supply than to him as a person. They knew he was *it* when it came to getting the good shit, but now that he had been busted, they had all disappeared into nothingness. Not his girlfriend; her absence, in particular, stung him, but he supposed he shouldn't be surprised about that either. Their relationship was more superficial than he cared to admit and was based more on his station in the underground than anything else. It's all fine when your man is such top shit, but when it all goes to hell, then he is the last person you want to be seen with.

Andy felt a heavy pall of depression weighing him down, a thick soup of weariness, anger, rejection, fear, loneliness.

Loneliness.

He sat here now in the clothes he had been found in: shirt, complete with torn-off buttons; jeans, rumpled and stained. At least someone had been kind enough to have them laundered for him, which had removed the worst of the blood and vomit. His battered khaki jacket helped to conceal the rest.

The experience had left him drained, even though - so they had told him - he had gotten off lightly this time. It was his second time.

Fucking idiot!

Andy DeVries was a dealer - a courier. A nimble young man who worked in the shadows of a dark underworld where illicit substances were coveted like precious jewels. There wasn't anything he could not obtain: Ecstasy, Ice, GHB, amphetamines. He was capable of laying his hands on just about anything. But more than that, Andy DeVries had garnered a reputation among manufacturers as someone who could move their product quickly and efficiently. He could realize handy profits, which made him highly desired. And though he was intertwined with the drug trade, Andy was not a product of it. Rather he had fallen into it through a combination of being easily led and the lure of a quick and lucrative income. He had started out as a mule but had progressed quickly. The perils of his chosen vocation had begun to take their toll on Andy. Like many who were drawn to it, Andy had become addicted to the product. And, as with any addiction, the highs were intoxicating. The 'Ice' was the key to nirvana, to unparalleled freedom. It unlocked your inhibitions, made you feel you could do anything. But the come-downs were earth-shattering if you didn't know how to handle them right. Andy always believed he was able to handle them.

Well, until now.

Suddenly Andy found himself close to tears. He shrank into his seat further and drew the edges of his jacket around him. He pulled his woolen cap down over his ears and allowed his long fringe to sway back and forth over his eyes. Even though there was no one else in the car right now, there could be up ahead. He didn't want to be seen like this.

Emilio Vasq was going to be pissed. The police had come to see Andy in the hospital and drilled him for a good couple of hours in an attempt to get him to talk. Where did he get the drugs from? Who was the dealer? Did he know anybody connected with the manufacture of the pills? Andy didn't yield, though, didn't reveal anything. He'd just played dumb and they'd bought it. In the end, all they'd slapped him with was a possession charge, which wouldn't go far. But now he was tainted, so far as Emilio Vasq would be concerned. Vasq couldn't risk using a dealer/courier, even his most successful one, if he'd been painted by the police. So Andy's other vocation, his other life, was now on shaky ground.

Andy became aware of an itching on his right forearm. He scratched at his arm absently then, turning his hands over in his lap, he inspected his fingers. The black nail polish had chipped on most of them and had been completely removed from a couple of them. He shook his head angrily and squeezed his hands into fists before relaxing them once again.

The L eventually ground to a halt at the station and Andy peeked out from behind his fringe. It was his stop. He got up and shuffled slowly towards the exit, past newly boarding passengers. He dared not look at any of them as he stepped out onto the platform and looked up and down the length of the train. It was bitterly cold out. In the handful of disembarking passengers there was no one here who looked familiar. His heart sank.

No one had come.

Slowly, sadly, Andy made his way from the drab station, down the ruddy sidewalks of the commercial district, then through the back streets and lane ways that he knew well. The sun struggled to shine through heavy clouds that threatened to dump down upon him. Not that Andy cared. He was single-minded in his purpose. He just wanted to get home. He trudged on through the uninspiring parks and public spaces and finally into the residential district, the apartments and houses.

With an overwhelming sense of relief, Andy turned his key in the lock, opened the door to the apartment and locked it behind him. It was dark inside. Nobody was home. His roommate, Beck, must be at work.

Probably pulling another long stretch, Andy figured.

He went straight through the darkened hallway to his bedroom where he unloaded his meager possessions. His wallet, his cell phone - upon which there were still no messages after four days - his keys and his cigarettes. He inspected the pack quickly and found there were only two smokes left - almost not worth the trouble. He stripped out of his clothes and tossed the ruined shirt into the wastepaper basket beside his bed. The bedroom was sparse. All that occupied the small space was his bed, a desk with a lamp - the only light source in the room - a tacky chipboard bookshelf that held a mishmash of magazines, books and folders containing sheet music. The walls around the room were adorned with posters of various bands such as The Black Crowes, Foo Fighters, Korn, Slipknot, Pantera and Metallica. An aged analog TV sat on an old crate at the foot of the bed. There were clothes all over the floor, and no order to anything. An expensive-looking Taylor guitar stood on a stand in the corner by the wardrobe. It was the one decent possession Andy owned, and it was central to the life he lived away from the drugs and the crime. He regarded it momentarily in the half light.

I need a shower.

Naked now, Andy stumbled into the bathroom and felt for the shower taps. He slumped down into the bath and let the water wash over him, let the sadness wash over him and finally, he let the tears wash over him. He sobbed and sobbed until he was spent and numb. He remained there, staring into the darkness, unable to move. Distorted images from the rave flashed before him like the shards of a broken mirror. Images of the people in his life peered at him quizzically as though they were on fast-forward. His girlfriend Cassie: all wild eyes, black lipstick and faux attitude. His father: distant, dismissive and alienated from his son. His friend and roommate Beck: solid and sympathetic to Andy's struggles but uncomfortable with many of Andy's activities and associates like Emilio Vasq and his posse of thugs. Then, suddenly, the images coalesced into something else - something unexpected. Andy squinted, even though his eyes were closed, trying to bring the image into focus. It was a face.

The face...

Well, not so much the face as the cheek of a woman's face. Soft porcelain skin, a delicate cheekbone. Andy tilted his head in the darkness, embracing the image, trying to capture more of it, intrigued by its sudden presence. A single teardrop trickled down over her skin. She moved her head. He could almost make out her eyes. But she turned away too fast.

Andy's eyes snapped open as that final image threatened to leave his stream of consciousness and become an echo. It stayed there, however. Somehow, he was able capture something of the image and keep it there.

His tranquility was broken abruptly, by a loud banging at the apartment door. Andy jumped reflexively in the bath. Dazed, he felt around for the sides of the slippery tub and scrambled to his feet. In the half-light Andy noticed the back of the shower curtain. A heavy layer of reddish-brown scum coated the curtain. The result of weeks and weeks of buildup from - Christ knows what.

"Jesus!"

Again the banging at the door, more insistent this time. Andy struggled to find a towel and wrap it around his still-glistening body while he searched around for the light switch.

The banging didn't let up.

"All right, all right already!"

He unlatched the door, but got no further after turning the handle. It fairly burst open at the hands of a lithe young figure who exploded into the hall and clawed enthusiastically at Andy, who could barely maintain his balance.

"Andy, honey!" purred the wild-eyed young woman as she leapt into his arms, wrapping her legs around his waist and plastering him with kisses. All he could do was back into the living room and flop down on the dusty couch.

Cassie.

Black hair with red streaks, dark eyeliner framing wild and overtly large eyes, too much pale foundation, thick black lipstick. A tattoo of a dragon poking up from her shoulder blades at the back of her neck. Her breath was the smell of mint chewing gum and marijuana. Her clothing was a derivative of early 80's Madonna. Fishnet stockings, ankle boots, torn denim shorts, black ripped T-shirt. She was chaos personified. And she was as horny as fuck.

Her hand immediately slipped down under the towel and grabbed his cock, masturbating him voraciously as he struggled for air. For a millisecond, Andy considered submitting to her. But then the anger surged once more and he grabbed her shoulders and hoisted her off him, tossing her to one side.

"Fucking stop!"

Cassie was confused and hurt. She remained crumpled on the couch beside him as he struggled to secure the towel once again.

"Jesus, Dev, I just wanted to give you a welcome home!" Cassie retorted angrily.

"A welcome home!" Andy croaked, exasperated. "Four days, Cee! Four fucking days! D'ya ever consider coming to see me in the hospital?"

"Oh, don't be so fucking stupid! You know full well if I or any of the others had gone to see you down there, the police would have collared us right away."

Cassie kicked herself up into a sitting position, legs drawn up at the knees, defensive. "Vasq is real pissed right now, you know. He thinks you talked."

Andy hissed and launched himself off the couch.

"Fuck Vasq," he growled as he made his way down the hall and into his bedroom. Stunned by his summation, Cassie was forced to follow him. "I didn't say nothin', and if I had, he'd have had cops all over him right now."

He paused, glaring at her intensely.

"Anyway, screw this! I was stuck there for four days and not you or anyone else cared enough to visit - regardless?"

Cassie feigned concern.

"Honey. You know I would have come if I could. I didn't want to put you in any danger, is all. I called the hospital a bunch of times. That's how I knew you were coming home."

She tried to wriggle in between his arms as he searched through the pile of clothes on the floor. His towel dropped away from his waist once again and she began stroking the insides of his thighs, running her fingers over his genitals. She smiled and licked her lips as he became hard, but it was short-lived. Again he brushed her away.

"I don't want it right now, Cassie, OK? I got shit to do. I need to be alone."

Cassie slumped back in a crouch on the floor angrily as Andy quickly threw on a T-shirt and boxers, then plucked out a pair of crumpled jeans from the pile.

"Look, Cassie. You need to go. I am not in a good mood and I need to get shit done. I... I..."

He searched his mind for a convincing reason to extricate himself from here. He noticed he calendar on the wall above the desk. Today was Wednesday.

"I need to go to work."

Wednesday was a work day, he remembered hastily. Pulling beers at The Pub.

"You're not serious?" she said with disbelief.

Andy rubbed his eyes with one hand then looked down at his girlfriend. His face was stony.

"Well ... can I call you later?" she asked.

He shrugged, then turned on his heel, grabbing his jacket and cap. He left the apartment.

Cassie remained crouched awkwardly on the floor of the living room, unsure of what had just happened.

Chapter 4

The Public House stood on the corner of a busy thoroughfare that fairly bristled with traffic. Surrounded by gray, lifeless monoliths of the modern-day urban sprawls, it was an old, stately building - almost Gothic in nature - so it carried some measure of authenticity about its characteristically Irish theme. Someone had once told Andy that it was one of the oldest establishments of its type in Chicago. To Andy, it was just a means to earn an honest income. Frankly, it was not a very good one.

As he stepped though the door to the dark, wood-paneled main bar, Andy hesitated, hoping like hell that no one here knew of his misadventure over the weekend. It was bad enough that his boss, the owner and a friend of Andy's father, suspected that Andy was hooked up in some clandestine shit but, to date, he hadn't called Andy out on it. If he *were* to discover the truth of Andy's overdose, Andy felt certain that he could kiss his job goodbye.

The front bar was busy but not crowded. Andy quietly slipped inside and dropped his head, trying to make himself inconspicuous.

He was regarded as a shitty employee, but Andy's boss was honoring an obligation to Andy's father by keeping him there. Whatever that obligation was, Andy didn't know other than it was a long story and it went back many years.

Andy hurried through the main bar, skirted the counter and slipped in behind it brushing past Samantha, a young, attractive female server who was attending to two customers.

As Andy disappeared into a cubbyhole at the back of the bar, the young woman exchanged a glance of disbelief with a large bulbous man, the owner of The Pub. Gideon Allan scratched one of his carefully manicured sideburns and checked his own watch before double-checking a clock high upon the wall behind him.

Andy DeVries had never been early to work. Ever!

Within a minute Andy emerged again, having swapped his shirt for a burgundy polo with an insignia of The Public House emblazoned on the left breast. Without a word, he had gathered up a tray and begun moving about the bar collecting empty glasses, taking orders for fresh rounds and wiping down the bar surfaces. All of them watched Andy incredulously as he went about his work.

As Andy swung around behind the counter armed with the fully laden tray, Gideon coughed and cleared his throat.

"Ummm ... Andrew?" he rumbled softly in a faint Irish brogue.

Andy deposited the glasses into a washer under the bar then began pouring fresh glasses for the orders he had taken. He regarded Gideon fleetingly.

"Are you ill?" Gideon continued, a note of sarcasm in his voice.

"No," Andy countered defensively. "Why?"

Gideon gestured with a thumb back over his shoulder at the clock on the wall.

"You've never been early a day in your life. I'm concerned for your well-being."

Andy looked up at the ancient timepiece. He was half an hour early. Shaking his head ruefully, he simply went back to pouring beers and placing them on a tray. Again, Gideon and Samantha exchanged glances.

That's how it went for the next few hours. Andy worked as he never had before, serving beers, taking orders for bar meals, getting them out to the customers quickly and efficiently and keeping the bar clean. He even quietly and subtly dealt with a couple of the rowdier patrons, diffusing a potential fight. Gideon studied Andy closely, with muted suspicion. Something was definitely up. The kid had never worked this hard.

Or this well.

Gideon regarded Andy as his worst employee. The kid was lazy, arrogant and frankly, a cock-head. What Gideon was witnessing now was bizarre and not a little disturbing. It was as though the young man was possessed.

Somewhere close to 6pm, Samantha slid a plate in front of Andy: Irish sausages on a bed of mashed potatoes with gravy. Andy looked at the plate indifferently.

"Whatever you've been taking must've had an effect on the boss," Samantha said in a Southern accent. "Take a break and have a bite."

Andy wiped his hands with a towel and tossed it to Samantha.

"Hospital appears to agree with you, huh? Although I wouldn't go around fixing anybody with that flat stare of yours - those baby browns are looking a little *too* bloodshot just now." She pointed casually at his eyes.

Andy quickly glanced in the mirrored panel beside him. His eyes were indeed puffy, the whites lined with red veins.

"You know, I'll bet your eyes are just full of useful information about what you got up to the other night."

Andy flashed her an angry scowl as he sat down to his meal.

Samantha had a penchant for alternative therapies. She was taking some sort of class for iridology in particular, and was constantly trying out her new techniques on her colleagues in The Public House. Andy, however, was in no mood for her quackery right now. His scowl intensified.

"Whoa!" Samantha said, throwing her hands up, mock-defensively. She leaned in close to him. "Don't worry, he doesn't know - none of them do. But you had better thank Beck and me for covering your ass for you - especially yesterday. The old man thinks you were actually home ill."

Andy's tensed shoulders relaxed and he glanced across at her but said nothing.

Samantha folded her arms over and appraised him, searching for a change of subject.

"So what is going on with you today? You're making me look bad."

Andy shrugged.

"Nothing's going on. I'm just - I dunno - feeling motivated."

Samantha's eyes narrowed, then she cocked her head slightly to one side.

"You nearly bought it the other night, didn't you?"

Andy chewed nervously on his food. He didn't respond, nor did he look up. Samantha could tell by the discreet twitch of his shoulder that she had hit the mark.

"That's it!" she crowed, trying to keep her voice down but attracting the attention of a few of the patrons.

"Look, can you just *fucking* drop it!" Andy snapped under his breath, his fork and knife clattering noisily on the plate in front of him. This time, when his glare drilled into her eyes, she saw something there that chilled her.

Immediately Samantha backed away and let him finish his meal in silence.

Andy regretted having snapped at Samantha so harshly. Though he would never admit it, he liked Samantha. She brightened up the smoke-filled bar.

Checking his watch, he gave the plate to one of the kitchen hands as they went past. He sighed, realizing he only had a couple of hours to go. He returned to his duties quietly and studiously.

Gideon sidled up to Samantha.

"So. Did you manage to find out what's up with the kid?"

Samantha shrugged without looking at Gideon. He could see she was uncomfortable with the question.

"I dunno. Why don't you ask him yourself?"

Gideon regarded her curiously, then shook his head before turning away.

"I think I liked him better when he was a lazy shit," he snapped as he left the bar.

The door to the front bar opened then, and a group of five young men entered, led by a particularly vicious-looking Latino. Despite the darkened interior of the bar, most of these new arrivals were wearing sunglasses and none of them made any move to remove them. Sporting slicked-back hair and expensive street clothing, including the bejeweled Stetson he held, the leader regarded the patrons absently, chewing gum before he spied Andy behind the bar. His companions were dressed similarly and appeared almost as menacing.

Andy felt their presence even before he looked up in their direction.

It was Vasq.

Emilio Vasq - smalltime crime-lord wannabe and self-styled stand-over man - approached Andy with theatrically outstretched arms as if to embrace him.

"Devvvvv - my friend! How are you feeling tonight?"

Andy's expression set like stone as Vasq's menacing tone chilled him. He did not know where to look. The patrons in the bar, attracted by Vasq's loud voice, all turned in the direction of the bar, studying Andy and the others with interest.

"What are you doing here, Vasq?" Andy said quietly.

"Awww, no reason, *dawg*. I wanted to be sure that you were feeling better, you know. After all, the word was that you were pretty close to the edge."

Vasq and his posse spread out along the bar.

"Look, guys, how about a drink?" Samantha ventured, sensing that this situation was rapidly becoming tense. Andy immediately brushed her away.

"These guys don't want anything to drink."

He set his bar towel down on the counter and moved past her. "Cover for me."

Vasq watched Andy slip through the far end of the counter and go immediately to the side entrance that led out onto the street. He disappeared through it, forcing Vasq - after several moments - to follow him.

It was chilly on the sidewalk, but Andy ignored it, pacing back and forth as Vasq and his crew emptied out from inside the bar. The sun was disappearing rapidly behind the L track nearby. His breath was visible in the cool evening air.

"I'm very concerned about what I've been hearing, Dev. You were visited by the police down in the city."

"That's true," Andy said cautiously. "But you haven't had any blue-and-white visitors to your door since the weekend, have you?"

Andy didn't know that for sure, of course, but the mere fact that they were standing here now was enough of an indicator for him to push forward with his supposition.

Vasq grinned broadly, his eyes narrowing as he nodded approvingly.

Andy's gone and grown a set, Vasq thought amusedly.

"True, true. But I...,"

"I said nothing, Emilio," Andy cut him off brusquely. "They kept at me ... but I didn't say anything."

Vasq approached Andy then, arrogantly stepping into his personal space and eyeballing him intensely. He often did that with his subordinates.

"It's got me worried. You see, I can't afford to have a marked associate. Yet no one would deny that you are my best courier. You can appreciate my dilemma."

Andy stood fast and eyeballed Vasq - something he'd never done before. As had happened with Samantha earlier, something within those eyes unsettled Vasq, knocked him off center. His shoulders relaxed ever so slightly; he stood back and stopped chewing his gum.

"There is no dilemma, Vasq," Andy said, his voice quivering upon the edge of breaking. "I have to go."

Abruptly, Andy turned on his heel and went back inside the bar, leaving Vasq standing there. One of his companions stepped forward.

"Man, are you just gonna let him *go* like that?"

Vasq said nothing. A dark cloud settled over him and he began chewing his gum again, angrily. He turned away from the others and walked off down the street.

***

Andy unlocked the door to the apartment and stepped inside. Blue light from the living room bathed the entrance hall. The sound of a cheering crowd emanating from the TV told him right away that Beck must be home. Sure enough, as he appeared in the entrance to the living room, there was Beck lounging in a Cubs shirt and boxers, balancing a bowl of Chinese noodles on his belly and a beer on the edge of the couch. The game was on.

Beck was tall and solidly built. He had a rugged visage that resembled a bulldog, with big eyes, a misshapen nose and a warm smile. Curiously, one of his most striking features was a set of almost perfect teeth. He was completely bald, having shaved his thinning hair as close to the skin as possible. Beck worked as a laborer on a construction site and, unlike Andy, had a work ethic worth its weight in gold.

"Hey man," he greeted cheerily through a mouthful of noodles. Beck struggled off the couch, spilling his beer as he did so. "Where you been at? I tried calling ya, but your cell was off *again*."

"Pub," Andy grumbled, taking off his cap and jacket.

Beck appeared genuinely surprised.

"Fuck, man, what are you doing working after being in hospital? You don't work even when you are functioning normally."

Andy wanted to be angry right then, but, of all the people who'd made some sort of jibe today, only Beck's carried no malice with it. And of all the people who'd stayed away over the weekend, only Beck had called regularly to check to see if Andy was OK. A fistful of message slips were still in the pocket of the ruined shirt he'd discarded earlier.

Andy settled upon a wan smile as Beck slapped his shoulder gently.

"Thank god you're all right. I thought this was it, this time - you know?"

Beck turned his head towards the TV and gestured with his head towards it.

"I'd ask you to watch the game, man, but ... ahhh..."

He hesitated a moment before gesturing with a nod towards Andy's room.

"You got company."

Andy winced.

"She's still here?"

Beck chuckled under his breath.

"Man, you better do somethin' with her quick. I thought she was gonna jump *my* bones at one point."

"Oh, man, she is the last person I wanna see right now. I just want to go to bed."

Beck took a swig of his beer and flashed Andy a mischievous grin.

"Well, I'm just gonna turn the game up loud and try not to get hard listening to you two fuck, OK?"

Andy scowled - but only half-seriously.

"Fuck you, man."

"Not likely, asshole."

Beck turned away from Andy, mockingly grabbing his own crotch as he plunked down again and went back to watching the game.

Though he thought he had little desire for it, by the time Andy stepped into his darkened room and saw her lying there in the half-light, his erection pressed firmly against the inside of his jeans. He supposed it was the fishnets that did it. He had a thing for her legs and feet, and the fishnet stockings she wore tipped him over every time. She was topless, except for the necklace and Gothic cross she wore. Her breasts were milky and smooth, her nipples erect.

The room was thick with marijuana smoke. Music issued softly from the laptop on the desk. She was smoking a joint, the smoke trailing up and catching the light from the laptop.

Cassie watched him as he stepped forward into the room and stood at the end of the bed. A smile tugged at her lips. She lifted her foot, placing it on his erection then moved it slowly back and forth. She offered him her joint. He hesitated, then took it, drawing back deeply, feeling the cannabis infuse through his lungs and into his body. The effect was almost immediate.

Andy closed his eyes and sighed at the sensation of her foot on his erection. Slowly he undid the button of his jeans, unzipped them and allowed them to drop to the floor, revealing his hardened cock. Taking it in both her feet she played with him for a while, expertly stroking his shaft while she massaged her breasts. Cassie slid one foot up over his chest and towards his mouth, pushing against his lips with her toes until they parted and he began sucking and licking her toes and the underside of her fishnetted sole. She licked her lips.

In his mind's eye, cast in shades of gray, he could see another body, a woman's body glistening with droplets of water. Her flat stomach, delicate navel, shapely hips. A man's arm - his arm - and outstretched hand moved slowly across her, his fingers touched her skin gently, stroking across her one way, then the other before moving down ... down...

Overcome by the waves of desire, Andy knelt on the bed as Cassie rolled over onto her haunches and crawled on fours towards him. She began licking and biting roughly at his belly, growling playfully. She stroked the insides of his thighs with her slender nails, digging into his skin, drawing blood. He shivered, but did not move away. She licked at the droplets of blood before cupping his genitals in her hands, taking his shaft in her mouth sucking him urgently, wantonly. He became more aroused as he looked down on her back, the elaborate tattoo of the dragon that extended across both shoulder blades.

Two mouths meet - a man and a woman's. Their lips part, tongues touch each other gently, lovingly, then passionately. They envelop each other in a lingering kiss. The lips are familiar. The taste is slightly salty, like the sea. He feels a breeze nearby. His hand explores her slowly, gently. He cups her delicate breast in his hand. His thumb slowly brushes her nipple. Her body reacts immediately...

Andy reached out and ran his fingers roughly down along the length of her slender spine, past her fishnets, down between her buttocks and further until he found her wetness. He rubbed his fingers over her swollen clitoris and her whole body shivered as he masturbated her eagerly. He penetrated deep inside her, feeling the walls of her vagina. Cassie gnashed her teeth together, feeling the waves of pleasure engulf her. She was throbbing with desire for him. Lifting her free hand up to his chest she ran her fingers down it, scratching at his skin with her nails. Waves of pain rippled through him, exciting him more. She withdrew him from her mouth and turned her body around so that he could have her from behind. He was drunk with an animal desire. Roughly peeling down her denim shorts and fishnets in one swift action Andy parted her buttocks. Feeling for her vagina with the head of his penis, he pushed deep inside her angrily, firmly. Cassie squealed with ecstasy as he fucked her deeply; she brushed her fingers against her swollen clitoris with each movement. Their bodies were bathed in sweat. The air in the room was stifling, but it only excited them more. She buried her head in the pillow before her, overcome with each penetration, moaning with desire.

Two bodies, entwined together, move rhythmically, synchronously under a silk sheet. Her gentle moan echoes in his mind as he makes love to her. His head is buried in her neck and she gently kisses his forehead. Slowly, he looks up at her ... at her slender lips, up ... at her porcelain cheekbones, up ... into her eyes. Perfect jewels, deep blue ... a world within a world...

Andy's eyes went wide as the single image of the woman's eyes lingered in his consciousness.

Who is she?

The question echoed silently in his mind, through the fever of his arousal.

He grabbed Cassie's hips in his hands and pushed deeper, feeling the climax building. Reflexively, he grabbed the back of her hair, pulling her up. Cassie ground her hips against him harder and harder, licking her lips and grinning maniacally. He held her around her neck, his grip tightening as the waves of orgasm approached, and then his breath was sucked from his lungs as he exploded into her. He let out a guttural moan. Simultaneously Cassie felt her whole body spasm, her vaginal muscles rippled, her clitoris throbbed so hard it took her breath away. She felt a satisfying gush within her as every single muscle fibre let go, and together they collapsed on the bed, bathed in sweat, bathed in smoke from the marijuana, totally and utterly spent.

In the darkness of the room, Andy gazed at the ceiling. The image of those eyes remained, those that had eluded him in the visions that had come to him.

Who was this stranger who was visiting his subconscious?

Was she a stranger?

Chapter 5

Andy sprinted across the lawn of the university fairly gasping for breath. He was horribly late and he knew it, but still he ran in some vain hope that it would make a difference. He gripped the unwieldy guitar case in his left hand, occasionally bumping it against his legs, cursing himself every time he did so.

This was the Conservatory where Andy studied classical guitar under the tutelage of some of the finest practitioners of the art in Chicago, if not the country. The guitar was the one thing of value to Andy. His talent had been discovered early by his grandmother, of all people. She had nurtured his gift, encouraging him and paying for lessons she could barely afford. Andy had been admitted to this institution on a scholarship, having continued to display a prodigious talent for the instrument during his senior years at high school. For someone considered underprivileged, Andy's talent was described as a revelation. He had been encouraged to go as far as he could with his gift.

But, as with other facets of his life right now, Andy's place at the Conservatory was under threat. Because of the overdose he had missed a crucial exam. It wasn't the first time. He'd missed exams and important tutorial sessions in the past for similar infractions. One too many hours at the raves, one too many drinks, one too many illicit substances.

As he ran, Andy was mentally working through possible scenarios to bullshit his way out of this mess. Though he knew the situation was dire, he deluded himself into thinking he would be able to sweet-talk his way out. His instructor, Veldtman, would be fuming.

He leapt up a flight of stairs, but the painful twinge of a stitch tugged ferociously at his lower right side and he had to stop.

Andy was a mess.

Because he was late, he hadn't showered this morning. He reeked of stale marijuana smoke and sex. His hair was greasy, his face was a mess of acne and what he thought was a developing cold sore. His clothes were the same ones he had worn yesterday - rumpled and in dire need of laundering. As he approached the doors to the lecture theater, he pulled his cap down a little further and checked his underarms. The cheap deodorant was simply that - cheap. It couldn't disguise his wretched body odor.

As he snapped open the door and stepped inside, he was confronted by a welcoming darkness. The class was in the middle of watching a documentary film. Andy found an empty line of seats at the very back of the amphitheater and huddled there, praying that she hadn't noticed him but knowing that she had.

Sorrel Veldtman, diminutive and somewhat earth-motherish, had been Andy's lecturer and tutor for the past two years. She was one of the few people he held in any regard. Veldtman had been a master of the classical guitar for more than 40 years, having brought her talent from a coastal village near Tel Aviv to the concert halls of both New York and Chicago. It was rumored that she had recorded with Jose Feliciano, though Andy had never been able to confirm this. Veldtman was a master of flamenco, a discipline Andy himself aspired to. She was noted for her loud head scarves and her deeply lined face that was harsh yet quite stunning.

The documentary film ended and the lights came up in the amphitheater. Veldtman clapped her hands together to rouse a handful of "dozers," then stepped out from behind her lectern to address the class.

"So!" her voice snapped. "The European Masters - Sor, Rodrigo, Giuliani - to name just a few. This introductory film is presented to give you a beginning point for the remainder of this semester. We shall be studying their history, their influence upon the modern discipline, and you will be required to learn *and master* some of the pieces."

Veldtman paused to allow her students to absorb her words. She scanned the auditorium, noticing the new arrival at the back. Her eyes narrowed imperceptibly, and then she nodded.

"That will be all for now."

Immediately the auditorium became a buzz as students began filing out. Andy sat in his seat, unconsciously biting at his fingernails and tapping his foot studying Veldtman, trying to gauge her mood. Something snapped inside him suddenly. He lost his nerve and got to his feet, trying to lose himself in a group of students who filed past him.

"DeVries!"

Andy's jaw locked like a vise and he knew the ceiling was going to fall. A few of his student colleagues regarded him with thinly veiled disgust as he turned around and shuffled past them, down the central aisle of stairs. One of them, a pretty young Japanese student named Michyko, seemed to look at him with pity, but he lowered his head before he could be sure. By the time he was three or four steps from the bottom, the auditorium was quiet again.

Veldtman was placing some notes in a folder before reaching for an oversized handbag.

"You missed my examination - again," she hissed.

Andy froze where he stood as she pierced him with a malevolent stare.

"What's your pitiful excuse this time?"

Andy opened his mouth to speak. The pre-rehearsed explanations circled around in his mind, but suddenly, they all seemed pathetic. He simply shook his head. His shoulders slumped.

"You were warned Mr. DeVries - *formally* - that if you missed another assessment task, the consequences would be dire for you."

Andy opened his mouth to speak. But he couldn't get the words out. The pre-rehearsed speech rang hollow in his ears to the point where to utter it would feel cheap, even to him. He simply nodded an acknowledgement. Defeat washed over him. He knew this was it. He was going to be dumped from the Conservatory.

Veldtman began pacing back and forth, arms folded.

"The decision rests with me now. I've discussed it with the faculty heads, and they have given me the final say - and *I say* I would dump you."

As she had with the class moments before, Veldtman let the impact of her words hang in the air between them. Andy felt as if he might throw up.

Veldtman forced air to whistle through her teeth.

"I am aware, however, that you've been in hospital."

Again, a theatrical pause. For the most fleeting of moments, Veldtman's icy facade cracked, her shoulders relaxed and she seemed to offer some sympathy through her worldly eyes.

Andy prepared to stammer a reply, but Veldtman brushed him away brusquely.

"You have an hour," she declared as she began gathering up her books. "You will be here ready to sit and you will take my exam. We shall see what you are capable of."

Before he could say anything, Veldtman strode from the room, leaving Andy floundering where he stood, trying to prevent himself from descending into wholesale panic.

Outside the lecture theater, Veldtman stopped before a man - an aging hippie with wild silver hair, a coarse beard and a pair of gold-rimmed glasses whose bridge was held together with a bandage. He regarded her with suspicion.

"So?"

Veldtman sighed, annoyed and rubbed her brow.

"I... I couldn't do it," she said scratchily.

Grantley Casper was not surprised. His satisfied smile said it all, and he clucked as though he had won a wager.

Veldtman considered slapping him in the mouth.

"I have given him an hour. He will sit the theoretical component this afternoon and that will decide his fate."

"I *knew* you wouldn't cut him loose," Casper taunted, with a self-indulgent expression that said: 'I-told-you-so'. "The faculty are going to be pissed, Sorrel. They're already fed up with your persistence about his suitability for the delegation to Australia. That's what this is really about, isn't it? You and I both know Andrew DeVries would be a nightmare for this Conservatory's reputation."

Casper could see Veldtman's jaw stiffen.

"There still a long way to go before we have to consider the final makeup of the delegation," Veldtman said. "I am more concerned right now with keeping Andrew in this school. The International Festival of the Guitar can wait."

She fixed Casper with her eye.

"Look. Do you honestly think you could live with yourself, knowing that you had denied a talent as potent as his?"

Casper opened his mouth, trying to think of an answer. He knew he couldn't. She had a point.

"Casper, I have not heard anyone elicit a more beautiful sound from the strings as I have from that young man. His technical ability borders on the sublime. He is a troubled soul, I'll grant you. But he has a gift such as I have never witnessed."

She paused, collecting herself as frustration threatened to well over.

"I know there is good in him. I am praying that the guitar will bring it out. I will not abandon that talent so long as it's in him."

Casper stood there, silently appraising the aged teacher.

"He's a fuck-up, Sorrel," he sighed, defeated. "You should've cut him and stopped denying the inevitable."

Shaking his head, Casper turned and sauntered away, leaving Veldtman to her troubled thoughts.

***

Andy hung his backpack on the hook just inside the door of the apartment and leaned the guitar case against the wall.

He felt sick to his stomach - and not just because of the fast-food lunch he had subjected himself to. The familiar pangs of withdrawal had begun to tease at the edges of his stomach again. He needed a hit. He had tried to resist it, but the urge was too much. It was always too much. As soon as he got home, he knew he would have to assuage it.

He knew he had blown the exam badly - he *knew* it. In the fall-out from the weekend he had completely forgotten to study - which wasn't anything new - but he usually made at least some sort of half-assed effort to cram before an exam. Though Veldtman had thrown him a fairly significant bone, he doubted it was enough to get him over the line.

The apartment was empty and Andy was relieved to have the place to himself. He checked the answering machine. There were two messages from Cassie. He considered calling her but he hesitated, deciding that he didn't want to talk to her right now. Instead, he went straight to his bedroom and stripped off his jacket, pullover and shirt in one effort and tossed them in the laundry basket in the corner. He lit a joint and smoked it absently for a few minutes, feeling the cannabis taking the edge off his withdrawal. But then, he took it out and considered the joint in his hand before butting it out on the leg of his bed. Suddenly, he found it tasted awful, even though it was the same stuff he'd always enjoyed. He felt uncomfortable smoking it.

Andy dropped to his knees and felt under the bed until his fingers brushed across the top of a hard metal object. He pulled out the small locked box and fished a key out of his pocket. Opening the box, Andy looked down at a thick wad of folded bills inside, his earnings. Though he hadn't counted it lately, Andy estimated that there was about two thousand dollars there, a considerable amount. He shouldn't have this money here. Despite his loyalty to Vasq, Andy didn't trust him. Andy was regarded with a certain amount of jealousy by the crew - even Vasq himself - and he knew that jealousy could be a dangerous weapon should any of them decide to act on it. He also found a couple of foil-wrapped pills in the box. He considered them.

But again, that feeling of disgust turned him off from taking one.

Andy shook his head as he considered his ill-gotten gains. Unable to look at it anymore, he locked the box again and shoved it back underneath the bed.

He remained crouched on the floor for several minutes, staring into the darkness before eventually deciding to shower - his odor was appalling.

Andy knew that, where the guitar was concerned, Veldtman considered him some sort of wunderkind. The grades he had achieved until now had given him the potential to top his class. But as with his other noble pursuits, he was arrogant, undisciplined and lazy. In his efforts to balance his two lives, Andy had come to rely far too heavily upon his raw performance talent to get him through the course work. Today, the earth-shattering realization dawned upon him that he could no longer charm his way through it.

Then there was the issue of the delegation. The International Festival of the Guitar in Melbourne, Australia, was an opportunity for students of considerable talent to perform among some of the finest practitioners in the world. The festival's highlight was the emerging talent concert series. This series, a competition, offered a prize that included a $10,000 cheque and a chance to record an album for worldwide release. Andy had considered applying for a place on the delegation but he knew the odds were stacked against him. The Conservatory's assessment panel was populated by the very people who wanted to expel him.

It was probably all for nothing now. The exam had been a disaster and he knew that - more likely than not - he was screwed. The thought of losing his place at The Conservatory, in itself, was a prospect too much to bear. It really was the only thing of true value.

"Jesus," he whispered despondently.

It was good to be clean again, Andy thought, as he stepped out of the shower and took the towel from the rail. He dried his hair off first, then his body. As he stood up, he caught sight of himself in the mirror.

Andy recoiled at what he saw there, and was gripped by a surge of revulsion that rolled through him like a wave. He felt sick, dizzy, and he was afraid to look back in the mirror. Andy tried to calm himself. He inched closer to the mirror. Slowly, he gazed upon his reflection.

A gaunt individual stared back at him. His cheeks were hollow, highlighting his prominent cheekbones, making him look emaciated. His skin - pocked with acne - was pale and pasty. His hair was stringy and ridiculously long in the front. His try-hard attempt at facial hair appeared mangy rather than *cool* and he shook his head, realizing that his whole appearance was appalling.

In his mind - a voice, foreign in accent and tone, spoke to Andy, echoing in his consciousness, causing him to flinch.

This isn't what I'm supposed to look like.

Andy felt his knees give way. He looked around him, searching for the source of the voice. *Where had it come from? Who was speaking to him?*

He turned back to the mirror, back to his reflection. Something in the reflection hooked him and he could not look away. It was as though he was looking at a stranger - a drug addicted stranger who was self-destructing. Andy blinked, shook his head, disoriented and

at that moment he was overcome by a wave of self-loathing so potent, he almost wanted to smash the mirror.

Is this where I'm supposed to be now?

Again that foreign voice sounded. Though he didn't know who it
was, Andy felt a strange familiarity about it.

Who was that?

But the voice didn't answer. Andy steadied himself, trying to
calm his frayed nerves until, finally, he backed out of the bathroom.
Ensuring that the apartment door was locked, Andy retreated to his
bedroom and shut the door. The room still stank of stale air, of per-
spiration and smoke. Andy screwed his nose up at it. It wasn't something that would usually have bothered him, but now he couldn't
stand it. Despite the cold outside, he unlocked the window and
opened it to let the crummy air escape.

Andy lay down on the bed and pulled the blanket up around him,
feeling afraid.

Where had that voice come from?

He lay there feeling disjointed, unable to sleep. And though he
was sure he was alone, Andy felt a presence in the room with him. It
did not move or speak, but he was sure it was there. Suddenly he felt
as though he did not belong in this city, in this life or in this
wretched body.

Chapter 6

His sleep was restless, plagued by bizarre nightmares. The people in his life - Cassie, Emilio Vasq, Samantha, Gideon, Beck and Veldtman - were all standing over him like a jury in a courtroom, passing judgment.

He dreamed of being back in the trauma room surrounded by the doctors and nurses, all of whom were laughing at him. Andy tried to move but he was shackled to the gurney, his wrists bound by thick leather straps that cut into him. Doctors and nurses grabbed his skin, pulling at it so hard they tore bloodied chunks of it away from his chest, exposing his ribs, his lungs and his blackened heart, covered in maggots. He tried to scream but he was unable to puncture the silence or pull himself from the depths of this horrible nightmare. He was trapped, taunted, mocked, ridiculed.

His father appeared out of the gloominess, standing alone on a dusty, gray highway, beside his Kenworth 18 wheeler, staring at him through black, emotionless eyes. Dust from a barren, inaccessible desert whipped up behind him. Shaking his head disapprovingly, Andy's father turned and walked off the road into the parched landscape, disappearing from view.

Then, somewhere in the deepest hours of the night, the disturbing imagery gave way to a nascent peace and suddenly Andy found himself immersed in a comforting warmth.

There was an ocean. Waves breaking on a sandy shore.

A grassy hillside.

He knew where it was, but he couldn't place it.

A dog was galloping across the grass, yelping enthusiastically. A cattle dog? A sheep dog? He couldn't tell. But he knew the dog. It was familiar. He felt a sense of companionship with this dog.

A woman's laughter, light and breezy, became audible in his ears and he felt his heart skip a beat as he tried to look towards where he thought she was. He couldn't manipulate his field of view, but he knew she was there, at the very corners of his vision.

Her presence was warm and pure. Her love was vital. And then she spoke. She called to him:

"Get the ball, honey! Before it goes into the sea!"

What was that accent?

He was sure he'd heard it somewhere, but its origin remained tantalizingly out of reach. The dog passed in front of him, and in that instant he recognized the black-and-white markings, the pointed ears, the sleek body of a cross-breed cattle dog. He tried to go to the dog but he was stuck fast where he stood, as though his feet were trapped in pools of cement.

He reached out with his hand...

But there was no hand.

He panicked, unable to breathe. As the image of the peaceful shore began to fade he tried desperately to focus on her.

Then, inexplicably, she was in his arms. Her touch sent electricity through him that was at once familiar and foreign.

Yet he knew it.

He could feel her skin upon his cheek; he could smell her hair. It was freshly washed and carried with it the scent of mint and something else. He searched his mind trying to determine what it was. A herb perhaps. An oven door opens. Roasted meat - lamb.

Damn, what is that?

It came to him suddenly, finally as an image of a herb with slender green shoots sporting pink flowers coalesced within his consciousness.

It was rosemary.

Rosemary and mint.

He felt her lips upon his and they kissed long and deeply. He tried to look into her face but could only see her lips as she drew back.

"I love you."

Andy awoke in the darkness of his room, her voice a fading echo in his consciousness. The warmth of the dream, and the bitterness of his nightmares conflicted until he sat up in his bed and shook them away. He stared into the darkness, the imprint of her voice fixed in his memory.

Quite unexpectedly, as though not of his own volition, he opened his mouth and whispered:

"Sonya."

***

Beck stumbled into the apartment early the next morning and collapsed down onto the sofa in the living room. He had pulled another all-nighter on the building site and was so tired he hadn't even bothered to change out of his work gear before he came home.

He felt blindly for the remote on the side table and flicked on the TV. In the light from the set, Beck suddenly noticed that the living room was absolutely spotless. The week-old pizza boxes were gone; the empty beer cans that had been piling up in the corner underneath the miniature Chicago Bulls basketball ring were also gone. The carpet had been vacuumed; there was no trace of crumbs or food of any sort on the floor. The battered wall unit that housed both Beck's and Andy's collection of books, DVDs, magazines and glassware was tidy, perhaps for the first time. The books were neatly arranged, as were the DVDs. Magazines - mainly copies of Maxim and FHM -

were lined up chronologically by month of issue. All at once Beck was bemused, impressed and disturbed. He suddenly felt guilty about having his dirty work boots on.

He got up and went into the kitchen, where he found a similar scene. It was spotless. The oven and stovetop were pristine. A pair of saucepans - one large, one small - sat on the hot plates, both of them sparkling. The benches had been wiped down, along with the small round table and chairs in the corner. The kitchen even smelled fresh.

It was then Beck heard the sound of scrubbing coming from the bathroom.

Poking his head around the door frame, Beck saw Andy down on his hands and knees, wearing only a pair of pajama bottoms, scrubbing the toilet - evidently the only remaining task in the bathroom.

"Umm - good morning, there," he said hesitantly, squinting in the half-light.

Andy paused and turned around. Beck noted that he was bathed in sweat and a trickle of blood from his nostril had dried on his upper lip.

Beck nodded, gesturing wordlessly at Andy's face. Andy wiped his nose with his hand and looked down at the flakes of dried blood on his skin.

"What gives, man? You turn gay all of a sudden?"

Andy smiled wanly, dropped the scrubbing brush into the toilet bowl, and collapsed back against the wall. Beck suddenly realized that Andy's stringy, greasy hair was gone. Andy had shaved it all off - crudely though. He now sported a crew cut similar to Beck's, only not quite as short. Beck noticed several nicks and cuts in Andy's scalp, some of which showed dried and crusted blood.

"Couldn't sleep," Andy wheezed. The fumes of the bathroom cleaner had infiltrated his nostrils. "Kept having bad dreams. I couldn't look at this fucking pigsty anymore."

Andy paused, pointing limply at the shower recess. The curtain was gone.

"I'll replace that. I'd hate to think how much *scuzz* was growing in that old one."

Beck nodded slowly.

"Fair enough, man. Whatever you think is best. Are you feelin' OK?"

Andy looked up at Beck and shook his head slowly.

"No. I've got the shakes. Got 'em real bad."

A long moment of silence settled between them. Beck had watched Andy fight his addiction before, knowing that he usually succumbed to temptation. Andy squeezed his eyes shut then opened them again, refocusing on Beck.

"I'll be OK. I just need to clean. I - uh - rearranged your DVDs. I hope, you know, that was OK."

Beck brushed it aside with a nod.

"No problem at all. You did an awesome job. I should've got off my ass long ago and done this myself."

Andy chuckled bitterly and he peeled off the rubber gloves he was wearing. His eyes drifted up to the ceiling.

"I can't go on like this," he said solemnly.

Beck sensed what Andy was getting at. He was struck by Andy's candor. He leaned his head against the door frame appraising his troubled housemate.

"Hmm," Beck replied simply. "You know - I've never judged, you man, because you pay your rent and bills. But - you're on a really shitty path. Those cocksuckers who hang off you, they're wrong for you, Dev. *They aren't you.* You can do a lot better."

Andy nodded and wiped his brow.

"I gotta get some sleep, man," Beck said, and he backed away from the doorway, about to turn towards his bedroom when he hesitated. He leaned back into the doorway of the bathroom and gestured with a nod at Andy's head.

"By the way - nice buzz cut, dude."

***

The following morning Andy arrived early at the Conservatory and went to his pigeonhole in the faculty office, where he found an envelope waiting for him. Sitting in the student lounge, Andy held the sheet of paper and stared at it. He was neither elated nor disappointed, just relieved. He had passed the exam - barely. The mark wasn't great, but it was a pass. For the time being, at least, Andy was still in the school.

Slowly he stood and put the piece of paper in his backpack. He turned to leave the lounge and his eyes fell across a large student notice board that hung from the wall nearby. It was filled with notices, student fliers, and posters advertising various musical events. Andy wandered over, drawn to one particular poster that hung in the bottom right-hand corner, set away from the others.

He leaned in close, scanning the poster.

MELBOURNE INTERNATIONAL
FESTIVAL OF THE GUITAR
VICTORIA, AUSTRALIA, 15TH - 21ST FEBRUARY.
FEATURING INTERNATIONALLY RENOWNED ARTISTS
INCLUDING SLAVA AND LEONARD GRIGORYAN,
DOUG DE VRIES, ANDREW YORK AND PAUL KELLY.

THE WEEK-LONG FESTIVAL TO BE HELD IN
MELBOURNE'S BEAUTIFUL FITZROY GARDENS
OFFERS THE OPPORTUNITY FOR
EMERGING ARTISTS TO
PERFORM ALONGSIDE THE MASTERS
OF CLASSICAL GUITAR.

A yellow rectangle of paper had been taped to the bottom corner.

Andy shook his head. This was the pinnacle event for students attending the Conservatory. To play at a prestigious international gathering and be recognized was the chance of a lifetime. One that he would have once aspired to, wholeheartedly. He knew he had no chance of being selected. His pattern of behavior had garnered him a reputation that made him the butt of jokes and the target of a faculty that wanted him gone. It was a lost cause - and he hadn't even applied. Finally, he turned away from the poster and left the building, unaware that a set of eyes had been watching him from the opposite corner of the lounge area. Veldtman watched Andy go, then shut the door to her office.

Andy attended all his classes that day and the next, only skipping a Friday afternoon lecture because he needed to get to The Pub for his shift. No one at The Pub mentioned his starkly different appearance. Andy just got in and worked hard, maintaining the momentum that had taken everyone by surprise a few days earlier.

His cell phone vibrated in his pocket during the afternoon and Andy slipped behind the bar and answered, crouching in the cubbyhole where he'd hung his bag. It was Vasq.

"I'm just checking in to make sure you're still good for the Warehouse job tomorrow night, Dev."

Andy hesitated, remembering that he had indeed committed to another job for Vasq.

"Yeah. I remember."

"I'll look forward to seeing you then. I gotta good feeling about this one, Dev. You're gonna make us a lot of money this time."

The way Vasq said that last sentence made Andy feel cold. Usually the mention of money was more than enough of a motivator for him. But he felt as though he was an instrument that belonged to

Vasq - a willing one, at that. Andy brushed the feelings aside as he ended the call and resumed his work.

***

Andy sat quietly at the end of the bar reading a text book during his break later that evening. Samantha brought a meal from the kitchen out to him.

"Thank you," he said quietly, and he turned the book over so as not to lose his place.

Samantha watched him curiously as he began eating, and after several seconds he looked up at her, making her shift her eyes away quickly.

"What?" he asked.

"N-nothing," she stammered. "It's just not like you to thank anyone for anything."

Andy eyed her briefly as he took a mouthful of food.

"I, uhh - your haircut looks good," Samantha offered. "You actually look pretty decent without all that crap hanging down over your face. I see you've dropped the nail polish, too."

Andy brushed his hand over his hair.

"It's OK," he said through a mouthful of mashed potato.

Samantha sensed she wasn't going to get anything more out of Andy, so she turned back to her work.

"This is probably the best meal I've eaten in months," he said suddenly. "If I'd known this was one benefit of actually working, I would've got my ass into gear long ago."

Samantha smiled at the comment and turned back towards him.

This was unusual, she thought.

"Well, if you keep this up you're gonna discover a lot more benefits in *actually* working here." She gestured with a nod behind her. "They're talking, you know. About you, trying to figure you out."

Andy shrugged.

"Nothing to figure out," he said.

Samantha eyed him skeptically.

"Something happened to you, didn't...," her voice trailed off as something caught her eye behind him. Her mouth opened in surprise.

Andy turned in his seat as a tall figure entered the bar. It was a man dressed in jeans, a thick, woolen tartan jacket and a grubby-looking trucker's cap bearing a Golden Breed logo. A match protruded from the corner of his mouth.

Bruce DeVries, Andy's father, regarded his surroundings dourly. His dark eyes fixed upon Andy for a moment, and Andy returned his father's gaze with a look of awkward hope.

Abruptly, Bruce turned sideways and walked through the bar, disappearing through the bistro entrance, completely ignoring his son.

Samantha felt a sharp twinge of embarrassment. Andy, clearly crestfallen, turned back to his meal and ate a few mouthfuls silently. She could see that his appetite had already left him and eventually he abandoned the dinner plate altogether. He got up from the bar and disappeared into the nearby men's room.

***

Bruce DeVries and Gideon Allan's friendship went back 20 years to the time of the first Gulf War. They had served together. Their friendship was an enduring constant in both their lives despite the failures of other, arguably more significant relationships.

Bruce had been drinking at The Public House for as long as anyone could remember. He often dropped by before heading out on the highway on his long-haul runs. He'd catch up with Gideon, have a bite to eat and then begin his run to the West Coast.

Rarely, if ever, did Bruce DeVries talk with his son. In fact, Bruce hadn't expected Andy to be here this evening. Had he known, he probably wouldn't have come. Their relationship hadn't been strong, not since Bruce had returned home from Iraq and the horrors of his tour there - horrors he had never spoken of. Once Andy's mother left, things became worse. Bruce withdrew further and had it not been for Bruce's mother stepping in to take on the care of Andy and his older sister, their circumstances might have been a lot worse. Bruce DeVries had taken little interest in his children. In recent years, he had patched up his relationship with his daughter - Andy's sister - who was living in San Francisco with her Army Officer husband. Bruce often stopped by there while he was in town. Andy and Bruce's relationship, however, was far more fractured. When Andy's talent for the guitar began to shine, Bruce dismissed it as a waste of time. Once Andy began living on his own and got mixed up with Vasq, the alienation between father and son became more acute.

So it was significant that Bruce DeVries reappeared at the bar a little over an hour and a half later, just as Andy was finishing up his last few jobs. Samantha nudged Andy as he unloaded a tray from the glass washer and nodded.

Andy set the tray down and wiped his hands with a towel. He looked up at his father: the square jaw with a five o'clock shadow, the dark thinning hair that was graying at the temples, dark eyes that avoided looking at his son directly.

Neither seemed able to open the dialogue. Samantha watched them from the other end of the bar, where she was serving.

Finally Bruce DeVries spoke:

"I'm heading to San Francisco tonight." His voice was gravelly and deep. "Be away maybe four, five days."

After a long moment, Andy nodded.

"Your sister called." Bruce continued. "She mentioned the hospital. They contacted her when you were brought in. Next of kin apparently."

"Yeah ... well," Andy rubbed his forehead and fidgeted nervously with his foot at a spot on the floor. "It was nothin'."

Bruce fingered his watch. Then he drew up his jacket zipper. The scowl that tugged at the corners of his lips was withering.

"Wake up to yourself. You're a fucking disgrace."

Bruce turned abruptly, strode from the bar and was gone.

Andy stood there, as expressionless as his father had been. His jaw tightened imperceptibly.

He felt crushed.

Chapter 7

The Warehouse stood in an industrial sector that was slowly being taken over by residential development - the kind that appealed to upwardly mobile career professionals looking for a cheap path into that chic, trendy inner-city lifestyle. The area was in a state of transition right now, though. Development was sporadic, untidy. The Warehouse sat well away from any of the new buildings. It was already owned by a developer, someone Emilio Vasq knew, so the trance parties that were routinely held there had been given an unofficial blessing. Also, there was significant money to be made. Vasq had cut the developer in on a significant piece of the action.

On Saturday nights this dilapidated building came to life. The Warehouse was fairly pumping right now. A dance floor occupied the center of the floor space, presided over by a raised stage upon which a DJ bounced around like some enraptured priest as he manned a massive soundboard and music station. The music was urban, primal, erotic. The dance floor was packed to capacity with steamy young revelers, hypnotized by the music's throbbing intensity. It was hot and stifling but overhead, a bank of sprinklers - part of the warehouse's original fire safety system - turned on and off intermittently spraying the party goers with cooling water, wetting them down. Clothing stuck to the skin. Clothing came off. The energy was arousing.

Elsewhere, a makeshift bar served beer, wine and spirits next to a group of lounges that sat in the remnants of an old office space and formed a kind of retreat where people relaxed, drank, smoked, took pills and took each other.

Andy, Cassie and a trio of Cassie's girl friends - all armed with long-neck beers - made their way through the throng of people awaiting service at the bar.

As he had done so many times before, Andy had spent the night working the venue for Vasq, selling product, collecting revenue, cultivating new buyers. He knew the regulars and the uninitiated who were yet to try. Andy knew how to sell. He was influential in his style without being pushy. He used his physicality, his eyes, his smile and sometimes his sexuality to procure a buyer regardless of their gender. He knew exactly what to say and how to say it. His gift was a potent one. His prowess was known to most of the partygoers here. Andy was admired, envied and desired.

Tonight, though, Andy didn't feel the rush he normally got when dealing. The call from Vasq had unsettled him. He was nervous, constantly looking over his shoulder, suspicious that he was being watched. He worried that the police who had seen him in the hospital might have somehow worked out who he was and decided to tail him.

But there was something else.

Somewhere deep inside him, he felt an alien disgust at what he was doing. He was dealing in drugs, dangerous drugs; it was wrong. Never before had he questioned what he was doing. He just did it, asked no questions and took his cut. As he dealt here and now, he found himself questioning them. He had no idea what this shit contained. For all he knew it could have been battery acid. It was destructive. It was lethal. He had his own experiences to vouch for that. Tonight, he regarded his clients with contempt. They were fools, just as he was a fool. He wrestled with a potent hatred for them and for himself.

But where were these thoughts coming from?

Andy felt that strange presence right now, moving with him through the room and silently taunting him, spurring his sense of disgust.

His remembered his father's words.

"Wake up to yourself. You're a fucking disgrace."

As they walked towards the lounge area he felt relieved that the job was over. All that was left was to liaise with Vasq, settle his account and have a few drinks. They stepped through what had once been a wall into the lounge area.

Cassie had been angry at Andy all evening. She wanted to know why he hadn't returned any of her calls and why he hadn't wanted to see her since they'd had sex earlier in the week. It wasn't enough for her to accept that he had fallen behind with his studies and that he'd had to work - even though he had apologized for not calling. The kicker tonight, however, was something far more petty. Cassie was angry with him for having cut off his hair. He no longer looked cool. She had bickered with him and taunted him; putting him in a foul mood.

They spotted Vasq's crew, who occupied a group of ripped and tattered leather couches in the center of the room and made their way over.

Vasq watched Andy as they approached. For a second there seemed to be a potent tension in his demeanor, but then he stood with arms outstretched.

"Dev! My man," he embraced Andy in a crude Latino imitation of Denzel Washington. "It's a testament to your spirit that you would return so soon after your ordeal."

Vasq pointed at each of the men sitting around him before gesturing at Andy.

"Learn from this guy. He should serve as an example!"

Vasq's crew glared at Andy while they made room so that he and Cassie could sit. Two of the girls paired up with men from Vasq's crew. The third girl, Alyson, a nubile young blonde, sat down beside Cassie and wriggled in close to her.

"I am glad you came, Dev. I hope I didn't cause any problems at your place of gainful employment."

Andy couldn't work out whether Vasq was being serious or not, so he just nodded.

"It's OK ... just don't do it again."

Vasq smiled, lowering his voice just enough to emphasize that he was talking to Andy rather than the others.

"I have to say, friend: it would seem this experience has changed you some, though. You seem a lot bolder in the way you present yourself."

Andy fidgeted with his beer and made an overly exaggerated attempted to relax back on the couch.

"Well - facing death will do things to you. It messes with your head."

"Hmmm," Vasq took a long swig from his beer then nodded outwards into the crowd. "We are doing very well tonight, my friend."

"There's more product out there than I've seen in a while," Andy replied. "The quality is good."

Vasq draped an arm over Andy's shoulders.

"I was thinking more in terms of your particular skills. Dev. Your ability to distribute. It is truly a gift."

Andy hesitantly reached into his jacket and took out a thick wad of cash. He handed it discreetly to Vasq, who grinned with satisfaction. He unrolled it, checked the amount then thumbed out several notes and handed them back to Andy.

"And how much was it that you earned pulling beers this week?" Vasq queried with another smile. He looked around at the crew, signaling for them to leave him and Andy alone.

Andy turned to Cassie.

"Why don't you go dance? Enjoy yourself."

Cassie looked at him with some contempt, but it quickly melted and she kissed him tenderly on the cheek. As she got up with Alyson and took her hand, Andy handed her a small piece of foil.

Cassie smiled, quickly unwrapping it to find two blue pills. She handed one to Alyson, who eagerly took it and slipped the other under her tongue.

Finally Vasq and Andy were alone. Vasq took two of his own foils out of his jacket and offered one to Andy. Andy looked at it coldly and shook his head. Vasq raised an eyebrow, but didn't push it.

"I was worried about you, Dev," he said. "I was beginning to think that experience of yours had damaged you. Why didn't you return my calls?"

Andy took another swig of his beer and shrugged. He surveyed the crowd on the dance floor, particularly Cassie and Alyson, who were already rubbing up against each other and kissing passionately. Though he was used to this kind of behavior from her in the past, Andy suddenly found himself inexplicably jealous.

"I have to say, man, your girl looks severely fuckable right now, doesn't she?"

Something clicked inside Andy and he felt as though he was suffocating. The room began to spin, and all he wanted to do was to get out of here as quickly as he could. He took a deep breath and turned towards Vasq.

"I don't know if I can do it anymore, Emilio," Andy said in his best attempt at sounding matter-of-fact.

The statement caught Vasq by surprise - so much so that he choked on his beer.

"Are you serious?" the Latino retorted. "You've conducted one of your best runs tonight, man. The product is good, everybody is happy. You're just still a little shaky from your ordeal."

"No, Vasq, I'm not. I've been doing a lot of thinking and I don't think I'm cut out for this anymore. I've been marked by the police now, so I'm a risk to you. And I'm losing the drive for it."

Vasq shifted in his seat, irritated.

"Andy, you are my best courier. No one can move around a room the way you do. None of the crew will measure up to your skill. If it's a question of money, I can cut you in on a better deal."

Vasq immediately drew out the wad of cash again, and thumbed out a few extra bills. Andy waved it away.

"It's not about the money, Emilio. Look, you've got two or three guys already who could take over. Chew's been working rooms, and he's got contacts with infrastructure. Sanchez is nimble enough. You don't need me."

Vasq's expression darkened and he gripped his beer bottle harder.

"But you see. I *do* need you, *dawg*," he leaned in close, lowering his voice until it was barely a whisper. "None of these fucks are gonna measure up. You're my best asset, my cash cow, baby. I can't just let you go that easily."

Vasq nodded across the room to the edge of the lounge where two large and imposing bouncers stood. Both were dressed in tight-fitting black tees, their meaty hands adorned with large jewelry. They were watching Vasq and Andy warily.

Andy's heart thudded noisily in his ears. The presence was there again, silently influencing him, directing him. Andy met Vasq's eyes with a piercing determination.

"Don't threaten me, Emilio," he whispered shakily. "It doesn't become you."

Andy got up off the couch and straightened his jacket.

"I'm done with this, *this ... bullshit*!"

He turned away. Instantly, Vasq's men approached him as he stepped through the ruined wall.

"Are you kidding me, Emilio?" Andy stopped, turning his back on the two men and facing Vasq. There was a fire in his eyes and, as he stood over Vasq, the normally cocksure man began to wilt.

"You want me to bring you down? I can, if you'd like. I can give the police everything - the suppliers, the networks, the crews you've got sucking your dick!" Vasq shrank further as Andy unleashed a potent anger. "I want to step away now before it kills me, Vasq! I've got no problem with you, but if you fuck with me, I will bring it all down. All of it!"

Vasq was stunned. His two lackeys appeared unsure of what to do. Andy spun around and marched towards the men as if to go through them. One of them put his hand up instinctively and shoved it into Andy's chest, but he slapped it away angrily, brushing the taller man aside. They looked to Vasq for guidance, but this time he shook his head, signaling them to back off.

On the dance floor, Cassie and Alyson continued their flirtations while others around them were getting similarly amorous. Cassie was aroused by the effects of the drug as much as the feel of Alyson's body, her skin, her lips.

Cassie saw Andy out of the corner of her eye, pushing his way through the crowd. She drew back from Alyson and watched him through her ecstasy haze, blunted concern tugging at her altered consciousness. Somehow her mind shook itself back to lucid attention once she realized that he was leaving.

"Wait for me," she told Alyson, kissing her lips softly before stepping away.

Andy pushed through a group of people at the entrance to the Warehouse and stepped out into the cold night air. He felt a nauseating panic rising from the pit of his stomach. Emilio Vasq had been sat on his ass, but Andy was under no illusions that Vasq wasn't capable of retaliating. Andy's emotions spun like a tornado as he tried to get the silent presence out of his head - the presence he was sure had influenced him in shutting the door on Vasq. He had to get away from here now - as far away as he could from this place, from this life.

As he crossed over a thoroughfare that had once been the Warehouse's parking lot, Andy glanced back over his shoulder and saw a trio of young women stumbling about in what he recognized as a drug-induced stupor. One of them was teetering on the verge of unconsciousness. Her companions tried to support her while she vomited in a gutter. She was pale, gaunt, sweating profusely. Andy stopped. The girl lifted her head towards him and in that moment, his eyes met hers. He was horrified by what he saw.

He saw nothing.

Her eyes were devoid of color. They were devoid of life. She was already dead.

Spying the fenced entrance to the Warehouse, Andy broke into a jog, heading towards a line of taxis that were dropping off and picking up partygoers outside the perimeter.

"Andy!"

He stopped suddenly at the sound of Cassie's voice and turned to see her walking unsteadily towards him.

"What are you doing?" she shouted. "Where are you going?"

"I'm going home. I don't wanna be here anymore."

Incredulity crossed Cassie's features as she stepped yet closer to him.

"What is going on with you, Dev? Something's seriously fucked you up."

Andy looked skyward with a pained expression.

"I don't want it no more, Cee. This ain't living! It's fucking slavery."

"What are you talking about, Dev? You're the one who's in control. Vasq and the others rely on you. *They're* the slaves! Not you!"

Andy shook his head in frustration and tossed his bottle to the ground. It clinked and rolled noisily across the pavement.

"I'm not in control of anything, Cee! My whole life is a fraud. *This!* All this…" He held his arms out to this world around them. "It's no good. I need to get out while I still can."

"You are so full of shit," Cassie spat. "What have you got to get away from? This is what you do. This is what you're good at. They love you in there! You're somebody in there! Outside you're *nothing!*"

Andy smiled bitterly at Cassie's revealing tirade. He turned from her, his shoulders slumped as he walked away.

Cassie, unable to comprehend his behavior, screamed after him: "What are you doing to me?!"

In an act of pure, reflexive rage she pitched her beer bottle at him. Her aim was true, striking the back of his head. Andy yelped in pain and he staggered, putting a hand up to the bleeding gash. He felt sick at the sight of his own blood.

He glared at Cassie, who fell to her knees, stunned at what she had just done. Then he turned away again and continued walking.

"Andy!" Cassie cried, breaking down in tears where she had collapsed. "I'm sorry! Come back!"

Andy had already disappeared into a nearby cab.

Chapter 8

"You've got to go gently, from the quick to the end."

They sat at opposite ends of the sofa. Denny was crouched over Sonya's left foot, cradling it in one hand and holding an applicator brush in the other. A small bottle of nail polish sat on the coffee table beside him and every so often, he delicately dipped the brush in and applied a layer of polish to her toes.

It was dark outside, even though it was only early afternoon. Rain fell harshly against the roof and the window panes of the old beach house; the sea beyond boiled and bubbled under the might of the storm. Angry white-topped breakers pounded the shoreline. Here inside, with a warm fire crackling in the potbellied stove in the corner of the living room, they were oblivious to it all. Sonya leaned back and closed her eyes, luxuriating in the sensual grip of Denny's hand as he gave his first pedicure. He sat deep in concentration, a slight quiver to his hand as he held the brush. He clenched his tongue between his teeth as he brought the brush down, attempting a delicate brush stroke of the rich burgundy polish across her toenail.

"Now, don't let it clump there, otherwise you'll have to wipe it off and start over," Sonya chided with a wicked smile.

She had been teasing him without mercy since they'd started this exercise. The rain had brought them indoors from working on the house. They'd showered together, making love underneath the water. He'd washed her hair with her favorite shampoo, rosemary and mint. He'd brushed it lovingly.

Denny flashed her a glower with his eyes, without altering the rest of his face at all. His tongue quivered at the corner of his mouth.

"Concentrate," she snapped, barely able to contain herself as she sipped at the glass of wine she held.

Denny calmly set the brush down in the top of the bottle, adjusted his grip on her ankle, then - without warning - he tickled the underside of her foot. She giggled furiously and bucked her leg wildly in his grip. She was unable to shake it.

"Denny, stop it!" she squealed. "You're terrible!"

"And you're a pain in the arse," Denny shot back, chuckling as he continued to tickle her.

Sonya felt dizzy, felt her breath leave her from her fits of giggling. Then Denny stopped tickling and began massaging her sole tenderly. Instantly Sonya caught herself and took a deep breath in before melting under his soft and delicate touch. She sighed, submitting to him, closing her eyes and laying her head back on the arm of the sofa.

"Now, do you want to try this again?" he asked gently, pressing his thumb into the ball of her foot, releasing a knot of tension.

"Mmm-hmm," Sonya whispered. "As long as you do it properly."

She opened one eye and grinned mischievously at him. Denny responded by tickling her sole once more, but this time with less fervor.

Sonya giggled softly again, and Denny dipped the brush into the polish and took it out, holding it up and glancing at her expectantly, as though he was waiting for her to give him permission to proceed.

Sonya nodded and gazed into his eyes, holding them in her own.

His eyes.

They were among his most beautiful features, and had caught her attention when they first met. They were wondrous orbs, full of intelligence and soul, filled with a kindness that radiated outward and influenced anybody who met him. They were filled with love. For her. For this life.

Denny looked back down at Sonya's slender foot and began painting her toenail again.

She smiled warmly, wishing this moment would never end.

***

Rain fell outside, pattering against the window. It was a gentle sound, not at all disruptive. It was peaceful, an almost perfect accompaniment to the sound of the guitar.

Andy sat on the bed in his pajama bottoms, his head leaning against the headboard, supported by a pillow. The bandaged cut on his scalp still throbbed painfully, but he tried his best to block it out. He was gazing through the window, not really focusing on anything. A pair of potted seedlings sat on the window sill. They were herbs - one rosemary, one mint - that he had bought from the grocery store on his way home.

He had never owned an actual houseplant.

The act of their purchase was bizarre enough, even to him. But their combined fragrance - subtle as it was - reminded him of something he could not put his finger on. Something familiar that, whatever it was, lay just beyond the edge of his memory.

It had maddened him.

Right now, his mind was attuned to the sound of the guitar he played.

He played the melody over and over, mentally adjusting his finger technique each time to perfect the chord progression. He was meticulous in that way. One of Andy's greatest qualities was the technical skill he brought to his guitar playing. It was a quality that had been evident ever since he had begun to play as a child. The song he played now, the opening interlude from the Foo Fighters' "Come Alive," wasn't especially challenging. It was just that he *felt* it, felt its mood, and it carried him along. The sensation was pleasant.

There was a certain irony to the ballad. To him, it was a story of reflection, of a troubled soul examining his life and realizing how much of it he has wasted. In the aftermath of the night before, Andy found himself examining his own circumstance.

He had existed in a monochromatic underworld whose color was illusory and sounds aurally bankrupt. The drugs just gave the impression that there was something better within it. It was all false - a simulacrum that drew you in like the web of a spider and snared you there.

His friendships were just empty acquaintances, relationships built on desperate need. They would destroy you as easily as nurture you, and they almost always did the former. There was no truth to them. All they wanted from him were the drugs. It was all so meaningless.

Closing his eyes, Andy felt something changing within him. This presence seemed to hover around him. He could feel it getting stronger, he was more aware of it. It scared him and yet, at the same time, he drew a strange sort of comfort from it.

Who was this presence that was speaking to him, showing him those potent visions?

Andy knew that wherever these dreams were coming from, the presence had something to do with them.

The music soothed him as he fingered the strings gently, expertly, the tone bouncing into the guitar and returning melodically without a hint of scratching. The hum was pure, more pure than any drug. It lifted him, carried him.

The guitar, a Taylor GS series model fashioned from Indian rosewood and cedar, was the one possession of real value to him. It had been a gift from his grandmother, before she had died, when he had been accepted into the Conservatory. His grandmother, who had essentially raised him in the frequent absences of his father, was the only person Andy had really cared for. She had loved him and nurtured him. She ensured that he and sister were well cared for, had clothes and food and even had decent medical insurance - another thing she struggled to afford. But she would not allow her grandchildren to suffer the indignities of a fractured health system.

The cell phone on his desk vibrated. He gave it a cursory glance, but made no effort to get off the bed. It was probably Cassie. He wasn't going to answer it. He wanted nothing from her. Vasq had called also, but Andy ignored him too. He wanted even less from him. Andy had retreated here and closed the door, locking himself away from everyone and everything.

Andy stopped, relaxed his grip on the guitar and leaned forward, wincing as his head throbbed painfully. He thought he should be doing something, but there was nothing to do. He often felt this way after a night working a room - the need to do something honest, cleansing. He wasn't required at The Pub today, though he half considered calling in and offering himself up for a few hours. That would really knock the stuffing out of Gideon. Instead, he relaxed back on the bed and considered his guitar once again.

Picking it up, he stretched his fingers and set them to the strings and fret board. He began tentatively playing *Deciso*, the first movement from Astor Piazzolla's renowned Tango Suite, an intricate and rapid-fire stanza whose opening refrain Andy had been practicing for some time. The piece required intense concentration, especially for someone unfamiliar with its movement. Though it was composed for a guitar duet, Andy played a single part, imagining the other as he played.

His natural gift allowed him to relax and he began to play more fluidly. He closed his eyes, concentrating. Then he was drifting - to a place he knew...

The beach house had a balcony overlooking the sea, the same stretch of ocean front he remembered from his dream. It stood at the top of a meadow bordered by the sandy shore.

It is an old house, a beach house. An aged retreat furnished lightly with the kind of second-hand accoutrements one would save for a holiday retreat rather than consign them to the rubbish heap. There's a slightly lumpy double bed in the master bedroom, bunk beds in the second bedroom, an old sofa in the lounge room - slightly moth-eaten, but sturdy - an ancient leather arm chair next to that with splits on the seat and broken springs.

The house smells of the ocean. A breeze wafts in from the open french doors that lead to the deck. Seagulls caw nearby. A dog barks, down on the sand.

A young man lounges in the old armchair. He holds a guitar in his arms, cradling it as though it were a natural extension of his body. Andy is in the room with him. He watches him from behind.

The young man plays the guitar.

Andy joins him. Together they play expertly, in concert with one another. For Deciso is a movement for two guitars.

They progress through the movement together, journeying through its lyrical dance. They play as though they have always played together; because in a way they have.

The young man looks up and out through the billowing curtains, through the balcony rail to the beach where she plays with the dog. What he sees, Andy sees, because Andy has become him. A woman is throwing the ball to the pup who chases after it eagerly, up and down the sand.

It is her.

It is Sonya.

Her shoulder-length auburn hair billows out and catches the breeze, blowing about her beautiful face. She wears an oversized knitted jacket over her bikini and pair of canvas shoes on her feet.

She is so vibrant, so alive, so beautiful. His heart aches for her.

She runs up the sand, across the grass and up the hill towards the house. The dog trails happily behind her, the ball in his mouth.

Then she is beside him, lounging back on the arm of the chair, a glass of wine in hand as she listens to him play. She gently strokes his hair and smiles ... listens to them play.

Andy watches, yet he is experiencing the touch of her hand on his skin at the same time.

How could that be?

He looks up at her, a loving gaze, and she leans down kisses him tenderly, fully on the lips. Her lips linger there.

Andy can feel her touch on his lips. The electricity of the kiss passes through him.

How could that be?

The guitar is set aside and she is in his lap now. They are passionate, lingering in an embrace, lingering in a kiss.

She whispers to him, "I love you, Denny."

Andy's eyes snapped opened and, for a moment, he was disoriented. He looked around urgently until he realized he was still in his bedroom, still in the apartment. The rain still fell outside the window.

"Denny?" He said the name out loud as if to test its sound on his lips. It felt instinctively natural.

He *knew* this name. How or why he knew, he couldn't explain. He just did.

Laying the guitar down on the bed beside him Andy got up and went to the bathroom, filled the basin with cold water and lowered his face into it, holding himself there for a good 30 seconds. His mind continued to flash images. Images of other people, of another place, another time. There was vibrant color and light, the fresh smells of the sea and the countryside and the sweet tastes in the air. They contrasted with the dull gray of his surroundings here and now.

Drawing himself out of the water, he wiped his face with a towel and looked in the mirror. Andy was sure he knew those people, and that place. But how?

He had never even ventured out of this city, let alone been to a place like that - a seaside town, an idyllic place.

He gazed at his reflection in the mirror. His gaunt features, his severely close-shaved head, his eyes.

His eyes.

He focused on them now, looking deep into the iris, studying the pattern of the green striations around his pupil; patterns that were as individual and as unique as his own fingerprint.

Except his eyes had always been brown.

Andy blinked, startled at what he was seeing.

They were green. And then they were brown.

Green - then brown. Changing each time he blinked.

Shocked, Andy staggered back from the mirror.

What was going on here?

He rubbed his hand over his forehead. He looked in the mirror again.

"Are you doing this to me? ...Denny?"

***

Dawn on the other side of the world. The early morning sun peeked up and over the horizon, heralding the new day. It rose slowly, languidly over the calm sea casting warm, golden rays across the water and the sky above, where it touched the underside of billowing clouds, imbuing them with a pinkish hue.

There was just a hint of a breeze. It was cool. The few denizens that occupied the beach were rugged up. Their breath was visible in the crisp morning air. The water was choppy, but not fiercely so.

A line of jacarandas that flanked a thin bitumen road above the beach swayed gently. The scent of nearby eucalyptus, melded with the salty spray coming off the ocean, giving the air a sweet earthiness.

This tranquil scene of the New South Wales south coast greeted a lone figure who appeared over a rise on the road above the beach. She paused briefly by the side of the road, putting her hand to her brow to take in the picture-perfect dawn.

A pair of sea birds soared lazily over the water, scanning for an opportunity to snare an early breakfast. On the beach, an elderly couple power-walked along the sand, past a couple of curmudgeonly fishermen who were bickering about something they'd heard on the morning news that was blaring from a battered transistor radio. A trio of young surfers sat on their boards, just beyond the breakers, engaged in an intellectual discussion about the water and weather conditions at this moment. A group of seniors practiced Tai Chi on the grass a little further up the beach, completely absorbed in the serenity of the early morning and the harmony of their movements.

The young woman, dressed in an oversized woolen cardigan, knee-length shorts and canvas boating shoes, adjusted her shoulder bag. She then continued along the road that wound down along the coast towards the sleepy seaside village that lay just a few hundred yards ahead.

A black-and-white cross-breed cattle dog trotted a few feet in front of her, wagging his tail.

Sonya Llewellyn smiled at the occupants on the beach, each of them engaged in their leisurely pursuits. It was peaceful. It made her heart feel light.

Simon the dog seemed unfazed by the activity and was completely oblivious to it all. Their early morning walk - their constitutional - was unmissable so far as he was concerned. If Sonya so much as brushed passed the dog lead that hung on the hook just outside the back door of the beach house, Simon would spin himself into a flurry of yapping that wouldn't let up until she diverted his attention with a special treat - or she relented. He was easy to please.

At 5 o'clock each morning, Sonya and Simon were up and out on the beach for their regular walk. Sometimes she resisted it, especially when it was cold out and the warmth of her bed was impossible to surrender. But this was a tradition begun during the first few months of this dog's life by his former "master," who would never dream of missing an early morning walk, no matter what the weather might be. Now that Denny was no longer here, Sonya felt it her duty to continue the tradition.

No longer here...

It had been a year since Denny's death.

Sonya couldn't quite comprehend it. It still seemed as though it had been only a few days since he'd died. Even now, part of her refused to believe that Denny, the love of her life, was gone.

The beach house Denny and Sonya had bought near the town of Hambledown was dilapidated, but it had perfect views and a quaint feel; and it was theirs. Everything was here in this little hamlet by the sea. Her work at her grandfather's law practice. Denny's career. Their house. Their *life*. It was to be their wonderful future. Now it was just Sonya and Simon. She had learned to function, but only barely.

Hambledown's General Store was already open at this early hour. A newspaper van sat outside idling as the driver unloaded several bundles of newspapers. He greeted Sonya as she approached.

"G'day, love. Nice morning for it."

Simon lowered his head and stiffened as the driver, Jim, approached him. He growled in the pit of his throat.

"Oh come on, pup. No one's going to hurt you," Jim chided gently.

Simon bared his teeth then and, as Jim went to put out his hand, the dog barked angrily, causing him to withdraw instinctively. Sonya dropped to her haunches and pulled Simon back.

"I'm so sorry, Jim. He still has this thing about men."

Jim chuckled and rose to his full height.

"It's fine, love. Some dogs are just hard to please, I guess."

Nodding, Sonya passed him, gesturing sharply for Simon to follow. Jim flashed a sympathetic smile as she passed him, then went back to his work.

At the entrance to the store, Sonya leaned down and pushed Simon's hind quarter down, forcing him to sit.

She gestured with an extended finger.

"Stay."

Simon whimpered softly and licked his chops, but he obeyed her.

Past the fresh vegetables and fruit, past neat aisles stocked with dry goods and condiments, past racks of freshly baked bread, Sonya made her way to the counter where she was greeted by a kind-faced man with neatly parted hair and a warm smile. He patted a newspaper and a loaf of bread that sat on the counter waiting for her. She smiled at his courteousness as he picked up a sealed cup from the counter behind him and sat it next to the items on the counter. The aroma of the freshly brewed coffee hit her nostrils instantly and she went straight for the cup.

The shopkeeper chuckled heartily.

"Don't laugh, Lionel," Sonya chided half-seriously. "I could kiss you right now."

Lionel Broadbent turned to a meat slicer behind him and switched it on. He shaved several slices of mild salami off a stumpy piece that hung in a group of similar smoked meats above his head. He wrapped the slices carefully and completed her purchase, placing them down next to the other items.

"There you are," he said, in a gravelly but very precise British accent. "Simon is set for the day."

Sonya regarded him with amusement as she took another mouthful of coffee.

"You know, it was *you two* who spoiled him. Simon is going to end up obese, I hope you realize."

Lionel chuckled softly at the nameless mention of Denny. He loaded the items into Sonya's shoulder bag while she sipped her coffee quietly. Realizing what she had said then, Sonya felt a twinge of emotion and she had to exert a great effort to stifle it.

Thankfully, she was distracted from her thoughts when a woman emerged from the rear of the shop and smiled upon seeing Sonya. Ruth Broadbent, Lionel's wife, sidled up to her husband and planted a kiss on his cheek then circled the counter to repeat the gesture with Sonya.

"How are you this morning love?" Ruth inquired breezily in a similarly precise British accent to Lionel's own.

Sonya returned the older woman's smile with her own and closed her eyes as Ruth squeezed her with one arm around her shoulders.

"Sleep deprived," Sonya replied dryly. "But well."

Ruth was slightly shorter than her husband, dressed in a billowing silk blouse and was adorned with large items of jewelry that framed her distinguished features. Her graying hair was cropped stylishly short.

Sonya noticed a large camera bag, hanging from Ruth's free shoulder.

"Off to capture some more images of beauty?"

Ruth regarded her bag with a lop sided grin.

"Sort of. I need to scout some locations for that wedding shoot this weekend. The Sallingers have expressed some concern about the old jetty. They think it's not aged enough."

"Ahh ... well. Mustn't do anything to upset the apple cart there," Sonya replied. "Jade Sallinger is some kind of *bride-zilla* so I've heard."

"Yes, indeed," Ruth responded malevolently. "Gillian down at the post office told me that Jade's mother is pushing her to see you about a pre-nuptial agreement. Can you imagine that sort of rubbish? It's ridiculous!"

"You know," Lionel began, searching for something to change the direction of their gossiping conversation. "People are talking about the practice; they are looking forward to your reopening. It'll be a relief for them not to have to travel down to the city to see a lawyer."

"Well, if I can get a second coat on the walls in the front area today," Sonya grinned knowingly at Lionel. "I'll be able to start seeing clients by the end of this week. It's just taken me a lot longer to clean up Harry's mess."

"Hmm," Lionel mused at the mention of her grandfather. "The old bugger died owing a lot of money. It was criminal for those creditors to come after you."

Sonya nodded as she downed the last few mouthfuls of her coffee. The hot liquid scalded the inside of her mouth.

"I guess they thought I was a soft target. I never did find out how much trouble Harry was in when he took me on. Fortunately, I've gotten myself back into the good books with most of his people. At the very least, they're taking my calls."

Sonya slung her now-full bag back on her shoulder and handed the empty cup to Lionel, along with a $10 note. Taking out the small parcel of sandwich meat, she flipped him a jaunty salute, then turned for the exit.

Both Lionel and Ruth watched her go.

"He - would have been proud of you."

Sonya paused and looked back at them as she put her hand to the door.

"Harry only ever cared about himself," she responded gruffly.

"Harry wasn't who I was talking about," Lionel replied.

Sonya wordlessly acknowledged his meaning. She turned the handle and slipped out silently.

Simon leapt up enthusiastically, pawing at Sonya's bare legs as she tried to tear an opening in the packaging and grasp a slice of the salami.

"Get down, you glutton," she scolded, dropping a slice into Simon's eagerly salivating jaws. He devoured the meat in seconds, then trotted along beside Sonya as she crossed over the street and walked a short distance along the path towards the center of the township, tossing him additional slices.

The old stone cottage stood in the main street directly across from the town's single pub. The sign that hung precariously from a rusted frame just near the gate said it all.

"Harold Llewellyn, Barrister."

Repainting the frame and replacing the sign was yet another item on her to-do list, but with everything else she had to get done just to start bringing in some income, this ranked very low right now.

So much to do.

She regarded the quaint cottage with a lopsided stare.

All of her energies were focused here on her grandfather's failed legacy. This was her life now: breathing life into a moribund practice.

At least it was the one life she could save.

Unlocking the door to the old cottage, Sonya ushered Simon through and stepped inside. She negotiated her way around a maze of painting equipment: two ladders resting against the wall, canvas drop sheets, cans of paint, brushes, rollers and other assorted paraphernalia of interior renovation.

Sonya surveyed the darkened former living room, which she had almost single-handedly converted into a smart reception desk and waiting area. It was quite an achievement given that, for the most part, she had no idea what she was doing. It was almost ready to be used now. It just needed a final coat of paint.

Sonya entered her office and made room on the cluttered desk to put her shoulder bag down. Simon trotted in after her and went for a battered wicker basket, filled with a pair of cushions, beside the desk.

Finally, Sonya flopped down in her own chair and kicked off her shoes, wriggling her toes with a sigh of relief. Simon sat up in his basket and pointed his ears towards her hopefully, noticing she still had one final slice of salami left in her hand.

Sonya regarded him sternly.

"You really are going to end up needing Jenny Craig for dogs, aren't you?"

Simon lowered his ears and whimpered plaintively, as he nudged her hand with his snout.

Shaking her head, Sonya allowed him to take the last slice in his teeth.

Then she checked her watch. It was still only 7 am - way too early to get cracking.

Sonya kept a supply of fresh toiletries here at the practice, so she did not need to worry about walking home again for a shower. Placing her feet on the corner of the desk, she leaned back and closed her eyes. It wouldn't hurt for her to have a power nap, she reasoned.

She allowed herself to drift. She lowered her head...

The darkness behind her eyes gave way to a smoky haze and, at first, she thought she was in a smoke-filled room that was on fire.

People surrounded her, chattering loudly. Glass clinked nearby. She wondered whether she was trapped in some stricken building, but as she got used to the haze, she realized the people were chatting and laughing and they were not under threat at all. The room was a smoky bar somewhere, but she didn't know where.

She turned towards the sound of an instrument nearby. Someone was playing.

A guitar, perhaps?

The people around her clinked their glasses as they drank and sang, joining in with whoever it was that was playing. The atmosphere was lively, warm and cheerful. She craned her neck to see over the people in front of her, to see who it was performing, but she couldn't make them out.

She began to work her way toward the front of the crowd. The sound of the guitar grew louder. Another throng of people prevented her from going any further, but now she could see past them to the guitar.

The arms that held the instrument were muscular, yet they held it with surprising delicacy. The fingers danced across the strings lightly, yet they elicited a sound that was pure and resonant.

Those hands.

She squinted in the half-light and saw the arm that held the head stock of the guitar. There, just above the fret board, she saw it. The inside of his forearm, just above the wrist. There was an inscription tattooed there.

Ancora Imparo.

Sonya gasped so loudly, she caused Simon to yelp and jump in his basket. She sat forward in her seat, as the fingers of the dream dissipated like tendrils of smoke. She grabbed reflexively at her chest, as if she were trying to slow her heartbeat.

The dream lingered and she shook her head to reorient herself. She looked down at Simon, who appeared a little spooked.

"That was intense," she whispered breathlessly.

Chapter 9

Changes...

Andy battled withdrawal like never before. The pall of his addiction came in the night and wracked his body with such violence and torment, he was sure he was going mad. For weeks and weeks, he denied his body the crystal meth that it had come to crave and it punished him dearly.

His head exploded in a firestorm of agony. His body sweated and cramped. Knives of pain assailed him, striking deep into his core. Night after night, he screamed into the darkness, clawing at his eyes, trying to reach whatever it was that was crawling around behind them. Night after night, he watched as the beads of sweat that bathed his skin turned into vicious, transparent beetles that crawled across his body. They clawed at his skin, burrowing into it and Andy could only watch in horror as they hollowed out bloodied craters in his abdomen and chest. He scratched at his body, trying to rid himself of the disgusting creatures, realizing through his fractured lucidity that they were figments of his twisted imagination. Night after night, he felt searing pain in his right arm, as though someone was taking a white hot branding iron and punching it into his skin.

He fought until he could stand it no longer - until he could feel it consuming him.

And then there was nothing. The torment gave way to serenity. He drew breath ... as did the presence.

He knew Andy had prevailed.

Waking to a new day, Andy rose early and did something he had not done in years. He went for a run. After putting on a couple of layers of clothing, Andy stepped out into the frigid morning air and jogged through the suburban streets of the city. His thoughts ran with him.

He felt numb. Empty. He could no longer reconcile himself to the life he had led, the depths to which he had sunk. In the pursuit of gaining approval from those who had sucked him into it and promised him so much, he had allowed himself to be used by them. He had been weak. He had so wanted to be like them that he would have done anything they had asked of him. In fact, he *had* done pretty much everything they had asked. And he had lost himself because of it.

Andy crossed over the street near The Pub and continued along the sidewalk under the elevated railway track. Once more, the incessant itching sensation rippled maddeningly through his right arm and he was forced to stop in order to scratch it.

"What the hell is that?" Andy cursed angrily as he forced back the sleeve of his jacket and woolen top.

He blinked in surprise at what he saw there.

It was a tattoo. An inscription had been inked into his skin in a cursive font that was beginning to blister as though it was brand new.

Ancora Imparo.

Andy studied the tattoo. He had no idea what it meant, nor could he remember, for the life of him, having gotten it.

Yet it was there, as new and as fresh as if he had gotten it yesterday.

The memory of the stoned girl at the Warehouse, being propped up by her friends, haunted him. He remembered her lifeless eyes. She had been so consumed by the drug, it had hollowed her out and poisoned her soul. She was empty. And, like her, Andy had become empty.

He had cared once. He had cared about his life, about himself and about his family. He had wanted more than an easy path to empty adoration. He had wanted the respect of others by earning it through hard work and effort. He had wanted to contribute to the lives of others. Through his own destructive selfishness, Andy had strayed from an honorable path and had lost himself.

It was time to find his way back.

Returning home from his run, Andy showered, packed his backpack and ate breakfast. He had a full day of classes at The Conservatory, then a shift at The Pub. He was solely focused on those two things.

As he sat at the table, he checked his phone. His message inbox was filled with voice mails and texts from Cassie and Vasq. He was less concerned about Cassie's messages than he was about Vasq's but, after considering them for a moment, Andy deleted them all without reading or listening to them.

On the train ride into the Conservatory, Andy watched the urban landscape pass by his window. As he drifted, he became aware of that presence again. Instinctively, he looked behind him. No one was sitting there. But someone was definitely here.

A hesitant idea formed in his mind. Andy closed his eyes, closed out all other sounds and distraction and listened to it.

He was aware now. Aware that he had not gone from this world ... that, indeed, it was not over. He didn't recognize this place or these people, but felt an affinity with this troubled individual to whom he had been given.

He knew every facet of Andy's life, had experienced every moment of it, in the short time he had been here. He sensed the ramifications Andy faced, if he were allowed to continue on his path of self-destruction. He had acted.

It was a second chance. A chance to effect change to help this man called Andy. And in the process, to help himself.

Andy's eyes opened, and he sat there as the echo of the presence began to dissipate. A curious smile tugged at the corner of his lips.

The presence was not around him. It was in him.

***

Andy noticed Samantha's troubled expression as she swung in behind the bar. He finished pouring a beer for Beck - who had dropped by a little while ago - and set it down on the counter top.

"What's wrong with you?" he asked.

"Ahhrghh," Samantha grumbled. She poured herself a beer and took an uncharacteristic swig. "Gideon is having a shit fit upstairs because the band for tonight pulled out at the last moment. He's letting *everyone* know about it."

Andy wiped down a section of the bar, then tossed his rag into the laundry basket behind Samantha as Beck took a long drink from his beer.

"Well, what happened, exactly?"

"Somebody's sick. Someone couldn't go through with it. I dunno. Gideon is ranting because he's been promoting this live music thing for weeks. He's barking at everyone and behaving like an asshole."

"Guess we better lie low, then," Andy said quietly, tossing a glance at Beck.

From the central bistro and entertainment area they could hear loud voices above the general chatter - voices engaged in an animated argument. Evidently, Gideon had descended from his upstairs office.

A few of the denizens of the front bar turned their heads in the direction of the din, though none of them broke ranks to go and butt in.

Andy, Samantha and Beck looked at one another. Andy quickly circled out of the bar. Samantha followed him, and together they stood off to one side of the entrance into the main dining area watching as Gideon stomped about - in front of guests - waving one arm as he bellowed down a cordless phone. The bistro manager and one of the bar staff trailed behind him, bickering at each other and at Gideon as he switched his rage between them and whoever it was at the other end of the phone.

A growing crowd of people was filling The Pub with the expectation that they were to see some traditional Irish music performed by a local trio whom Gideon had been negotiating with for several weeks. Though it was understandable that he should be upset at the last minute, venting his frustrations so publicly was ill-conceived.

"How do you expect me to explain to my patrons - some of whom expressly booked tickets - that the act they were expecting to see this evening has been canceled?!" he shouted.

Gideon listened to the response from the person at the other end of the phone with a stony face. For a moment his eyes met both Andy's and Samantha's. They cringed and retreated back to the bar.

"He's an idiot, that's for sure," Samantha remarked bitterly as she poured another beer for one of the regular barflies.

"Well, it's his Pub, I guess, so it's for him to deal with and no one else if everyone chooses to walk out," Andy said.

Samantha flashed him an icy stare.

"Although, you *are* right. He is making an ass of himself."

Samantha turned around to the doorway and noticed the familiar bulk of Andy's leather guitar bag. She stared at it momentarily as a light bulb clicked on in her head.

"Andy...?"

He glanced across at her, and saw immediately what she was looking at.

"Oh no..." he exclaimed, before she had a chance to respond. "No, no, no. I am not going to bail the old bastard out of this one."

He backed away from her suddenly looking for something, *anything* to do.

"But Andy, you play and I've heard you play really well," she looked across at Beck, holding out an open hand. "Isn't that right,

Beck? You live with him. Andy, you could offer to play in place of the others."

Andy shook his head, clearly spooked by the suggestion.

"I am *not* going to play for a Pub crowd who are expecting to hear Irish music. Besides, I don't play that style. No way!"

"But you wouldn't have to play that style," Samantha persisted. "They would appreciate any form of music, so long as it was played well. C'mon! It would be perfect. What are you afraid of?"

Andy looked to Beck, pleading wordlessly for him to jump to his defense. Beck merely tilted his head to one side and swirled the beer in his glass.

"She's got a point, man," he said, winking at Andy.

Andy was cornered.

A few of the other bar denizens had started taking an interest in the conversation and were now looking at Andy expectantly.

"*Jesus,*" he hissed. "I don't know how to play for that kind of audience. They'll laugh me out of the bar."

"How do you know that until you give it a try?" one of the old men sitting further down the bar from Beck piped up.

Andy glared at the old man incredulously.

"How would *you* know? You don't even know me."

The old man smiled behind his beer glass and nodded towards the guitar case he could see in the doorway behind the bar.

"Because, smart ass, if I'm not mistaken that's a Taylor guitar you've got hiding back there. Anybody who carries around that type of hardware has got to be a better than average guitarist."

The old man reached into his pocket and slapped a fifty-dollar bill down on the bar.

"So why don't you stop bein' a goddamned pussy and try it out?"

Beck and Samantha looked at each other wide-eyed while Andy stared at the cash on the bar.

Then Beck reached into his own pocket and fished out a twenty, placing it beside the other bill.

"C'mon, guys," Andy whined, scratching his head nervously. "This is not fair."

Another couple of patrons added to the pair of bills on the bar, taking the amount up to $150.

Andy was shocked.

With a confident grin, Samantha stepped out from behind the bar, gesturing for him to follow.

"C'mon ... pussy."

Andy shook his head dejectedly and followed.

"Of course," the old man said as Andy shuffled past, "You get none of this if you don't go through with it."

Gideon had hung up on the caller and was trying to come up with an explanation he could deliver to the full bistro and central bar of The Pub.

Samantha approached, with Andy trailing a few feet behind her.

"Boss," she said, tugging at his elbow.

Gideon Allan spun around to face her. He was clearly irritated.

"What do you want? I thought I told you to get back to work."

Samantha bit the inside of her lip to keep herself from slapping the sanctimonious prick.

"We have a proposition for you," she replied through clenched teeth. "If you're prepared to listen."

Gideon eyed her quizzically, letting his shoulders relax.

Samantha turned to Andy, grabbed his arm and pulled him next to her. "Andy can play the guitar. *He* could replace the band."

Gideon coughed and blew a raspberry through his lips, chuckling sarcastically.

"Don't make me laugh. You're suggesting he could entertain this crowd? Bugger me."

Gideon's colleagues shared in his snickering laughter, regarding Andy with thinly veiled ridicule.

"You may have gotten your act together, Dev, but I don't think your death metal music is what this Pub needs right now," Gideon chuckled, dismissing them both with a wave of his hand. "Go back to the bar where you belong."

A knot of anger twisted in Andy's stomach as Gideon turned his back on them.

"I can play, Gideon," he said firmly.

Gideon Allan glanced back over his shoulder, then turned slowly back to face Andy. He sized him up and down, grabbing at Andy's work shirt.

"Are you serious? You're barely capable of pouring beers, let alone entertaining a crowd."

"Gideon," Samantha shot back, flashing him an angry glare. "Andy is a good guitarist. He can salvage you from this mess you've gotten yourself into."

Gideon was taken aback by Samantha's sudden boldness. He appraised Andy again for a moment. Something was definitely different about him - something he couldn't put his finger on.

His eyes narrowed.

"OK." Gideon said, finally. "Go get out of that work shirt. And wash yourself up."

Samantha's eyes widened and she looked to Andy with excitement. They stood back from Gideon and went back to the bar.

"This should be a laugh," Gideon said to his bar manager.

"This is going to be a fucking disaster," Andy hissed as he quickly stripped off his polo and replaced it with a wool sweater. He splashed water on his face and checked himself in the men's room mirror, then fetched his guitar from behind the bar.

"I'm gonna need a beer," he said as he sat down on a stool beside Beck and hurriedly began checking the strings, making sure they were tuned.

Sensing his anxiety, Samantha placed a pint glass down on the counter top. He gulped down a couple of mouthfuls.

"You'll do fine, man," Beck encouraged him with a gentle nudge on his arm. "You play like no one I've ever heard. *Seriously.*"

"Yeah - well, strumming a guitar in the privacy of my own bedroom is a little different than performing for a pub crowd. Expectations are going to be way different."

He fiddled with the guitar for a minute longer then, satisfied with its sound, he finished off his beer. Feeling the pleasant warmth of the alcohol coursing through him, Andy stood up and ventured into the central bar.

It was a mixed crowd that had packed in here on this chilly Friday evening, an all-too-different demographic to the type Andy had become accustomed to, in his other life. Different again from the regular barflies and miscreants that populated the smaller front bar. These were normal working people, urbane city people, honest people.

A fire crackled in the old fireplace and a few people stood near it, warming their backs against the generous flames, laughing and chatting and drinking. A stool had been set up on a raised stage with a microphone stand adjacent to the fireplace. Gideon stood there waiting for Andy to appear. When he did, Gideon cleared his throat, adjusted the buttons of his blazer and thumbed the switch of the microphone. His lack of enthusiasm stood out like a sore thumb.

"Ladies and gentlemen!" he announced, adding a layer of thickness to his already thick Irish brogue. The level of tumult in the room died away. "Thank you for coming out to The Pub this evening as we present our first foray into live music."

He paused for a polite round of applause before continuing.

"I have to apologize to you all in advance, but the musical act we had intended to present to you tonight were unable to be here due to unforeseen circumstances."

A ripple of mock groans passed through the audience, followed by laughter.

"However, all is not lost, *apparently,* as we have instead, for your listening pleasure, a local lad who I'm told is fairly handy with a guitar. Would you please welcome to our stage, Andrew DeVries!"

Andy approached the stage and stepped up as Gideon stood aside for him. He squinted in the spotlight.

"Now, I'm warning you, Dev, I don't want any of that death metal shit. Do you understand?" he grumbled in Andy's ear above the applause.

Andy ignored him, settling down on the stool and adjusting the microphone stand downwards towards the guitar. As he looked out into the room, he felt himself becoming increasingly nervous and he had to take a few deep breaths to calm himself. The lights went down while the single spotlight softened just a little.

He rubbed his fingers to ensure that he would not fumble on the strings.

What the hell am I going to play?

The room was silent, waiting in anticipation. Andy looked across the room towards the doorway, seeing Samantha and Beck standing there. He glanced over at the fireplace, saw the dancing flames, saw the people there, warming themselves on this cold Chicago night.

He bowed his head.

Andy launched into a piece called "The Sounds of Rain Part 3," a composition he had picked up when he'd first begun playing the guitar. It was a piece that had first drawn Andy to the instrument. He recalled hearing it on an album by one of his favorite artists, a Kazakhstan-born virtuoso named Slava Grigoryan. It instantly drew everyone's attention to the stage, as if there was no one else in the room. The soft notes characterized the gentle beginnings of rainfall, capturing his audience. His fingers danced effortlessly across the fret board negotiating the lyrical melody, delving into it with graceful ease and confidence. It transported everyone from the chill Chicago winter to a place of warmth, where a summer rain might fall, pattering on a tin roof in a tropical locale by an ocean. They were transported to a verdant countryside, where cows might graze in a meadow on a hillside; where morning fog rolls down from a mountain range to settle just above the tree tops; where rain falls through the leaves onto the pasture or into a meandering brook swelling its banks.

The presence was with him, beside him. It didn't manipulate him at all, rather it influenced his emotions, helping him to visualize the soft imagery of the rain and deliver that into his performance. Andy closed his eyes and felt himself transported. He was floating with the music, leaving behind the city.

Across an ocean, towards a late afternoon sun, to a place on the other side of the world. To that little house overlooking the sea. To her.

It was captivating.

Gideon, who was standing at the bar, lowered his glass, revealing a slackened jaw that was opened in stunned surprise. He could not believe what he was hearing. Samantha almost squealed with delight and had to stop herself from jumping up and down, while Beck wore a knowing smile.

Andy's playing was passionate, intense and tender all at once. He moved with the piece, bowing his head into the lower registers then climbing up again on the back of the lyrical melody. There was nothing more beautiful than the sound of the guitar.

As quickly as it had begun, the piece ended with a flurry of complex finger movements and Andy finished with a theatrical swish of his hand. The crowd erupted with enthusiastic applause and cheers and whoops of appreciation.

They were ecstatic.

Both Samantha and Beck clapped furiously and Beck pointed directly at Andy, mouthing, "You're the man!"

Gideon Allan, dumbfounded at what he had just witnessed, applauded, too - his previously slackened jaw breaking into a grin of appreciation. He raised his hands and nodded respectfully - approvingly - at Andy.

Andy sat in front of his audience, a polite smile creasing his lips as he said "Thank you," a few times. He was as equally stunned by their reaction to him.

For the next sixty minutes Andy played for his audience, taking them on a rich journey through some of his favorite sonatas and fantasias. He performed a sprightly Caprice in A minor by Nicolo Paganini, and then attempted a somewhat more challenging variation on a theme from Mozart's "The Magic Flute" that had been first performed by Fernando Sor. He included in this performance a work by one of his favorite artists, Mauro Giuliani, whose interpretation of Handel's "Harmonious Blacksmith" Andy executed with a surprisingly artistic flourish that surprised even him. His audience responded enthusiastically. It was a performance unparalleled for this part of the city which was, perhaps, used to a much different musical sound. During his performance numerous patrons went to the stage and dropped coins and bills into an ashtray that sat at his foot, nodding at him appreciatively as they did so.

Andy stepped off the stage after a final ballad to which a group in the audience supplied respectable, if a little rusty, vocal accompaniment. He was exhausted but exhilarated. He made his way through the crowd, who congratulated him with sustained applause, a few back-slaps and handshakes until he slipped through into the front bar, encountering more of the same.

"That was awesome, man!" Beck enthused as Andy flopped down on a bar stool, handing the guitar over the bar to Samantha. "You *killed* in there. They were eating out of your hand."

Andy blushed bright pink and grinned as Samantha passed over a couple of beers.

"You were fantastic," she said.

Andy felt someone tapping his shoulder, and he spun around to face Gideon, who stood before him with a blank expression. Slowly he extended his hand and his poker face gave way to a smile of genuine warmth.

Andy took the older man's hand.

"Andrew, that was unbelievable," he said. "I had no idea."

As Andy acknowledged Gideon, he thought he saw the older man's eyes misting.

Gideon took out some folded bills and placed them in Andy's palm.

It was $100.

Gideon stepped back and extended his finger.

"Your father would have been proud of you tonight."

Chapter 10

Hands slide over a ruler, a pencil, an eraser on a page. The drawing board holds the paper steady as lines are drawn, faint at first until he is happy with his progress. Then he fills them in more heavily giving the drawing more definition, breathing life into the design. As he works he makes calculations both on the paper itself beside the developing floor plan and on a battered old calculator - the scientific kind, one he has owned since high school. The numbers are almost completely worn away from the buttons now, but it doesn't matter. He knows the device intuitively. He sips coffee from a chipped cup with a fancy pattern. The coffee is good, fresh from the grinder. There is nothing in the world like a great coffee. He is sure it helps his creative impulse.

He has been at it for hours, working on the project - the assignment. It's due in a couple of days and he knows he is way behind on it. He must get it done, so he sits in the front room of the house, having gotten away from the city so he can finish the project without distraction. He feels alone, however. No one else is here, not even his dog.

He can hear the ocean, the waves breaking gently on the shore outside. Music plays quietly in the background. It is the guitar: a selection of soft, languid tunes that help him work. He is lost in concentration.

He has failed to sense her presence. She slips into the house quietly, through the doors that open out onto the balcony. She wears a mischievous smile, a figure hugging long summer dress, flip-flops. She covertly slips out of those flip-flops now, places the basket she is carrying down in the old chair and tiptoes the last few feet to where he is working. Still he hasn't sensed her; such is his concentration.

And then...

The scent of her hair, the freshness of its perfume is unmistakable: rosemary and mint. He feels her cheek against his as she leans in close to him. Her lips press his cheek tenderly. The kiss lights up his face and he leans back in his chair. She falls into his lap, wrapping her arms around his neck. She gazes at him, her eyes filled with love.

"I couldn't stay away."

He wants to scold her, but he can't. They agreed he needed to get this assignment done without distraction. But he is so glad she's here.

They kiss, long and tender, tongues meeting and embracing.

"I'm glad you came."

***

Changes...

Andy became The Pub's house musician. In addition to his duties behind the bar, once a week he would perform whatever he wanted for the evening crowd who were now frequenting The Pub in increasing numbers, just to hear him play. Word was quickly spreading about this young virtuoso that played pieces of rare beauty and they responded enthusiastically, tipping him generously. Gideon, surprisingly, began paying him extra for his expanded role. For a man who had previously regarded Andy with contempt, the gesture was significant. In fact, Andy noticed a tangible change in the old man's behavior towards him. He sensed in Gideon, an appreciation for his playing, a deeper understanding of music than Andy might previously have given him credit for. It was as though Gideon had heard these beautiful pieces somewhere before. In this harsh, urban place, far from the soft inspiration for the kind of music he was performing, Andy had created a sort of musical sanctuary. A rather beautiful, unspoken conversation had been allowed to flourish between him and the patrons.

Andy's performances had attracted another observer, but he remained carefully out of sight so as not to alert Andy to his presence. Bruce DeVries spoke to no one while he watched his son play. He simply observed in silence, then left before anyone noticed. Not even Gideon knew he was there. Once Andy's performance was over, Bruce disappeared into the night as silently as a ghost.

Sometimes Andy would play as the opener to another act, or sometimes he would play impromptu duets with whomever happened to be in The Pub at the time. If they were halfway decent, then they were welcomed up onto the stage. It might be a vocalist or someone with a guitar of their own. Gideon had a few authentic Irish instruments scattered about the walls as ornamental pieces, and even these were recruited into service: a dusty old Irish drum, a battered but still usable mandolin, even an old fiddle. It was wild and raw and a little crazy, but somehow it worked.

Within it all - the music and the people, the euphoria of the music and the smiles on people's faces as they made music together - Andy began to feel peace. His confidence grew. He adapted his style to embrace a broader palate of music. He was enjoying his new role so much that his enthusiasm spilled over into his bar work. He derived greater satisfaction from it. He even began experiencing a feeling he wasn't used to in anything he had ever done: pride.

He no longer missed any classes at the Conservatory, which didn't escape the notice of Veldtman or Casper or any of the faculty heads. They watched with quiet astonishment at the turnaround in this troubled virtuoso. He seemed to be driven by something very powerful: a desire not only to excel but to attain something that had been missing. Veldtman had never seen anything quite like it. She worked with him in the group tutorials and in one-on-one sessions, marveling at his technical brilliance. It was a quality that had previously lacked an emotional core. When he had played before, Andy was single-minded in his approach. He played the music flawlessly, but he did not move with it. He didn't feel the emotion that the music was supposed to evoke. Suddenly, from out of the shadows, Andy had begun to display an unprecedented soulfulness in his playing. It was as though a door had been unlocked to an expressiveness that had long lain dormant. It had become a central dimension now, that was even more staggering in its artistry than even Andy had ever thought possible.

In their sessions, the teacher and the student found a dialogue that had been, for too long, suppressed by his self-destructiveness and her inability to reach him. They shared a renewed energy towards fostering more of his ability - that investment in his music that was truthful, that laid bare his regrets, his frustrations and his hopes. Andy was drawn to the events in the trauma room as a beginning point for his change. Increasingly, he sensed that there was another cause for it. The sense of the presence was becoming stronger. The visions, the dreams were becoming more vivid. As though they were not so much dreams now as they were memories. Memories that were not his own.

Yet they were.

Andy became less of a loner at the Conservatory, and had even begun to strike up tentative friendships with some of his classmates, some of whom he'd never talked to before, though he'd been in class with them since the beginning. They practiced together, discussed assignment work on the campus lawns and sometimes gathered at lunchtime.

He changed his diet, taking advantage of a nearby grocer that stocked fresh fruit and vegetables daily and he began cooking. He found he was actually quite a decent chef, turning out meals that both he and Beck enjoyed immensely.

His appearance began to change. He put on a little weight, filling out rather than fattening up. His gaunt face became a healthy, clear and surprisingly handsome one with vibrant eyes, a squarish jaw and a healthy head of hair that he had allowed to grow out just a little.

He ran every morning, rising at the same time each day and taking the same circuit around the local neighborhood. Somewhere along the way he had managed to bring a training partner with him: a mongrel pooch belonging to the old Italian lady who lived in the apartment across the hall. She was too frail to handle the dog outdoors anymore and so she offered him payment for helping her out. Andy wouldn't take money, so instead, a steady stream of delicious Mediterranean cuisine began making its way across the hall.

His relationship with Cassie ended. There had been no contact between them for some weeks. Her calls to his cell trailed off and, though he tried several times, he didn't get through to her either. He felt disgusted with himself for having let it go in that fashion, but she represented a link to Vasq and the life he wanted to leave behind.

His father remained painfully aloof. Bruce visited The Pub as he usually did but he ignored Andy. A couple of times Andy attempted to talk to his father, even offered him a drink, but Bruce dismissed his approaches. Samantha witnessed these exchanges and felt awful. It was clear Andy was trying to reach out to his father but he was slapped down each time.

***

Andy arrived at The Pub late, having had to stay back at the Conservatory to finish an extended tutorial. Gideon hadn't booked anyone so, once again, Andy was going to perform for the Friday night crowd.

Stepping into the front bar a little after five, Samantha was relieved to see him. She had been staffing the bar all by herself.

"Where have you been?" she asked, clearly harassed.

"Sorry, I missed the train," Andy said hurriedly as he slipped in behind the bar.

"There's a good crowd in tonight. Bigger than usual," Samantha remarked. "Gideon is already rubbing his hands together. You've become his little cash cow, I think."

Andy grinned and took orders for drinks from a group of city workers, who had stepped into the bar behind him.

"The old bastard's created a monster with these live gigs, I think. I should consider asking for a raise."

"Ppffft!" Samantha retorted. "Do you honestly think anyone could release a sphincter as tight as his?"

Andy smiled warmly as he served up the beers for the group before him. His smile caught Samantha's attention, so much so that she stopped what she was doing and looked at him quizzically.

"What *is* going on with you, Andy DeVries?"

He met her gaze and held it for a moment before shrugging his shoulders.

"Nothing. Nothing's going on. I just - I dunno - I'm feeling different. Everybody's entitled to an epiphany every now and then, aren't they?"

"That's some epiphany."

"Maybe. But when you come *that* close...," he raised his hand, bringing his thumb and forefinger together, indicating just how close he had been.

Samantha nodded her understanding.

Beck appeared in the entrance to the bar, and Andy smiled in greeting. His smile quickly faded, however, when he noted that Beck's expression was tense.

Beck sat down at the bar and took off his cap. Samantha and Andy exchanged concerned glances.

"Are you OK, man? You look like somebody stole your car."

Beck tried to offer a smile at Andy's words, but failed miserably. Samantha poured him a beer and set it down in front of him.

"If I *owned* a car ... then, yeah," Beck replied. "Nah. It's nothing. Just had a hard shift on the site, is all."

His explanation was lame. Andy frowned suspiciously.

"C'mon, Beck. You are *the worst* at bullshitting. What's really up?"

Beck looked away. He was clearly struggling with whatever was burdening him. Eventually, he scratched the back of his scalp and looked up at Andy solemnly.

"I had a couple of visitors to the site today," he said. "They were, uh, interested in knowing where you were at."

Andy's stomach dropped, and he felt as though he was going to be sick.

"What did they want?" he asked.

"Well, they weren't really specific on the details, but they did take the opportunity to subtly threaten me. Told me that they knew my cell number, where I like to hang - shit like that."

Beck rubbed his hands together then took a large mouthful of beer from his glass.

"We moved them on pretty quickly," he said with a hint of sarcasm. "But I would consider watching your back, Dev - just in case."

Andy exhaled and stared off into the distance. He should have known Vasq was going to make things difficult. Not only for him, but for his friends as well. Andy shook his head, then turned towards Samantha and Beck.

"Well, are you gonna do something?" Samantha asked with concern.

"I don't know," Andy replied hesitantly. "I'm not sure if there's anything I *can* do. He'll back off eventually. Vasq won't risk exposing himself, for fear that he'll draw attention. He can't afford that."

"I hope you're right, Andy," Samantha said. "He sounds like a persistent SOB."

They were both quiet.

It was time for Andy to begin his set. The moment he appeared on the small stage, there was a round of applause from the audience, which caused him to blush. He hadn't gotten used to this kind of reception, but he enjoyed it nonetheless. He had yet to fully understand how a guy playing classical guitar in an inner city pub in Chicago could so appeal to an audience he wouldn't have picked as having such eloquent tastes.

Gideon patted his shoulder on the way through and handed him a jug of beer to take up to the small stage. He smiled approvingly, the way Andy wished his own father would smile at him.

He played an hour-long set, mixing it up a little by playing pieces that he was most familiar with. He performed several guitar concertos by composers such as Gabriel Faure, Sor, Paganini and Spanish composer Joaquin Rodrigo. The audience was as appreciative as always. The music was an elixir, taking them out of their day-to-day lives and delivering them to a place of sanctuary.

During this first set, a lone figure slipped into the front bar from the chilly outside and sat as far back as he could. He looked across cautiously to where Andy was performing, but couldn't quite see him over the heads of people who were standing in the entrance. Samantha approached Bruce DeVries with a barely contained look of disdain and poured him a beer. She said nothing to him.

Andy took a break and retreated to the front bar where Samantha had a beer waiting for him. He wiped his face with a towel as he sat down on the stool. Beck and Samantha were looking at each other awkwardly. The men's room door had just closed behind Bruce.

"What's wrong?" Andy asked, lighting up a cigarette. "Do I sound bad or something?"

"No. Not at all," Samantha answered hastily. Her reflexive response didn't convince him. Andy turned to Beck, who shrugged and hid in his beer.

"You're sounding great out there," Samantha said, changing the subject. "You're definitely growing in confidence."

Andy smiled bashfully and examined the crowd in the main bar.

"They are a good audience," he said.

Samantha kept one eye on the door to the men's room, hoping Andy's father wouldn't suddenly appear. Andy butted his cigarette and stood, much to her relief. He returned to the stage and settled onto his stool just as Bruce emerged gingerly. He scanned the room, then stepped forward.

"OK," Andy began, plucking the strings of his guitar to check it was still tuned. "At around this time, I like to invite people from the audience to come and join me if they think they can perform."

There was little response from the bar as the murmur of conversation continued.

"Hmmm. I usually like to have at least one person come up here. A vocalist, perhaps? C'mon - anyone is welcome. Except for you karaoke wannabes. I don't do karaoke."

There was a faint laughter from the audience, but after a few moments there were still no takers. Andy shrugged and prepared to launch into something.

"I'll play with you," came a familiar voice from the audience.

Andy squinted in the spotlight to see where that voice had come from. A woman stepped into view and approached him.

It was Sorrel Veldtman.

Dressed in a battered black leather coat and her trademark loud head scarf, she stepped up onto the stage and nodded at Andy, smiling as he stared at her dumbfounded.

"I've enjoyed listening," she said breezily as she took up her place on the spare stool.

Unsure of what to say in return, a shocked Andy handed her the spare guitar and she began tuning it.

"Uhh ... thank you," he said, watching her awkwardly.

Veldtman caught his stare.

"Are you OK?" she asked teasingly. "You did ask for anybody, after all."

Andy shook his head, embarrassed, and smiled.

"Sorry," he stammered. "I just didn't... I wouldn't have picked you for a ... pub-goer."

"Ahh," Veldtman nodded. "There are a lot of things that you don't know about me."

Andy picked up his glass of beer, swallowed a mouthful too quickly and very nearly spluttered.

Veldtman dragged her fingers across the strings, assessing its sound. It was clear she wasn't overly impressed with the battered instrument, but her expression was one of "It'll do."

"What shall we play, Andrew? You seem to have brought a little culture into this place recently. Why don't we give them something best suited to a duet?"

Andy nodded, genuinely impressed.

"OK ... how about *Deciso*?"

Veldtman grinned broadly, and together teacher and student launched into a quick-fire rendition of the first movement from Astor Piazzolla's famed Tango Suite. The general chatter in the bar died away and the audience turned towards the stage.

The worldly experience of Veldtman's playing contrasted beautifully with Andy's technical brilliance which, it was clear, was something very special for somebody so young. Together they conjured intense imagery from the music of *Deciso*, a piece that bristled with a controlled erotic energy of the legendary Argentine dance.

Andy felt a satisfying rush as he played through the piece, every now and then watching Veldtman for cues to step forward and deliver the solo parts of it. He was just as absorbed by Veldtman's exquisite skill as the audience. Her fingerings were flawless. She led him perfectly, the two guitars capturing a harmonic synergy. Samantha and Beck smiled as they watched their transformed friend.

Andy and Veldtman reached the end of the piece and the audience responded with terrific applause. Andy was buzzed, laughing joyously and he turned towards Veldtman as she slapped her hand into his, nodding approvingly.

"Very nice," she said. "There is certainly more to you than meets the eye, isn't there?"

Andy didn't know what to say.

"Why don't we play some more?" she said.

"Oh. Most certainly."

Together they played, showcasing a group of compositions suited to a duet. Then they changed tack, launching through some very eclectic pieces. They included the classic Jose Feliciano interpretation of The Doors' "Light My Fire," which Veldtman sang with surprising effectiveness. They played some blues standards that had the audience clapping along enthusiastically, then Veldtman finished off with some passionate ballads from her homeland.

By the time they finished, Andy felt elated. It was the most satisfying musical experience he could recall having had. He was struck not only by Veldtman's technical mastery but also by the emotional investment she delivered into her playing. It was that same emotional investment that he so aspired to - the key to a performance that transcended the music and attained perfection.

"That was amazing," Andy gushed as he gestured to Samantha, at the main bar, to get them a couple of drinks. "Thank you - thank you very much."

"Oh, it was a pleasure," Veldtman replied as they stepped down from the stage and went across to the bar. "You certainly haven't been wasting your time. You have brought *wonderful* music to this place."

"Well, I don't know if it's always appreciated. But they seem to have embraced it," Andy said.

"Embraced it?" Veldtman replied as Samantha set two beers down in front of them. "Andy, they have accepted you unreservedly here. You only need to see the appreciation on their faces. I am sure you wouldn't derive that sort of reward from *others* in your life."

Andy nodded, considering Veldtman's words as she studied him keenly.

"Those *others* aren't going to be a fixture in my life anymore," he said. "I've made some decisions about that recently."

Veldtman smiled.

"That's good to hear," she said. "Hopefully, it will have given you some clarity to reconsider some other opportunities."

Andy shook his head slowly.

"The Concert Series?" he exhaled wearily. "Look, you and I both know that the Conservatory will laugh any application I make."

"What makes you so sure of that?" Veldtman challenged him.

"Well, I dunno," Andy said. "The fact that the council want nothing more than to drum me out of the school? I know they have it in for me, that they don't want me there."

Veldtman nodded as she sipped her beer.

"Seems you have it all figured out."

"Well, it's true, isn't it?" he said.

Veldtman merely offered him a wistful smile.

"I think you should seriously reconsider your suitability. I think it would be a tragedy if you didn't at least submit an application."

Veldtman paused and finished her drink. "Don't let it slip away, Andy. You have a chance to achieve real greatness."

Across the room, Bruce DeVries stepped discreetly through the crowd, watching Andy and the woman talking. He slipped through the door and disappeared outside.

Veldtman stood and touched Andy's shoulder. She reached into her jacket with the other hand, took out a folded piece of paper and set it down in front of him.

"Reconsider, Andrew. I think you'll be surprised. You're more suitable than you realize."

Andy looked at the piece of paper and unfolded it. It was an application form for the concert series. His eyes widened, noting that Veldtman had already filled in parts of the application, including her endorsement, which was a requirement for selection. She was challenging him - he knew that. Veldtman had championed him, even when he was at his worst depths.

Veldtman regarded him a moment longer, her eyes filled with encouragement. Then she turned and left the bar. Once Veldtman was gone, Samantha sidled up to Andy.

"That woman was incredible," she remarked. "Who was she?"

Andy smiled distantly.

"A good woman ... a *really* good woman."

"She seems to have made a good impression on you," Samantha said.

Andy left his beer unfinished on the counter as he stood and picked up his guitar. He seemed a million miles away.

"Yeah." He nudged Beck on the shoulder. "I'll see you at home, man." He left the bar.

"What was that all about?" Samantha muttered to Beck.

***

Andy walked home, his surprise pairing with Veldtman still buzzing in his mind. It left him energized, eager for another experience like that. Her last words to him stuck in his head as he passed underneath a street lamp.

'You have a chance to achieve real greatness.'

He shook his head as another thought crossed his mind about the Festival and about its location. That far-away continent - so far from here.

"Australia," he said to himself. "Is that where these dreams are coming from?"

He fished the application out of his jacket and examined it in the light from a street lamp.

Melbourne, Australia.

What was it about that city that felt so familiar?

He turned into an alleyway he often took as a shortcut home and drew up the collar of his jacket higher around his neck. He adjusted the weight of his guitar bag on his shoulder.

From behind him came the sound of a car's engine revving hard as twin beams cut into the darkened alley. Andy turned around to see a white sports car coming towards him and he moved to one side to let it pass.

Only it didn't pass him.

Instead, the car screeched to a halt a few feet away and its doors opened, expelling several figures.

It was Vasq's crew. Andy felt a sudden knot of dread in his stomach.

He stood fast as Vasq stepped out last and held his arms out in that arrogant, theatrical greeting of his. Though he was silhouetted in the darkness, as Vasq moved to stand in front of the car's headlights Andy could make out his sinister grin.

"Yo *dawg!*" he greeted sarcastically.

Vasq and the trio accompanying him were brandishing steel bars and knives. Andy looked beyond them to the car, and spied Cassie and the girl from the warehouse, Alyson. Even in the poor light from the street Andy could see that Cassie was affected. She was looking at him through bleary eyes.

"I'm very disappointed that you haven't returned my calls, Dev," Vasq said, walking towards Andy. The others surrounded him. Andy stood fast.

"I wasn't aware I needed to return your calls, Emilio. I told you already, I'm done. I'm not working for you anymore."

Vasq clicked his tongue against his teeth.

"Dev, Dev, Dev. You don't realize that you can't just make that decision on your own. You have to consider how it will affect others - namely, me."

"It's not my problem, Emilio," Andy said flatly, steeling himself as the crew spread themselves out.

"Hmmm." Vasq moved towards him until he was standing toe to toe with Andy. "No. No, it's not. It's very much my problem, *dawg*. My competition is taking advantage of this. Your ... recalcitrance is only ... exacerbating my problem."

"Wow, Emilio," Andy commented. "You learned two whole new words this week. I'll bet that took some effort."

Blindingly fast, Vasq smashed the steel bar in his hand across Andy's right cheek, splitting his skin down to the bone. Andy reeled backwards, but Vasq's colleague was there, brandishing his own steel bar. Holding it like a baseball bat, he swung hard, hitting the guitar on Andy's shoulder. The sickening crack spun Andy like a top. The guitar inside the bag splintered and broke in half. Andy fell to his knees before Vasq. He felt sick to his stomach, his head throbbed. Blood poured from the gash in his cheek.

"You can't just walk away, you *fuck!*" Vasq screamed, tearing the shattered guitar from Andy's arm and tossing it aside. "I won't let you!"

He grabbed at Andy's collar, pulling him close, then spat in his face.

"Fuck ... you!" Andy croaked, vomiting unexpectedly all down Vasq's front.

Vasq's features contorted with rage and he exploded, slamming Andy in the side of the head with his flattened hand, then kicking him to the ground.

In the car, Cassie, gasped. Tears filled her eyes and she turned away, unable to watch.

Vasq set upon Andy, beating him and kicking him so violently that he vomited again, this time all over one of the gangsters' shoes. It enraged the thug so much that he kicked Andy in the stomach. He then tore open the guitar bag and pulled out the shattered instrument, using it like a club to beat Andy's flank. Andy could only curl himself up in a ball to protect himself from the worst of the blows.

Soon he lay unconscious on the pavement. Vasq signaled for them to stop. They fell back to the car as a gate opened nearby. An elderly Chinese man, armed with a handgun, emerged with his wife beside him.

"Let's go!" Vasq called. The crew fled to the car. Vasq looked down at Andy's lifeless form and spat on him.

"I own you!"

The car's tires screeched and smoked as it took off, crushing the shattered remains of Andy's guitar and disappearing down the alley.

The elderly couple ran over to Andy's crumpled body, the wife already dialing 911 on her cell phone. Her husband dropped to his knees beside Andy checking him for any signs of life, horrified at what he saw. Andy's face was already beginning to swell up and he was bleeding heavily. The man's wife pleaded into the phone for someone to come.

Quickly.

Chapter 11

The Doctor enters the office with a folder in his hand. He circles around the desk, slides out his chair with deliberate care and sits down, placing the folder in front of him. He doesn't immediately look up at the couple sitting opposite. Rather he turns over the cover of the manila case file, runs his hand down the inside seam. It is not a very thick folder at all. It is crisp and new.

Finally, he looks up at the patient before him and takes a sheet of paper in his hand. He passes it over. Denny studies it momentarily, closes his eyes, squeezes Sonya's hand entwined in his.

"I'm so sorry, Denny," the Doctor says in a subdued voice.

Denny simply nods. He is too stunned to speak.

He had been given his answer.

***

Each week Denny visits the clinic. An intravenous cannula is inserted into his arm and through it he receives the chemotherapy drugs. He knows they won't save him, that they will only stave off the inevitable. But deep down, he holds onto some spark of hope. He often jokes with the nurses that he could pass for a drug addict now, so marked has his arm become. They make a lot of jokes together at the clinic. Usually dirty ones, because they are the ones that crack them up the best. Sometimes he'll bring his guitar with him and play for the staff and the patients. His music brings a beautiful atmosphere to the clinic, making the days for the patients attending treatment here and the staff caring for them much more special. Rumor has it that the other patients have been trying to swap their treatment days to be there at the same time as Denny, just to hear him play.

Sonya is always with him. She sits with him, reads a magazine, listens to her iPod, holds his hand. Sometimes they share the iPod - each of them wearing an earphone so they can listen along to a favorite internet podcast of theirs - Keith & The Girl. When Denny is overcome by waves of nausea, the awful metallic taste he gets in his mouth after vomiting, the anger and frustration that sometimes overcomes him, she is never impatient, never frustrated. Sonya is Denny's rock. Sometimes she'll bake fruit muffins to take into the clinic for the nursing staff. The nurses adore her.

Week by week, Denny changes. His hair begins to fall out. He loses weight dramatically. The dirty jokes don't come as easily and though he still brings the guitar, he no longer has the strength to play it. The nurses never fail him, though. They retain their outwardly happy, supportive and professional selves. He knows it's a facade. One day he caught one of them struggling to hold back her tears at the desk after she had put in his I.V.

When he makes the decision to end the chemotherapy, Sonya supports him unfailingly, even though he knows her heart is breaking, watching him die.

The day comes when he no longer attends the clinic at all.

He lies in bed, looking through the window at the garden. He likes to close his eyes sometimes and listen to the birdsong. It distracts him from the pain. He listens to his own heart beating, trying to reason why he should have to die. His heartbeat feels so strong.

***

The first thing Andy became aware of was the sound of his own heartbeat - strong in his ears. He heard birdsong nearby, and in his mind he smiled. His mind slowly, sluggishly swirled back into consciousness. He became aware of an awful metallic taste in his mouth and an intense throbbing in his cheek.

Have I had chemo today already?

He grimaced, and with a great effort he opened one eye. He was confronted by darkness. He tried to focus, blinking furiously. He became anxious. His mind wallowed on a lumpy sea, and he felt as though he might fall overboard, until he realized that he was in a darkened room, that it was night time. He sank back into the pillows and tried to slow his breathing, collecting himself once again.

Blinking into the darkness, he discovered his right eye was puffy and swollen completely shut. A large bandage encircled his head, partially covering his affected eye. He felt cuts and bruises on his scalp. Andy tried to work out where he was. The room smelled of crisp sheets and disinfectant. It was a hospital room.

Am I alive?

The sound of a radio talk show punctured his disorientation from somewhere nearby. It was the kind of late, late night, lonely hearts variety that catered to terminal insomniacs.

"And to those of you who are just joining us, I'm talking tonight with paranormal psychologist and lecturer Dr. Michael David," the syrupy voice of the male talk show host announced. "And we're discussing the phenomena of past lives, the concept of reincarnation - of spirits co-existing simultaneously within us."

Reincarnation? Andy thought sluggishly.

"Dr. David - you discuss in your new book a concept based upon conventional physics suggesting that energy - in this case our spiritual energy - doesn't just dissipate after we die. Rather, it transfers?"

"That's correct, Drew. We have theorized that our spiritual self, just like our physical self, has an atomic structure as tangible and as real as, say, our skin or our hair. But unlike those physical attributes, our spiritual self has an electrical potential that - if harnessed in the right way - can be sustained beyond our own mortality."

"So what you're saying is that this potential can allow for the reincarnation of an individual in a living person provided certain conditions are right ... a sort of spiritual symbiosis of sorts?"

"Indeed, Drew. We have interviewed a number of subjects who report this sort of phenomenon most acutely after near-death experience. That through the process of being revived they have unwittingly become a lightning rod for these disparate energies to attach themselves to, after which the subjects begin to recall experiences and memories that are not their own. Rather, they have absorbed the life imprint of these spiritual entities..."

Andy was distracted from the radio discussion by the presence of a figure in the corner of the room, beside the bed, huddled in a chair. A woman.

He strained to see her in the darkness.

"Sonya?" he croaked. "Sonya, is that you?"

The figure in the chair woke with a start and reached up above her head for a switch on the wall. A light snapped on and Samantha sat on the edge of the bed.

"Dev? Hey," she said, blinking the sleep from her eyes. "Welcome back."

Andy shook his head and tried in vain to open his eyes. His face felt so swollen. He managed to open his left eye and look up at Samantha. For a moment, as he stared blankly at her, Samantha sensed that he didn't recognize her; it was as though he were expecting her to be someone else.

Everything spun back into focus. He was gone from the room overlooking the garden. He was gone from Sonya again. He was back in Chicago, The Pub, his apartment, Samantha sitting here. Then he remembered.

Vasq.

Andy's last recollection was Vasq striking him with something hard.

'You can't just walk away, you fuck!' Vasq's words echoed. *'I own you!'*

Andy struggled to sit up in bed until Samantha placed a firm hand on his shoulder.

"Hey, hey. Just take it easy, there. You've got a couple of busted ribs - not to mention bruises all over you. You need to rest."

He slumped back, flustered, frustrated, suddenly aware of a dull ache in his side that was evidently masked by morphine.

"Sonofabitch," he said, feeling as though he was trying to talk with a mouthful of marbles. "This is not good."

"You're telling me," Samantha agreed. "You got jumped pretty good. Those friends of yours left you for dead in an alley not far from your house. You took a hell of a beating."

"What time is it?"

"It's early," Samantha replied. "The nurse let me sneak in since I accompanied you into the hospital. You've been here three days."

Andy groaned ruefully and blinked his eyes, trying furiously to open his bandaged one, but failing. Eventually he gave up.

"I knew Vasq wouldn't let me go quietly."

In the soft light from the overhead lamp, Samantha noticed his good eye. Something about it made her frown curiously. It was different, somehow, but she could not determine what exactly it was that was different.

"You have to talk to the police, Dev," she said, brushing the thought away. "If you *know* it was them, you've gotta stop them now before they do it again."

Andy's face contorted into a mask of pain.

"They are a protected species, Sam. I don't have the coziest relationship with the police, either. I doubt they would act on my sob story," he looked back at her. "You've been here all this time? Every day?"

Samantha nodded.

"Gideon has been really good about letting me come down. It's almost as if he's really worried about you. He's even paying my cab fare and not docking my pay. Generous of the old bastard, isn't it?"

Samantha watched him sympathetically before a curious frown furrowed her brow. She remembered something Andy had said just a few moments ago.

"Who's Sonya?"

Andy blinked with his one good eye and Samantha tilted her head slightly.

There it was again, that *something* about his eye that she couldn't quite discern. She leaned in closer to him, her iridology interest coming to the fore. As he looked towards the ceiling, Samantha tried to get as close a look at his pupil as she could. But whatever it was, it eluded her.

Brushing the thought aside, Samantha smiled curiously.

"Andy? Who's Sonya?"

The mention of her name from anyone else's lips sounded strange.

"Dev?"

Andy turned his head slowly, painfully, back to Samantha.

"She... I...," he struggled to come up with an answer. Eventually he settled on a simple diversion. "Nobody."

Samantha's frown softened.

"C'mon," she pressed. "Didn't sound like nobody to me. I've never heard you mention that name before. You've got me curious."

Andy shook his head.

"It's nothing. Nobody. It was just a dream."

Samantha wasn't at all convinced.

"C'mon, Dev," she said with a quizzical grin. "I know you've had a few more irons in the fire than you let..."

"Let it go, will you?" he shot back suddenly. Samantha flinched. He immediately regretted it.

"I'm sorry."

Samantha was stung. Her cheeks flushed and she looked away from him.

"I should leave you to get some rest."

She rose from the bed and collected her jacket from the chair. Feeling awful, Andy reached out and took her hand in his.

"No, Sam. Please stay. I..."

Samantha paused. She looked down at her hand in his, but made no move to pull it away. His hand was warm, his grip firm. Slowly, Samantha sat down again. An awkward silence settled between them for a few moments.

"I have a habit of being an asshole to you, huh?" Andy finally said. "You don't deserve that. You deserve much better than that."

Samantha blushed and squeezed his hand. Still she didn't pull away.

"Have you ... ever felt like you've known a place ... somewhere far away, like, intimately?" he asked. "Yet you know you've never been there?"

Samantha tilted her head to one side.

"What are you talking about?"

Andy closed his eyes. He spoke haltingly.

"Ever since the overdose, I've been having these dreams. About another place, another life. It's like - I know this place. I've *always known* this place. But I've never been there."

In the darkness behind his closed eyes, he saw her.

"I've never even met her. It's crazy. But I know her. It's like - I've *always* known her."

Samantha withdrew her hand. He didn't notice.

"She's beautiful, Sam. We're in love. Like, *really* in love. We have a house together - a dog. We have a life together - or at least, we *had* a life. Something happened. I'm not there anymore. Something happened to me. But I don't know what."

"It sounds to me like you've taken one too many pills, Dev," Samantha mumbled.

He continued, unaware she was growing uncomfortable.

"I know it sounds crazy. But it's so *frigging* real. I can't explain it. It's like - something happened in that trauma room. It's like I *absorbed* the memories of someone else's life."

Samantha stood up again abruptly, and this time she put her jacket on.

"Andy, you need to rest," she snapped. "You've had the stuffing kicked out of you and you're not thinking straight."

She leaned over the bed as if to plant a kiss upon his forehead. But she caught herself, hesitated, then turned away briskly and left the room.

Andy stared dumbfounded at the door that shut noisily behind her.

In the hall, Samantha paused and glanced back at the door to Andy's room. She shook her head and cursed under her breath.

***

Two days later, Andy sat propped up in bed, contemplating the breakfast tray in front of him. He had been moving the cereal around the bowl for nearly half an hour, hoping that, miraculously, his appetite would magically appear.

It didn't. He wasn't the slightest bit hungry.

The swelling in his face felt as though it had improved significantly in the time since he'd first awoken in the ICU - yet it still felt incredibly painful. Every time he so much as twitched his lower jaw, sharp, intense pain pierced through the sutured gash in his right cheek. Once he was moved to the four bed bay on the ward, his sleep was terrible. He tossed and turned - as much as the awful bruising would allow him to. Often he found himself seeing out the pre-dawn hours mulling over his predicament, thinking that he must be going crazy. The police had been and, once again Andy had stonewalled them, as he had done so in the past. This time, the detective had left him a card encouraging him to consider making contact if Andy's memory came back to him. Strangely, Vasq was of little concern to him right now. He had no idea what the hell was up with Samantha. She hadn't returned to the hospital after the other night and she hadn't called either. Her behavior was a mystery to him.

The curtain to his cubicle ruffled quietly and Beck's head appeared around it.

"Hey, man," he greeted.

Relieved by the diversion, Andy pushed the tray table aside and gestured feebly for Beck to come in.

Right away, Andy registered that something was not right. Beck's face was pale. Dark rings circled his eyes, as though he hadn't slept in days. He was still in his dirty work clothes.

"Hey yourself," Andy said, taken aback by his friend's disheveled appearance. "Jesus, you look worse than I do."

Beck nodded with a wan smile and stood at the end of the bed.

"I'm just glad you're OK, man," he said flatly. "Those pricks sure did a number on you."

Again a moment of silence. There was definitely something not right.

"What is it, Beck? What's wrong?"

Beck fidgeted.

"We got broken into, man," he said. "Same night those fuckers jumped you. The apartment's been trashed. I found it that way when I got home, after I left The Pub."

Andy's shoulders slumped and he sank into the pillows. Suddenly his head was incredibly heavy and he felt a rush of nausea.

"I just got through with the police," Beck continued. "I suggested that whoever it was that got to you probably did over the apartment."

Andy nodded slowly, painfully. A knot of anger twisted in his stomach and he grimaced. He knew right away who they were and what they had done.

"I'm so sorry, Beck. First they come after you, and now this. I never meant for this to happen. How bad was it?"

Beck brushed it aside and sat down on the chair.

"Look, don't worry about it right now. You need to rest. I'll take care of things."

"I walked away, Beck. I turned my back on that bullshit."

Beck patted Andy's arm awkwardly. He did not want to betray the frustration he felt.

"I know you did, man. I know it. But I guess this is the blow back, huh? Of having gotten caught up with that shitty crowd in the first place."

Andy closed his good eye, knowing Beck was right.

"Hopefully the police will be able to do something," Beck said.

"Did they take anything?"

Beck shook his head wearily.

"Seems as though they wanted to cause damage to send a message, rather than take anything. It's a mess, but it's fixable."

Beck was prudent enough not to tell Andy yet the extent of the vandalism. The structural and property damage was bad enough, but the perpetrators had gone further by defecating in the bedrooms, spreading feces across the walls and leaving graffiti tags in red spray paint.

"When are they gonna let you go?" Beck asked, changing the subject.

"I dunno," Andy replied. "I think maybe in a day or so but I haven't seen a doctor yet today. I want out of here as soon as possible, though. I'm not sure if my insurance covers me for this length of stay. Besides that, I'm getting sick of being a repeat visitor."

Beck managed a smile, leaned back in the chair and put his feet up on the corner of Andy's bed.

"Mind if I hang for a while?"

Andy gave Beck a gentle punch on the arm.

"Would you, man? That'd be cool."

***

By lunch time the doctor still hadn't come, so Andy sent Beck home and decided to go for a walk - the first walk of any kind he had been capable of taking in days. Lost in his thoughts, Andy wandered the hospital corridors. He stepped out onto a balcony that overlooked the Chicago skyline. He sat alone in a stark and cavernous patient lounge. He thumbed through just about every trashy magazine on the rickety coffee table. One of them, a particularly tattered edition that was minus its cover, was dated 1992. As Andy thumbed through it, the beginnings of a headache tugging at the corners of his temples, he came across a full-page ad featuring a pristine coastline, a bejeweled sea, a brilliant sun hanging in an azure sky. It was a travel advertisement.

"Visit the Sapphire Coast, New South Wales, Australia."

A boom went off in Andy's mind and his one working eye went wide. He recognized this place! He had been there! A cacophony of black-and-white images erupted like camera flashes across his consciousness as though they were on fast-forward.

He remembered the words of the radio announcer from the early hours of the morning.

"...our spiritual self has an electrical potential that - if harnessed in the right way - can be sustained beyond our own mortality..."

A question began to form in his mind. Andy tore the page out of the magazine. He folded it and stuffed it in his pocket, then got up from the lounge. In the corridor, he inspected a sign on the wall showing directions to various departments.

He was only interested in one.

Trauma & ER.

Andy hopped an elevator and found his way to the ER on the ground floor - the very ER he had been brought into on the night of his overdose. It was unsurprisingly busy with staff: nurses and doctors rushing here and there, orderlies moving patients in beds, on gurneys and in wheelchairs through the bustling reception area. The waiting area was chaotic with yet more people being seen by staff or waiting to be seen. The noise didn't help his headache.

Andy scanned the reception area and beyond to the trauma rooms. Searching. Searching.

A familiar doctor in a green lab coat and scrubs stood before a gurney, upon which lay a lifeless, elderly African-American man. The doctor was signing a form on a clipboard while shouting orders to a team of staff nearby. He wore gold-rimmed glasses and sported a neatly trimmed salt-and-pepper beard.

Andy watched intently as the doctor checked the patient with a stethoscope then signaled for a pair of orderlies to wheel him away. The patient appeared to have died.

And then the doctor stood alone, rubbing his brow with thumb and forefinger wearily. Seeing an opportunity, Andy approached him. The doctor looked up at him.

Andy knew he gotten the right man. The name tag hanging lop-sided from the lanyard around his neck left him in no doubt.

It was Ellis - the doctor from the trauma room.

Ellis studied Andy curiously.

"Can I help you?"

"You're Ellis, right?"

Ellis nodded tugging his lanyard.

"That's what it says here. This is a restricted area. Are you lost?"

Andy smiled inwardly at that question.

"You probably don't remember me. I was here a while ago. You saw me. I was in a pretty bad state."

Ellis squinted at him.

"Look, I see a lot of people in here, kid. I couldn't possibly..." his voice trailed off and he raised his finger towards Andy. "Wait a minute. Overdose - crystal meth right? Pulled from an inner-city trance party."

Andy nodded evenly and said, "Good memory."

Ellis folded his arms and studied Andy more intensely.

"I see you've managed to grace us with your custom once again," he observed cynically. "What was it this time? More of the same?"

Andy smiled and shook his head.

"On the contrary, Doctor. You'll be pleased to know I've had a change of direction. Unfortunately, in the process I've made a few enemies. It's been more difficult to leave that life than I anticipated."

Ellis seemed genuinely surprised. Somebody called out his name nearby, and he looked across to see the team wheeling yet another new arrival into one of the trauma rooms.

Ellis turned to leave. Sensing that his opportunity was slipping away, Andy stepped forward.

"Dr. Ellis, I have to know something."

Ellis paused in his turn, signaling to his team to go ahead.

"That night. When I was brought in. Did I ... die ... at any stage when you were looking after me? Did I have to be revived?"

Ellis nodded.

"Yes. You were in cardiac arrest when we wheeled you off the ambulance. The paramedics said that you had been out for about five minutes. It took us another two to bring you back."

Ellis couldn't stop any longer. He hurried away to the trauma room.

Andy had been given his answer.

Chapter 12

Sonya sat at her desk in the freshly painted office examining a thick sheaf of documents. She grabbed at the collar of her crisp, white business shirt trying to get some air across her skin. Although the air conditioner was finally installed and ready to go, it hadn't been connected to a power supply. The small fan that sat on the bookshelf behind her was woefully inadequate, but at least it kept the air circulating in the room. Sonya was thankful for the short business skirt she wore. In the rush to get the practice up and running this week, she realized belatedly that she didn't own any sort of appropriate suit for the summer weather. A rushed drive up the coast to Wollongong had her searching desperately until a small boutique came through for her at the eleventh hour. It was an uncharacteristically warm day, so early into the season.

Across from her sat an elderly couple. The husband was dour, slump shouldered and balding, with an overgrown mustache and a crumpled suit that smelled of mothballs. He daubed at his perspiring forehead with a handkerchief and constantly tugged at his tie. His wife was a large woman in a loud floral dress, the nylon type that made her sweat so profusely her body odor filled the room. Her hair was pulled back in a severe bun. Sonya could have sworn it had smoothed out all the wrinkles on her face. She sat, arms crossed, her lips pursed as though she had been sucking on a lemon.

"So, to be clear, Phyllis: what you're looking for is a divorce from Bernard here," Sonya began. "Because you allege he had an affair five years ago with your sister - even though he has assured you repeatedly that nothing ever took place."

Phyllis shifted in her chair and nodded forcefully, while Bernard seemed to shrink even further into his own.

"That's correct, Miss Llewellyn. Despite what Bernard here says, I have evidence - hard evidence - that *proves* his infidelity."

She pointed a meaty finger at the papers before Sonya for effect.

"Yes," Sonya said. "I've reviewed the phone records that you have obtained, as well as the statement from your sister, who is now living in a Sydney nursing home - in a dementia ward - that states that she and your husband did 'carry on a bit' a number of years ago."

"So it should be a forgone conclusion, then, shouldn't it?"

Bernard did his best to stifle a sigh of frustration as he let his eyes wander to the window.

Sonya quietly put her pen down and glanced discreetly at Simon, who was curled up in his basket. He regarded her with an expression of complete indifference, before dropping his head down and closing his eyes.

"Look, Phyllis. I'm not here to pass judgment on your actions," Sonya paused, considering her words carefully before proceeding. "But - I think you should consider carefully whether this is what you really want to do."

Phyllis blinked.

"What do you mean?" she asked indignantly.

"Well, is it not true that you were having coffee with Mrs. Marks on Tuesday morning?"

"Well, yes, I was."

"And that during that coffee you were showing her travel brochures for the Seychelles..."

"I - I was?" Phyllis sat upright in her chair now, the indignation on her face melting into uncertainty.

"And you were overheard remarking that, like Wanda Brickham, who divorced her husband and pocketed a substantial amount of money; you could do the same and be able to afford to go on that group holiday the women's group has been planning for the past 12 months."

The blood appeared to drain from Phyllis's face. Sonya waited for her to respond.

"I - I..." Phyllis stammered, switching glares between Sonya and her husband.

"Lionel and his wife have exceptional hearing, Phyllis," Sonya added. She opened her drawer, took out a card for a local marriage counselor and handed it to Phyllis.

Phyllis abruptly stood up, clutching her handbag close. Her lips seemed to purse even more severely as she turned on her heel.

"I'll be waiting in the car, Bernard!" she snapped as she left the office.

Bernard stood wearily and offered his hand to Sonya.

"I'm not sure whether I just made things worse," she ventured sympathetically.

Bernard brushed it aside and shook Sonya's hand weakly.

"Thank you for your time, love. I'm sorry to have wasted it on such ridiculousness."

Sonya smiled and accompanied the old man out of the office and into the reception area, which was still in a state of partial renovation.

Bernard turned to Sonya.

"I'll be sure to bring down a supply of vegetables and eggs from the farm in a day or two, for your troubles."

"Bernard, you don't need to do that," Sonya reassured him.

The old man managed a smile for the first time this morning.

"I insist," he said.

Sonya watched from the door as he trudged towards the ancient Morris sedan parked out front. Phyllis sat in the passenger seat, silently fuming. Sonya didn't envy poor Bernard.

As the car pulled away, Sonya noticed Lionel approaching from the other side of the street pushing a small trolley that contained various lunch orders, including Sonya's own.

She smiled warmly upon seeing him and waited as he crossed the street. No matter what the weather, Lionel always wore a neatly pressed business shirt and smart trousers. He was always well groomed, proud of his appearance.

"You are a sight for sore eyes," she said as Lionel stepped up onto the curb.

"Am I to assume that there's trouble in paradise at the Salt residence again?" Lionel asked, fetching Sonya's mail from the letterbox as he maneuvered his trolley through the gate.

Sonya shrugged.

"Sorry, Lionel - lawyer-client privilege. I could tell you, but then I'd have to kill you."

Lionel scoffed as he handed Sonya her mail and parked the trolley on the porch of the converted house.

"She got sprung big time, didn't she?"

"Well, put it this way: if she had pushed ahead with it, I would have called you and Ruth as witnesses for poor Bernard. I don't know how he puts up with her. Have you got time for a coffee?"

Lionel reached into the lunch trolley and revealed a pair of lidded cups along with a brown paper bag.

"I already came prepared."

Sonya grinned, taking her bag and cup and gesturing for him to come inside.

"The office is coming along," Lionel said as he inspected the reception area. The drop sheets, ladders and painting equipment occupied the waiting area, in readiness for the remaining work Sonya needed to complete.

Sonya nodded, surveying her handiwork.

"Aside from the wacky divorces, the contentious will preparation, small businesses administration, claims and probate duties, yeah," Sonya replied as they went into her office. "It is. I'm just relieved to finally be working. It's starting to pay off."

Simon peered up from his basket and growled, a low rumble in the pit of his throat, upon seeing Lionel. Sonya glowered at the dog and gestured for him to stop.

"I see he's just as charming as ever," Lionel joked as he sat down and sugared his coffee.

"Hmmm," Sonya said, continuing her glare until Simon relented. "I honestly don't know what to do with him, Lionel. I've had obedience classes suggested to me, but I think he's too set in his ways now. This animosity towards men in particular is becoming embarrassing."

Sonya flopped down in her chair and put her legs up on the corner of her desk. She eagerly fished the contents of her lunch bag out and unwrapped an overtly large salad roll.

"Well, like I've said before," Lionel remarked. "I think it's a relief to have a legal practice in the town again. It will make life a lot easier for a lot of people."

"I don't mind saying that I've been busting my chops for this, though I didn't expect that I'd be running my own practice so soon."

Lionel nodded as he sipped his coffee.

"And it's good to finally have mail that doesn't include warning letters from other law firms," Sonya added, nodding towards the pile on her desk. "Though I'm sure there are plenty of bills in amongst that lot."

She sighed and chuckled lightly.

"At least I'll have plenty to keep me occupied this weekend."

Lionel fixed Sonya with a half-serious frown.

"Sonya, you really should start socializing again. Why aren't you getting out and enjoying yourself? You're a beautiful young woman."

Sonya returned his disapproving look, adding a lopsided smile. She'd heard this line from Lionel before.

"Lionel. Stop trying to stitch me up. I know how your mind works."

"Well, it's true," he argued. "You can't continue to squirrel yourself away in that lonely old house like a hermit with a mongrel. You'll become an old and twisted spinster with no teeth and a funny smell."

"Lionel!" Sonya gasped theatrically, screwing up a piece of paper and pitching it at him. "That's terrible."

"It's true," Lionel chuckled. "No man will want you then. Look, Ruth and I care about you, is all. You're like a daughter to us. We just hate the thought of you spending all of your time alone."

Sonya laughed in spite of herself, taking another bite out of her salad roll.

"Lionel, I'm doing all right. I don't need any extra complications in my life right now."

"OK, OK. I'll drop the subject - for now."

As she glanced over the contents of the pile, one particular envelope suddenly caught her attention - a bright yellow business-sized envelope.

Sonya removed her legs from the desk and sat forward in her chair, plucking the envelope from the pile and inspecting it closely.

Lionel's brow furrowed and he set his cup down on the desk.

"What is it, Sonya?"

"A letter," Sonya replied flatly. She appeared to have paled considerably. "It's for Denny," she said.

There was a long silence as Sonya stared at the envelope, unable to move. She had not seen a letter addressed to Denny for at least three or four months, let alone anything that had his name printed professionally on it.

"I thought I had taken care of all his mail - all of his contacts. I guess I missed one."

"Well, who's it from?" Lionel asked gently, immediately following it up with a bashful, "Sorry. You've piqued my interest."

Sonya finally looked up at Lionel. Her eyes were misty.

"The Arts Council. In Melbourne."

Slowly, Sonya turned the envelope over in her hands and ran her finger through the gap, opening it. She unfolded the letter inside, whereupon two tickets fell out from the middle. She placed them to one side and read the letter.

"It's an invitation. For Denny to attend the concert series at the Melbourne International Festival for the Guitar."

"Oh, my." Lionel said, doing his best to stifle a gasp.

"He loved the Festival Series," Sonya remembered wistfully. "He looked forward to it every year."

She scanned the letter. Her eyes widened as she approached a particular sentence on the page. She had to read it once more to convince herself she'd read it correctly the first time.

"He has been invited to play."

"Sonya..." Lionel didn't know what to say. He felt suddenly very awkward and wished he could find the right words - any words.

"No, no, it's OK," she reassured him, her voice quivering. "It's OK. It's just caught me off guard."

"That would have been wonderful for Denny," Lionel offered, sipping the remainder of his coffee. "I do miss hearing him play."

"Yeah."

Gathering up the envelope abruptly, Sonya stuffed the letter and tickets inside it, then dropped them in the wastepaper basket beside her.

Lionel frowned.

"Are you sure you want to do that?"

Sonya quickly wiped at her eyes, trying hard not to break down in front of Lionel.

"I don't need the tickets. I won't be going to the Festival."

"Maybe so. But you might want to at least let the organizers know that Denny won't be able to attend."

Sonya's cheeks flushed red, and she reconsidered the wastepaper basket.

"You're probably right," she said quietly, suddenly feeling awful.

Sonya fished the envelope out of the basket again and hastily smoothed it out with her hand. She looked down on Denny's name for a long moment, then set the letter on the desk before her, next to a picture frame.

A picture frame containing a photograph of her and Denny together.

Sonya and Lionel sat in awkward silence.

***

Andy felt almost afraid to open the door of the apartment. He hesitated, key in hand, in the darkened hall. Taking a deep breath, he inserted the key into the lock and turned it. Inside he flicked the light switch on the wall.

"Jesus."

The hallway leading into the apartment appeared as though someone had set off a small explosive. There were great holes in the walls, some the size of a basketball. Long gouges had been dug into the plaster, as though someone had dragged a sharp object like an ax or even a sword along their length. Accompanying these, crude spray-painted tags had been left on the walls and doors.

Andy shook his bandaged head, seething with anger.

He noticed the faint smell of feces as he went deeper into the apartment. Although it was apparent Beck had cleaned most of it off the walls and floor, the foul odor lingered, melding with the smell of disinfectant.

Setting his bag down, Andy went into the living room, threw open the blind and opened the window, allowing fresh air in from outside.

In the hall, Andy noted that Beck had already cobbled together some tools, plaster filler, paint, brushes and rollers to begin repairing the damage. Andy picked up a paint roller and considered it.

Then he looked up at the graffitied door of his bedroom. Andy stepped up to it, hesitating, not wanting to see what was inside. He knew it wasn't going to be good.

The room was utterly devastated. The bed had been upturned, the mattress shredded to the point of uselessness. His desk had been smashed in half. There were splinters everywhere. On the floor, lying in pieces, was his laptop, its darkened screen smashed. His television set had been kicked in and lay lop-sided on its face on the floor, still plugged into the wall socket. As Andy surveyed the ruin, his eyes fell across his shattered guitar case, which Beck had retrieved from the alley and had placed in against the wall just inside the door.

Andy's heart sank. He knelt down gingerly, appraising the damage, clutching at his broken ribs painfully. He opened the zipper and, upon seeing the wrecked instrument, he squeezed his eyes shut, fighting to hold back tears. His grandmother's legacy, her gift to him from so long ago, was devastated. The guitar was irreplaceable.

And then he remembered something else. Through tear-filled eyes Andy looked across the room, blinking furiously, searching amongst the mess until he saw it.

The locked box.

Upturned and lying on its side, the steel box had been pried open with considerable force. He knew it had been emptied. All the money that Andy had put away, the earnings from his dealing, his wages from The Pub. All of it was gone. All that remained were a couple of tattered photographs, which lay away from the box.

Angrily wiping at his tears, Andy snatched up the remaining contents of his locked box. One of the photos was of his mother posing alone under a tree in a garden. He looked upon this stranger's face, a woman he hardly knew. The other photograph was of his father, much younger. Dressed in a military uniform, he wore a broad smile, and was looking up at a very young Andy - he must have been about five - who sat astride his shoulders. Andy's sister stood leaning against her father, holding his hand.

Andy smiled through his tears, remembering when the photograph had been taken. It had been another time, another place. When he had been happy.

He looked up and saw the wall in front of him where the bed head had been.

Scrawled in black paint, was the crude inscription: "I own you."

Andy stared at the words. A black pall settled over him. He remembered Vasq standing before him in the alley, threatening him; his crew surrounding him, preventing his escape; Cassie watching indifferently, hating him.

'I own you.'

Andy grabbed the ruined locked box and pitched it at the wall with a guttural scream. Then he collapsed back, burying his head in his hands.

***

Beck opened the apartment door a couple of hours later to find Andy armed with a paint roller applying a second coat to the hallway wall. Large drop sheets covered the floor and the apartment smelled - thankfully - of fresh paint. He blinked upon seeing Andy in paint-smeared clothes, his head bandage also splattered with paint.

Andy paused, nodding wearily at Beck.

"Hey, man. Do you think you should be doing that in your condition?"

Beck's voice trailed off as he realized that Andy had managed to completely repair the damage in the hall, remove the graffiti and patch up the walls in the living room. The devastation was already almost completely gone.

"Holy shit, man! You did all of this?" He set down the two plastic bags he'd been holding. "I never had you figured for any sort of handyman."

Andy smiled faintly and nodded.

"Neither did I. I just felt I should get in and try to clean this mess up before the landlord discovers just how bad it was. I'm discovering that I can do a lot of things I never tried before."

"Jesus, let me give you a hand. I got some fresh supplies." Beck fished a pair of brushes out of one of the bags and began helping, finishing the detailing around the door frames. "What time did they let you out of the hospital?"

"I didn't wait," Andy admitted. "The nurse told me the doctor wouldn't be able to see me until the morning, so I checked myself out. I took the train home."

"Are you sure that was a good idea?" Beck asked. "You took a hell of a beating. What if something happens, like you start bleeding from your brain or something?"

Andy shrugged, running the roller over a spot in the middle of the wall.

"I feel fine, Beck. I'd rather be here, anyway. I couldn't handle sitting around there doing nothing. I tried calling Sam, but she wouldn't answer her cell. I think she's pissed at me or something. I've got no idea why."

Beck glanced sideways at Andy, adjusting his grip on the brush.

"You sure about that?" he said from the corner of his mouth.

"What do you mean?" Andy asked, stopping in mid-roll.

"Well, I'm no expert, dude, but I think she's sweet on you. You only have to see how she looks at you."

Andy's breath caught in his throat. He blinked at Beck.

"I ... never ... picked up anything from her."

Beck chuckled and flicked his brush at Andy, hitting him with splatters of paint.

"That's because you're a douche bag," he said. "It's the worst-kept secret in the world. Since you began cleaning up your shit, she's definitely been taking more of an interest in you."

"But why would she be so angry, then?" Andy asked, more of himself than Beck.

"Maybe it's because you started talking about this chick Sonya in the hospital. It raised those little green hackles on the back of her neck, I guess."

Andy flinched at the mention of Sonya's name.

"Wait ... she told you?"

Beck nodded simply.

"She was bitching about it in the bar yesterday afternoon, making herself heard just a little too much, in my opinion. She reckons you were saying some weird shit. Talking about spirits and past lives. I told her it must've been the painkillers."

Andy slowly continued painting. For several minutes he was very quiet.

"You wanna talk about it?" Beck finally asked. "I've never heard you mention this Sonya chick before. Who is she?"

Andy shook his head and kept on painting.

"She's nobody," he scowled. "A figment of my imagination."

"Whatever you say, man."

Sensing Andy's discomfort, Beck was prudent enough not to pursue the conversation any further.

"Well... I think this is a great job, man, Maybe too good a job. Hector may choose to jack up our rent once he sees this."

"It wasn't your mess," Andy said, inwardly glad for the change of subject. "It was mine - all mine."

"Your mess?" Beck said. "You can't keep blaming yourself for this."

Andy laughed bitterly.

"Seriously," Beck continued, more forcefully. "You should stop punishing yourself. Look - you wanted to get out of that shit with Vasq. He'll get bored with you, eventually, and move on."

Beck noted a wry smile crease Andy's lips.

"What is it?" Beck asked.

"Oh, I'm sure Vasq will be moved on. *Very soon.*"

Andy gestured with a nod to the wall beside the door. Beck turned around and saw, pinned to the door frame, a small business card.

"DETECTIVE M. SORENSEN - NARCOTICS."

The phone number below it had been circled in red pen.

Beck grinned at Andy.

"You made the call?"

Andy nodded.

"Seems I have a friend amongst the police after all. I took care of it. All of it."

***

Two squad cars flanking an unmarked van pulled up quietly outside a ruddy clapboard house, catching the attention of an overweight Hispanic youth who sat on the porch playing a Nintendo.

Instantly he sprang to his feet, feeling for the small bulk strapped down low on his left ankle as several uniformed officers emptied from the squad cars on the street. He panicked and scrambled towards the front door.

"Stop right where you are!" shouted one of the detectives as he sprinted onto the lawn, weapon drawn.

The young henchman burst into the kitchen of the house where Emilio Vasq and members of the posse were sitting around a table. Numerous weapons lay on the table top, among beer bottles and ashtrays as well as clear plastic bags containing newly manufactured pills.

Vasq saw his lackey standing in the doorway with an expression of pure, paralyzing fear.

"We're fucked!"

Before any of them realized what was happening, the house was overrun by police brandishing their weapons menacingly. The stupefied Vasq and his counterparts at the table were caught completely off guard. They had nowhere to go. Within a few minutes, more vehicles had arrived out front. Emilio Vasq was led from the house in handcuffs. He wore a bitter, defiant grin as a gray-suited detective shoved his head down and pushed him into the police car.

A growing audience of neighbors had gathered in the quiet suburban street as, one by one, other members of the gang were frog-marched from the house and bundled into waiting vans.

***

At the disused Warehouse in the industrial precinct, a trio of police vans burst through a roller door and screamed into the center of the building, followed by a squad of heavily armed and uniformed tactical response officers.

A group of people sat in the lounge area. One of them, a slick businessman, stood up. He looked with contempt at the police officer who approached him.

"What is going on here?" he demanded.

"You're Victor Varnado?" the officer asked.

"Yes."

"You're under arrest, sir," the officer replied as he holstered his weapon and slapped a pair of handcuffs on the businessman. He was the owner of the property upon which the Warehouse stood. He was also Vasq's financial backer, the man behind the trance parties.

"On what grounds?" Varnado protested, glancing from the police officers to the group he was with - one of whom was Cassie. She got up from the couch where she had been canoodling with a young man dressed in expensive-looking street wear.

The police officer didn't answer. A second officer began reciting his rights. As quickly as Emilio Vasq had been spirited away, Varnado and his associates were cuffed and put into the police vans.

The officers only briefly considered Cassie and her partner. They did not arrest either, but turned and left without another word. Soon, the Warehouse was empty, except for the stunned couple who sat in the lounge area.

Cassie watched them go, and a feeling of dread slowly filled her.

Chapter 13

In a dream Andy finally met the presence: the soul who accompanied him. Curiously, the soul did not reveal his face to Andy. It was tantalizingly just out of reach, blurred by the boundaries of his dream state. But Andy could hear his voice as he spoke, and he had a sense of who this soul was. It was as though Andy were looking in a mirror, seeing himself, yet seeing this stranger.

This stranger was a friend. He had always been a friend. His name was Denny.

They walked across a quiet meadow. They learned about each other, though there was nothing really to learn, for they were one and the same. Yet Andy had many questions. How had Denny come to be here? Why had he chosen Andy? Why had Denny not gone to that other place where all souls go to find peace?

Denny was unsure of the answers to those questions. Little of what had happened had been of his own volition. He was an involuntary participant in his journeys: the journey before, when he had battled cancer, and the journey now - this place beyond the pain, beyond the tragedy, beyond the loss.

Denny had never wanted to die. He never wanted to leave Sonya, and so he fought the illness hard until all that was left was his indestructible spirit. Even in death, he had refused to accept his mortality - refused to accept that he could be lost from Sonya forever. It wasn't his time. He had watched Andy; the trauma of his self-destructiveness, the alienation from his father and the brilliance of his gift. Denny supposed that, somehow, a decision had been made by someone: a decision that Andy was worthy of redemption, and thus he was chosen to become a vessel within whom Denny could live on.

Andy recalled the shame of his own journey, one signposted by weakness and cowardice. The experience in the trauma room had enabled him to look upon his own wretchedness and rebel against it. Somewhere inside Andy was the seed of a proud young man. It had always been there. Andy just needed the means to nurture that seed and grow it beyond the things that had kept him shackled. He had cast off his avarice. In its place was the potential for a new beginning.

As they sat down together by a brook underneath a weeping willow, they talked about their mutual love of the guitar and the potent influence music had been in both their lives. They strummed together under the peaceful shade of the willow tree, sharing their music, enriching each other with the sounds of the strings.

And as Andy continued his conversation, he suddenly realized Denny was no longer beside him. Setting the guitar down he searched around for him, worried that he had gone so abruptly. He felt an incredible sadness. But it was then replaced by an enveloping warmth. Denny wasn't gone. Andy could sense him close by.

Beside him.

Within him.

Separate individuals had become singular. Andy breathed deeply and felt himself being infused with Denny's soul.

And with that symbiosis came a new sense, a new feeling. It was a longing for home, that place by the sea that he knew so well. It was also a longing for her, for Sonya - a longing to hold her again, to kiss her lips and to tell her that he loved her.

Andy knew that he had to find her.

Andy sat at a computer terminal in the library of the Conservatory, staring at the screen, the cursor blinking in the input field of the search engine as if it were waiting patiently for him. The library was quiet, much more so than he had anticipated. Not that he had ever spent much time in here. It was a novelty that he'd had to book time for the computer he sat at. With his laptop well beyond repair and the likelihood that he would never see his stolen money again, Andy had few options.

Andy adjusted the garish baseball cap he wore, conscious of the bandage underneath it. He had gingerly tested his affected eye this morning and found it to be functional, but he couldn't tolerate looking through it for any more than a few minutes at a time. He had replaced the dressing on his cheek with something a little less ostentatious and found the look more natural.

The dream still lingered at the corners of his consciousness - the conversation with Denny, the reverie they had shared. He had awoken this morning with a single focused thought. The morning's classes seemed to take forever, and he had found it difficult to concentrate - so eager was he to get to the library. Now that he was here, however, he was unsure of how to proceed.

All he had to go on were the disparate memories and flashes of insight from that other life which had now become his own. What was clear to him were his memories of Sonya and his burgeoning knowledge of Denny. They were two names, and only first names, at that. There must be thousands of similar Dennys and Sonyas on the planet. There was also the affinity he felt for Australia - a country so remote from Chicago that it might as well be Mars. He had the tattered magazine ad beside him now, but there was nothing more significant to it than its description of the Sapphire Coast.

"Let's start there, then," he reasoned silently.

Pulling his attention to the screen, Andy's fingers hovered over the keys, wiggling hesitantly. Then he typed into the search field "Sapphire Coast, NSW."

Results flashed up almost immediately: thousands upon thousands of pages devoted to this faraway place on the other side of the world.

There were detailed descriptions of tranquil rural countryside, robust agricultural economies tied to a popular tourist industry that offered wine, cheese making, gourmet dining and fresh seafood. There were images of verdant hills and lush meadows sprinkled with dairy cows next to a majestic coastline with pristine white beaches and gentle waves washing up on the sand from an azure sea. There were fishing boats that plied the water searching for the culinary delights of the ocean: oysters, mussels and prawns. There were picture-perfect villages inhabited by carefree locals like a scene out of *Gilmore Girls,* where friends and families mingled, and shopkeepers and business people ran trendy cafes, quaint boutiques and successful tourism enterprises. Children played with family pets, swam in the sea and roamed free in lush countryside. It was idyllic and appealing.

But none of it touched off anything in particular in Andy. It was all very pleasant, but ultimately boring. He cradled his chin in one hand as he tapped the keys with the other, scanning through the various websites, image galleries and streaming videos.

He was getting nowhere.

His gaze drifted down to the magazine ad beside him. Andy picked it up and gazed at it, trying to recall what it was about it that had struck him when he first saw it. The image of the coastline here on the page was so familiar to him. It was what he had seen in his dreams - but what about it was so significant? He scanned the text, searching until his eyes fell across some small print near the bottom of the page: "Photography by R. Broadbent, Hambledown, NSW."

Hambledown!

Andy felt a bolt of recognition. He reached down and fished through his backpack for a notepad and pencil, whereupon he scribbled down the name of the town. He returned to the search engine and was immediately rewarded with a plethora of results for the small coastal hamlet, a tranquil fishing village situated in the center of the Sapphire Coast region.

Andy browsed the place that had become their home, the place where Denny and Sonya lived. The peaceful seaside town with its quaint main street, populated by businesses and cafes, shops and services. A butcher, a pharmacist, a garage, a pub, the general store.

The general store!

It was where they went for their fresh fruit and vegetables, smaller grocery items that could be purchased conveniently at a moment's notice rather than having to drive to the supermarket in the next town over. It was where he used to stop on his morning run with the dog to take a break, have a coffee and treat his dog with some slices of sandwich meat the shopkeeper used to cut especially for him. These were vivid recollections. The sounds of the shop, and the conversations with the shopkeeper echoed in his mind. Andy's pupils dilated; he'd unlocked the door to yet more memories. He noticed a laser printer at the end of this row of terminals, and he began printing out pages of information.

Andy clicked through more photos of Hambledown's main street, identifying its post office, local bank branch and a small, seemingly ramshackle cottage that was in serious need of repair. Andy hovered over this image: an old double-fronted cottage with a lopsided sign that hung precariously from a single chain attached to a pole next to a gate.

"Harold Llewellyn, Barrister," Andy read.

Llewellyn.

"I know that name," he whispered in amazement.

Andy scribbled the name down on the page beside him. As he did so, his eye fell across the name Sonya immediately above it. And then he realized...

"Sonya Llewellyn!"

That was it! That was her!

He sat forward and examined the faded image of the house of the former barrister. This was the practice Sonya had hoped to re-open, the practice that her grandfather had run into the ground through a combination of poorly handled legal cases and a love affair with a 12-year-old single malt whiskey. Denny had met him only a handful of times, but Harold Llewellyn was mired in local infamy. Andy smiled, shaking his head, remembering the conversations about the curmudgeonly old piss-pot that used to hang out in the Pub at Hambledown.

He found himself drifting towards a number of real estate web pages displaying properties for sale in the Hambledown area, as well as properties that had been sold in the recent past. He continued, taking notes of street names, descriptions of the houses that he came across and names of the agents representing them. He was looking for something but couldn't put his finger on what it was.

Suddenly, he stopped.

A description of a property sale about 18 months ago. He looked at an image of a small house overlooking a quiet stretch of beach just outside of the township. "A renovator's delight", "A family get-away", "potential first home" were the descriptions attached to it.

It was the beach house. Their beach house.

He clicked on an icon that opened a gallery in a new window. Andy stared at it, hypnotized.

The beach house was just as he had seen it in his mind. The ruddy weather board that was in desperate need of a coat of paint, the terra cotta tiled roof with green moss growing in patches, the balcony that gave a glorious view across the beach and the bay away to the south where Hambledown was just visible, the overgrown garden with its once beautiful collection of plants and shrubs that just needed to be coaxed back to life from the maelstrom of weeds and glory vine.

It was the beach house he'd planned to renovate into a chic and modern coastal residence, where they dreamed of a life together, where they would start a family. He was going to set up his studio there, his drafting business. He remembered it all. He had already drawn the plans for it.

Already drawn the plans.

Andy remembered the drawing, the lines on a page that came together to form a detailed plan of what they'd hoped to achieve in renovating the old house. He knew how to draw. Denny had been studying it, at university.

They had been to university together, he and Sonya. That was how they had met and fallen in love. She was studying law and he was working towards a degree in architecture.

Andy blinked, absorbing a flurry of new memories now, trying to make sense of them. He saw a large, domed building in a park somewhere close to a city. The Exhibition Building! A bright green tram trundling down the middle of a busy thoroughfare. Swanson Street! A tall spire near a river lit up at night by colorful spotlights. The Yarra River!

Andy recalled the image of a tram and a spire next to a river on the poster for the Festival that hung in the student lounge. Reaching into his bag, he took out the application form Veldtman had given him. The logo for the Festival stood out on the page.

Melbourne.

Andy tapped in a new search query, looking for higher education facilities in the southern Australian metropolis of Melbourne. A list of descriptions came up. He scanned through the listings until his eyes fell on one part-way down the page.

Melbourne University - Home.

It was the University where both Sonya and Denny had studied. Melbourne University. As Andy clicked on the link for the University's website, he remembered.

He remembered studying hard for his degree, participating in the music society - the perfect outlet for his guitar, playing university cricket in the summer, swimming competitively for the swim team, playing football in the winter, drinking beers with friends at the Uni Bar, the parties and the life. And being in love with Sonya.

Andy navigated through the website, browsing the courses available for study, the facilities available on-campus, current news and events, images of the campus ground and the student services directory. Then he was drawn to a small icon in the right-hand corner of the page, underneath the student services link.

REMEMBERING DENNY.

He rubbed his forehead as he was taken to a new window. It was the Facebook login screen. Andy strained to remember his long-unused password. It was "Lotus." He logged in. A page loaded.

Andy felt as though all the air had been sucked from his lungs.

There on the screen in front of him was an image of Denny Banister. His profile had become a memorial filled with hundreds upon hundreds of Wall posts from family, friends, colleagues and acquaintances.

"Dennis Banister. Student, Guitarist, Lover, Friend. Passed away October 18th after a short battle with cancer."

"Denny - you were a diamond. God bless you brotha!!" "RIP Denny - We will never forget you"; "Denny - you were the worst slips fielder ever, but the finest cover drive in a generation - love the game, love you!"; "Denny - your music made us love more"; "Denny - Stevie Ray saved a spot for ya."

Andy scrolled through myriad profile pictures attached to the posts, his eyes welling with tears as he recognized the faces. Denny's kid sister Jocelyn, whom he'd nicknamed Joss since they were toddlers; his mother Lucy, a recent convert to the social networking phenomenon; his best friend Anthony Llewellyn, Sonya's brother. There were friends he had studied with, friends he'd played guitar with, friends with whom he'd grown up who were now living abroad.

He remembered all of them. Andy felt overwhelming waves of grief twist inside of him. All of these people, so much a fixture in Denny's life, had expressed their love for him and expressed their own grief at his passing. For this wonderful young man had been lost from them. The tears came quickly and fell down over his cheeks. Andy's heart ached for these friends who had enriched Denny's life, this place so far away that Denny had called home, this life that was so full of promise - that was so *good*. He struggled to comprehend the strength of the emotions he was feeling.

Although Sonya didn't have a page of her own, she was well represented in Denny's image gallery. There were photos of them together posing for a romantic couple's shot, photos of them camping with friends from university, lazing on the beach, swimming in the water, hamming it up at a theme park.

Andy had lost track of time. Suddenly a pair of fingers tapped his shoulder, and he jumped in his seat. He spun around quickly to find a young woman standing behind him.

"Excuse me. Your time's up," she said, a little awkwardly.

Andy blinked furiously and hurriedly wiped his eyes with his hands, hoping she hadn't noticed.

"I'm sorry."

Andy quickly gathered up his things while the woman waited patiently. He gazed at the screen one last time, at Sonya and Denny together, then closed the window as if it had never been.

***

Andy stumbled from the library trying to collect himself as he stuffed the print-outs into his backpack. It was Denny who had re-acted in there, not himself - he knew that - but still, he was confused and frightened by the power of those dormant emotions, his power-lessness to separate them. His heart was racing.

He crossed an expansive lawn, fastening the zipper of his back-pack and taking some deep breaths. By the time he reached the faculty building he felt a little calmer. His mouth was dry, and he decided to get a can of soda. Entering the faculty building and the student lounge, Andy spied a vending machine and approached it. Some students from his classes were milling about near the large notice board and they regarded him curiously as he passed by them. He hoped he didn't look as strange as he felt.

Lifting the can from the machine, Andy opened it and downed a generous gulp of liquid, relieved to soothe his parched throat. He turned from the machine and saw the notice board once more. The poster in the bottom right-hand corner was still there.

MELBOURNE INTERNATIONAL FESTIVAL
OF THE GUITAR,
VICTORIA, AUSTRALIA
15TH - 21ST FEBRUARY

The yellow rectangle of paper that was there previously had been replaced by a white strip of paper upon which an inscription was scrawled in red marker.

"Last days for applications. Closing Friday!"

Melbourne.

"Still weighing it up?"

Andy flinched at the sound of Veldtman's voice. She was standing right beside him.

"What?" he stammered before composing himself. "Oh. No. God, no. I was just daydreaming, I guess."

Veldtman looked Andy up and down and shook her head, tsk-tsking at his bruises and bandages.

"What have you gone and gotten yourself into this time, Andrew?" she questioned in the way a disapproving aunt might interrogate a naughty child.

"Nothing," Andy replied weakly. "Well ... it's what happens when you try to walk away."

Veldtman was caught off guard by his frank response. He had returned to studying the poster.

"You've heard this all before, Andrew, I know, but may I remind you of just how prestigious this event is?" she said. "One of the finest music gatherings in the world."

Andy nodded without looking away from the poster.

"Why, then, are you still procrastinating?"

Andy became flustered. He tried to speak, but could not find the words. He met her with a pathetic smile.

"There's no *way* I could possibly go to an event like that," he said weakly. "It's gotta be, like, 12,000 miles away from here. It would cost a fortune just to get there."

"There are means of addressing issues of cost, Andrew DeVries."

Andy turned to face her.

"Nobody wants me on this, Ms. Veldtman. You know it and I know it. Decisions have already been made; I'm sure of that."

Veldtman folded her arms over her chest. Her eyes pierced through him as though she could see his innermost thoughts.

"What makes you so sure? I think you underestimate those who are more qualified than you to assess a person's ability. Especially when they have seen the effort that person has undertaken to better themselves both in the classroom and ... on a certain stage, in a certain part of town."

She leaned in close to him and lowered her voice.

"For god's sake! Submit an application and do it *quickly*. There are only four places available and there is not a lot of time left."

Andy blinked at her, bewildered. In his mind Denny's voice spoke to him.

This is your chance.

He considered the poster again, then, slowly, he reached into his pocket and took out the folded application form. Veldtman almost snatched it from him and examined it.

Andy had completed it.

***

Jochen Zinski rushed through an expansive hallway in the Melba Memorial Conservatorium of Music - a quaint group of buildings situated in the leafy Melbourne suburb of Richmond. He juggled several books and folders in his arms, while desperately keeping his left arm cocked in an effort not to lose the strap of his laptop bag. Various colleagues and students greeted him as he passed by; he managed to acknowledge every one, even though it was a rather harried greeting at best.

It had been an incredibly busy morning for Zinski. He had attended four meetings in five hours, and not all of them had been in one place. Having to contend with Melbourne's perpetual peak-hour traffic was enough to fray anyone's nerves, and Zinski, who was renowned for his quiet way and exquisite patience, was close to wanting to strangle somebody.

As was often the case with Zinski, a Hamburg native and artistic director of the Melbourne International Festival of the Guitar, he steadfastly refused to acknowledge any suggestion that he couldn't manage. At times like these, when the demands were seemingly insurmountable, he reminded himself of the prestige his appointment carried. The festival was steadily gaining renown as one of the finest gatherings of international artists on the calendar, and the significance of this was not lost on him.

He would kill for a coffee right now, however.

Zinski was praying his secretary had been able to clear his schedule for this afternoon; otherwise there simply would not be any time for him to digest any of the information from the morning's meetings. There were numerous venue and scheduling conflicts to contend with, city council logistics and politics to wade through, guest performance line-ups for the week-long festival to finalize and a multitude of applications from candidates hoping to perform in the emerging talent concert series to consider. He dreaded the prospect of having to take home yet another pile of unfinished work tonight. His wife would surely kill him.

Though he had finally submitted to the enthusiastic sales pitch of his eleven year-old daughter and purchased a BlackBerry, he had no idea how to use the blasted device. He was thankful that he hadn't pitched his notebook into the rubbish bin. Though it was fairly bursting at the seams with additional sticky notes, scraps of A4 paper that had been stapled inside and business cards, Zinski would be utterly lost without it.

Zinski rounded a corner and arrived at his office. Passing by his secretary he issued a comical expulsion of air up over his face as he sprinted the last few steps into his office, where he literally tossed the contents of his arms across his desk.

His relief at having unloaded his burden was brief, however, because almost immediately, the phone on his desk began ringing.

Zinski found the inside of his bottom lip with his teeth and bit hard. It was all he could do to prevent himself from cursing out loud.

The ringing stopped as his secretary, Grace, picked up the call from her desk, giving him the desired moment to collect himself. He flopped down in his chair just as Grace came into the office with a coffee cup in one hand and her other hand perched at her ear, balancing a headset there. She took a quick mouthful from the coffee then handed it across to Zinski, who mouthed an appreciative 'Thank you' as he took the cup.

He sipped away while his secretary nodded in response to the caller on the other end of the line. At first he was absorbed in catching himself up, until he noticed the expression on Grace's face change subtly from her usual, professional demeanor to one of concern.

Finally, putting her hand over the microphone, she looked at Zinski.

"I think you'll want to take this," she said quietly, pointing at his own telephone, which was buried under papers.

Sitting forward, Zinski placed the cup down beside him and dug out the telephone, clutching at the receiver.

"Good afternoon," he greeted in his suave German accent as Grace transferred the call and stepped away. "Jochen Zinski; can I help you?"

"Hello, Mr. Zinski," a woman's voice replied at the other end of the line. "My name is Sonya Llewellyn. I'm calling on behalf of Dennis Banister."

Sonya sat in her office, holding the letter from Zinski and staring at it as she spoke.

Zinski immediately recognized the name. He had taught Denny years ago when Denny was still in high school, and they had become good friends. He had been instantly transported by the young man's talent with the guitar and though Denny had chosen a university degree in architecture over the instrument, Zinski regarded him as one of the finest virtuosos he had ever heard.

"Yes, of course, Ms. Llewellyn," he responded cheerily. "I trust that he received my invitation, then."

Sonya nodded absently, adjusting her grip on the handset.

"He - I mean, *I* did, thank you, Mr. Zinski. However, I am afraid that I am calling you with some rather sad news," she paused, her words threatened to catch in her throat as she prepared to deliver the sad little speech yet again. "Denny passed away last year after a short illness. He was ... diagnosed with cancer, but it was untreatable."

All the maelstrom of thought that had accompanied Zinski's busy morning suddenly dissipated as the import of Sonya's news struck him. He sat forward in his chair and rubbed his brow with his free hand.

"Oh, my dear. I am - so very sorry to hear this. Please accept my sincerest condolences."

"Thank you, Mr. Zinski. The invitation you extended to Denny was lovely. He would have been so thrilled to attend the festival. I know he loved it very much. I - I just wanted you to know."

Zinski was unsure of what to say next.

"I - it was my pleasure. He was a beautiful exponent of the guitar. I know he will be sadly missed by us here. I will be sure to pass on this news to the Conservatorium."

"Thank you, Mr. Zinski," Sonya said finally, her voice flat. "Goodbye for now."

Sonya hung up the phone and sat there numb, the familiar sadness of loss creeping through her once more. She laid the letter down before her, the two tickets paper-clipped to its top border, and glanced over at the photograph of her and Denny together. As she gazed into the joyous eyes of her lost love, Sonya felt her emotions threaten to crumble around her. His warmth, his voice, his conversation, the way he held her, the way he kissed her. How Sonya missed his gentle touch. Before she could allow herself to break apart, however, Sonya pulled herself back from the precipice of her grief; she stifled her tears and closed down her heart.

Zinski re-cradled the receiver of his own telephone and swiveled in his seat to gaze out through the window across the lush green lawn outside. He considered the sad news that had just been delivered.

Grace gingerly poked her head around the door.

"Everything OK?" she ventured warily.

Zinski nodded but did not speak.

"I managed to clear your schedule for the afternoon," she said, sensing he was more affected than he was willing to admit. "Grant has offered to take your tutorials, so you have a clear run until the end of the day."

Zinski smiled wanly. He regarded his coffee for a moment but suddenly found himself not wanting it anymore.

"Thank you, Grace," he said distantly, returning to his thoughtful gaze out through the window.

Chapter 14

There was a tension between Andy and Samantha, but he tried to ignore it. She had barely said a word to him from the moment he'd arrived at The Pub, apart from offering him some of her foundation so he could cover up some of the nastier cuts and scratches that were still visible on his forehead. Andy had ditched the gauze bandages entirely and replaced the Band-Aid over his cheek. In the subdued lighting of the front bar, he was mostly able to conceal the fact that he looked like shit. Gideon had tried to send him home, but Andy insisted on staying. He needed the money and desperately. For the first time in a long time, he found himself worrying about money.

Gideon allowed Andy to borrow the guitar they used for the random guest performers Andy had been encouraging up onto the stage. But it wasn't the same. The guitar was like wearing a left-handed glove on a right hand. It was unwieldy and difficult to tune. It just didn't fit.

After a couple of hours, things hadn't improved. Samantha was frustrated that Andy apparently hadn't noticed she was pissed with him. He seemed distracted, as though he had something on his mind. She didn't know what to say to break the ice. Andy sat at the corner of the bar during his evening break, eating his meal quietly and reading some documents. It piqued her interest and she made a rather ham-fisted effort of trying to see what it was that he was reading, but it remained tantalizingly out of reach.

An opportunity opened up when Andy stood up from the bar and went to the men's room. She quickly stepped over to the unattended documents on the bar and surveyed them, keeping one eye on the door to the men's room. There were dozens of computer printouts of web pages, reams and reams of abstract, scribbled notes and photographs of buildings, a strip of coastline and faces of unfamiliar people. None of it seemed to make any sense at all. The door opened a couple of times, causing her to flinch, but it wasn't Andy.

"What the hell is he up to?" she wondered.

He'd circled passages of descriptions of a town, as well as pictures of an old house sitting on a rise. In the soft light of the bar Samantha shifted a couple of pages around, hoping to see more of the handwritten scribble Andy had produced. Then she recognized one of the names on the page: Sonya, the name he had spoken in the hospital.

Samantha felt a twinge of jealousy seeing the name on the page. Just under that sheet of paper was another printout. It was an image of a young couple posing together. She fingered the edge of the paper, hoping to see it better, while her eyes darted between it and the men's room door. The couple stood in front of a hedge that was full of pretty pink flowers and appeared very much in love. Samantha looked deep into the eyes of the young man. She saw something there that was familiar, but she couldn't work out what it was.

The door opened again and Samantha skittered back down towards the other end of the bar as Andy stepped into view.

***

Towards the end of the evening, when the bar was nearly empty, Andy decided he could no longer avoid Samantha. As she unloaded a tray of beer glasses from the washer, he saw an opportunity and took it.

"So what's going on, Sam?"

Samantha shrugged her shoulders brusquely as she carefully plucked out individual glasses and began to wipe them down.

"Nothing is going on," she said tersely. "You haven't exactly been all fluff and bubble tonight. I could ask the same thing of you."

Andy looked tired.

"C'mon, Sam, let's cut the shit. You've been pissed at me since the hospital. I just want to know what it is I'm supposed to have done."

Sam pursed her lips, clearly uncomfortable. She couldn't look at him.

"You haven't done anything," she answered feebly, to which she added under her breath. "That's the problem."

Andy stared at her, having caught that last jibe.

"What's that supposed to mean?" he pressed.

Samantha stopped what she was doing and put her towel down on the bar. She fidgeted on the spot for a moment then let the tension in her shoulders dissipate.

"It's nothing, Dev," she said, her voice resigned. "It's my problem, not yours."

"I don't buy that, Sam," he challenged her, shaking his head. "You don't lie very well."

Samantha fixed Andy with an almost pleading gaze.

"What's going on with you, Andy? For the longest time you've been this ... lost soul *douche bag* or something. Nobody could reach you. Then the moment you start becoming ... interesting, you start acting all weird."

Andy squeezed his eyes shut and shook his head, trying to work out what the hell Samantha was getting at.

"I have no idea what you're talking about," he said exasperated.

"Oh, c'mon, Dev. What's with all this bullshit about souls speaking to you and mysterious women on the other side of the world?"

Andy was completely sideswiped by Samantha's escalating tirade until he realized what she was getting at. He glanced over at his backpack hanging up in the alcove behind her. The penny dropped. She had been looking through his stuff.

"Sam, my bag and what's in it is my business. No one else's," he said angrily.

Samantha shifted uncomfortably, stung by his barb.

"Andy, I just don't understand why you're doing this," Samantha was exasperated now. "You're inventing all of this ... this ... *shit,* so you don't have to face up to the realities of *this* world"

"Samantha you have no *friggin' idea* what is going on with me right now," Andy hissed.

He glanced sideways then, noticing that their increasingly heated exchange had attracted the attention of the few remaining patrons in the bar. He lowered his voice as much as he could. "I don't even understand it myself. I confided in you because I thought I could. But you didn't want to know about it then, so why should it matter to you now?"

"It matters, Andy." Samantha blinked; her cheeks flushed a bright pink. In that moment, when she looked into Andy's intense gaze, she noticed something about his eyes that caused a shiver to pass through her. She turned away from him, unable to meet his gaze any longer. "Because *you* matter. To me."

Abruptly, she turned away from Andy, pushed past him and disappeared into the men's room.

Andy stood there stunned.

Son-of-a-bitch, he thought.

***

Late in the evening The Pub was quiet. The bar was closed, most of the staff had gone home and Gideon was discussing the day's take with the bar manager. The door behind him opened and he turned to see Bruce DeVries step in from the cold. Bruce nodded a wordless greeting to Gideon and unzipped his jacket, welcoming the open fire that crackled brightly in the corner.

"Look what the cat dragged in," Gideon said, gesturing for his old friend to join him over at the bar. He signaled for the bar manager to serve them a couple of drinks.

Bruce removed his cap and placed it down on the bar beside him.

"It's friggin' freezing out there," he grumbled hoarsely, swinging his leg over his own bar stool and ruffling his matted-down, graying hair. The barman placed a whiskey tumbler in front of him.

"You just get back into town?" Gideon queried, eyeing his watch discreetly. "That's a bit late for you, isn't it?"

Bruce shook his head wearily.

"I got back a couple of days ago. Been down at the yard dealing with some engine trouble."

"Have you eaten anything? I can open the kitchen for you, if you'd like."

Again Bruce shook his head without speaking.

Gideon regarded his friend with concern as he sipped his whiskey.

"You get my message, then?"

"I got it," Bruce nodded, sipping his whiskey thoughtfully. "Is the ... kid still here? I called his apartment, but his friend said he wasn't home yet."

Gideon lowered his glass and held it still. Bruce DeVries wasn't given to asking anything much from anybody, especially when it came to his son. This was definitely a rare show from him now, Gideon thought.

"You just missed him by a few minutes," Gideon answered. "I suspect he's probably home by now."

Bruce nodded once. Gideon swore he noted disappointment in his friend's expression.

"You went and saw him, didn't you?" Gideon ventured.

Bruce considered his glass for a long moment before nodding silently.

"I went to the hospital the night he was brought in. I stayed for a few hours. When I went back yesterday, the shit had signed himself out."

Gideon smiled, which brought a frown from Bruce.

"He looked a little worse for wear when he turned up for work today. I tried sending him home, but he wouldn't have it."

"And of course you couldn't resist the opportunity to have more money coming in over the bar by workin' him, could you?" Bruce said.

Gideon feigned being hurt by Bruce's jibe, grabbing at his heart before chuckling sardonically.

"What's goin' on with him, Gideon?" Bruce asked, his tone becoming serious.

"You tell me. All I know is that he turned up here for work one day and worked like no one I have ever seen work. It blew me away. Blew us all away. He hasn't missed a shift in three months, he's always punctual and he's probably one of my best barmen. It's a mystery to me."

Gideon paused as he fished around in his jacket pocket for a half-cigar he'd been saving. He lit it and puffed away.

"I don't get it," Bruce muttered sourly, shaking his head slowly. "One moment he's mixed up with that bunch of lowlifes, the next he just - changed. No one just changes like that, especially not a kid like him."

"A kid like him?" Gideon asked.

"Yeah, a kid like him. A fuck-up, a do-nothing. Spends more time with that damned guitar and swallowing pills than applying himself to anything useful."

"Hmmm," Gideon nodded thoughtfully, suddenly feeling a little defensive. "Those are strong words for a father to describe his son. Especially when he hasn't been around to know what the fuck his son has been doing."

Gideon saw Bruce flinch, almost imperceptibly, and he smiled inwardly.

"From what I've seen lately, that guitar-playing of his is pretty bloody special. Almost as special as what we heard back in Nasiriyah," Gideon paused as an old memory hovered between them.

"And I've noticed you sneaking in here to watch him perform," Gideon took a drink from his glass then pointed directly at Bruce. "So you haven't written him off entirely, have you?"

Bruce bristled, flashing Gideon an icy glare.

"I *never* wrote him off, Gideon. I just never understood him. I still don't." Bruce's shoulders seemed to sag as though a heaviness had descended on him. "I know I haven't helped things much."

Gideon reached out with a meaty hand and patted his shoulder.

"Dev, I've never criticized you for any of the choices you've made. You did what you felt you had to do after Clare left. Your mother did a fine job with both Andy and his sister," Gideon took a moment to think carefully about how he was going to frame his next sentence. "But Andy's been lost for a long time. He's needed a father and, sadly, you haven't been around for him. He's desperately wanted someone to be proud of him, to show an interest, but no one really has."

Bruce felt a painful twinge of guilt and he took a large mouthful of his whiskey. He knew that Gideon was right. Not that he would let Gideon see that.

"That still doesn't explain what's happening with him right now, though, does it?" he said.

"No, it doesn't," Gideon acknowledged. "But I guess, again, we've all underestimated him, haven't we? The boy is no fool, Bruce. He's a bright kid. I guess that overdose was enough for him to realize that he had to change his direction, and quickly."

Bruce shot Gideon a surprised look. He hadn't said anything to Gideon about the overdose and, so far as he knew, no one else in The Pub knew about it, either.

Gideon took another puff on his cigar.

"Look. Talk to your son, Dev. Whatever it is with him is welcome enough on its own, but it's only a side note to what he really needs right now..."

"And what does he *need* right now?" Bruce echoed with a tinge of frustration.

Gideon shook his head and smiled as he stood up from the bar.

"You really are a slow one tonight, huh?"

***

At the sound of knocking Andy trotted to the front door of the apartment and peered through the peep hole. His eyes went wide when he saw his father standing a little off to the side so that he was only partly in view.

"What the hell?" Andy muttered, alarmed.

When the door opened, Bruce stood back a little, probably not expecting anyone to answer. Andy poked his head around the door and looked at his father blankly. There was an awkward silence between them.

"Hello," Bruce finally offered, trying to look at his son but unable to find the courage to do so.

"Uhh - hi," Andy stammered, unsure of what to do or say next. His father rarely came to the apartment. "What are you ... doing here?"

Whaddaya mean, what are you doing here? You idiot! Andy cursed himself.

Bruce shrugged and fidgeted on the spot. He loosened the woolen scarf he wore under his trucker's jacket and removed his cap, holding it tightly in his hand. Andy noticed he had a newspaper rolled up under one arm.

"You - want to let me in, perhaps?"

Andy quickly opened the door as if he had forgotten his manners.

"Shit. I'm sorry. Of course."

He ushered his father inside. Bruce noted the drop sheets and paint cans on the floor in the hall, as well as the partially repaired holes in the living room wall. He pointed at the damage.

"This from your friends?"

Andy nodded.

"Yeah. Beck and I are fixing it up."

Bruce raised an eyebrow as Andy passed him and went through into the kitchen.

"*You*?" he said, surprised.

"Yeah, *me*," Andy shot back. He scratched the back of his head, wincing that he'd been too defensive. "I've - uh - just made a fresh pot of coffee. You want some?"

Bruce nodded and sat down at the table, placing his newspaper down without unrolling it. Andy studied his father suspiciously out of the corner of his eye as he poured two cups of coffee. For his part, Bruce sat nervously at the table, unsure of himself, not knowing whether he should stand or sit.

"I missed you at the hospital the other day," he said finally. "Nurse said you checked out against medical advice."

"Yeah," Andy responded flatly, transferring the two cups to the table, shaking his fingers vigorously from the heat of the ceramic. "The doctor kept delaying and delaying. I just wanted to be home here."

Bruce nodded once as he sugared his coffee and added milk.

"You think that was a good idea?"

Andy shrugged as he sat down at the table, splinting his injured ribs with his arm as discreetly as he could so that his father would not see.

"Probably not, but I'll deal with it."

"Like you dealt with those friends of yours, huh?" Bruce ventured, without looking up.

Andy sat back in his seat and appraised his father.

"Look, what do you want, Dad? What are you doing here?"

Bruce finally looked up at Andy with that hollow stare he was so good at.

"I'm just ... here!" he said evenly. "I was concerned. I know what happened the other night with that gang of yours - I know they ambushed you. I just wanted to know ... that you're all right."

Andy relaxed slightly and took hold of the cup in front of him. He didn't lift it up.

"I'm all right," he said simply.

Moments ticked by.

"So. What's with all this turning things around for yourself?" Bruce asked.

"I dunno," Andy's tone was noncommittal. "Guess I've just had enough of drifting along."

Denny observed the tension between father and son, lamenting their alienation.

"Well, that's good. That's good."

Bruce was floundering and he knew it. His son sat across from him fidgeting, unable to look at him directly. This was how it had been for so long. Andy could barely remember a time when it had been any different. The years spent longing for his father when he went away, the disappointment of trying to win his father's affection, only to have it dismissed out of hand, when Bruce was around. All of it clouded his emotions now. He did not know how to react to his father's presence here and now.

He is trying to reach out, Denny suggested. Listen.

"There was this kid out in the desert," Bruce began, relaxing back slightly in his seat. "Near Nasiriyah. He had a beat-up old Spanish guitar. Looked as though it had been run over by a truck."

Andy looked up at his father. Bruce DeVries had never spoken of the Gulf War or his time in Iraq.

"Nassar used to play all the time, whenever we were on down time. It was a beautiful sound. We used to listen to him play all these classical pieces that he knew by heart."

Bruce's eyes lifted towards the ceiling as he recalled the 20-year-old memories.

"Nassar wanted to study in Europe. He was saving up to leave Iraq. We chipped in each time he played for us, and he used to busk on the street in the town. I guess he made a decent sum of money over time."

Andy listened, suddenly transfixed.

"Our supply unit got caught in a firefight, late one night. The camp was overrun by insurgent fighters. As we were trying to defend it, there was a lot of crossfire. People were running everywhere."

Bruce looked down at his son again. This time, Andy was sure he could see tears welling in Bruce's eyes.

"He got caught up in it. Gideon and I were marshaling civilians to safety. We had to take cover from a mortar attack. I - mistook him for an insurgent fighter. And I shot him."

Andy was stunned, unable to move or speak. He could barely comprehend the guilt that his father had harbored, let alone that he would be so open with him now. That he would lay bare such a terrible truth, a burden he had carried with him for two long decades...

"I haven't been able to listen to so much as a Willie Nelson record in, maybe 20 years," Bruce said. "And I haven't heard anyone play as beautifully - the way he did - until - well, you know. Until now."

Bruce gestured awkwardly towards his son. Andy felt overwhelmed, recognizing the compliment for what it was. The significance of this moment was not lost on him. Then Andy remembered something from long ago. A memory from when he had lived with his grandmother. The memory of a beat-up old guitar she had stored away in the attic. He had found it one day, as an inquisitive seven-year-old, and begun to play.

"That guitar," Andy said. "The one I used to play around with at Nana's house. That was his, wasn't it?"

Bruce nodded wistfully, not wanting to speak for fear that he might break down in front of his son. Andy looked down at his hands in his lap, balled them into fists, then relaxed them again.

"I've stopped with all that shit, Dad," he said. "I ended it. They - the crew - weren't real happy about it."

Andy circled his face with his hand for effect, before cupping his hands in his lap.

"What are you going to do about it?"

"I already took care of it," Andy said, allowing himself to smile bitterly. "The police took down the crew yesterday. Busted them wide open. They won't be a problem for me anymore."

Bruce sipped his coffee and looked across through the entrance into the living room.

"I'll bet that's cost you a lot."

A trio of worry lines creased Andy's brow.

"Too much."

Bruce smiled wryly at his son, downing the remainder of his coffee.

"Would you like another?" Andy offered hopefully.

Bruce considered it a moment, then nodded with a smile.

"Yeah. Why not?"

He slid his cup across the tabletop towards Andy, who refilled it and his own.

"Gideon tells me that you've got an opportunity to travel overseas - to some sort of gathering of guitarists?"

Andy nodded hesitantly, pointing to a flier that was secured to the door of the refrigerator. He took it down and handed it to Bruce.

"Australia," Bruce remarked with surprise. "That's a long way to go. Can you even afford this?"

"There's talk of a sponsorship arrangement, if I'm successful," Andy replied, sitting down at the table again. "I haven't been interviewed yet."

"Oh? Well, when does that happen?"

"I don't know yet. I don't even know if they'll want to interview me."

Bruce gazed at his son with a curious expression. A question began to form in his mind. *Who was this young man who sat across from him?*

He was unable to put it into words.

Bruce stayed for several hours, and together father and son talked - more than they had in a long time.

Chapter 15

Andy stood behind the bar wiping a glass when the side door opened and Beck appeared. Andy greeted him with a smile as he stepped inside and took off his jacket.

"Hey, man."

"Hey yourself."

Beck's greeting wasn't especially enthusiastic - not unusual for him, such was his quiet way - but there was something in it that made Andy consider his friend with concern. For a moment he feared someone associated with Vasq might have threatened Beck again.

Beck sat down at the bar and Andy poured him his usual beer right away. Beck definitely had something on his mind.

"Are you OK?" Andy ventured as he set the beer down in front of Beck.

Beck nodded without looking up.

"Yeah. Well - I dunno, man."

Andy gave him a quizzical eye as he picked up another glass and began wiping it over.

"Please tell me someone didn't harass you again."

"Oh, god, no!" Beck retorted reassuringly, forcing a smile. "Not at all."

Beck surveyed the bar distractedly as though he were looking for someone.

"Where's Sam?" he asked.

"She's not working today," Andy replied, growing impatient.

"She still pissed at you?"

"Yeah. I think. Beck, you're stalling," Andy fixed his gaze directly at his friend. "You wanna tell me what's up?"

Finally, Beck looked up at Andy and his expression became serious. He rubbed his mouth with his hand nervously.

"I got some bad news today, Dev. There's a whole mess of trouble brewing between the financiers and the project heads on the building site. The money has dried up. There's gonna be a court case, but for the time being, they're shutting us down."

Andy stopped what he was doing and focused his attention fully on Beck.

"That's shitty, man. When are they..."

"End of next week," Beck finished for him. "Unless they can work their shit out - and I'm pretty sure they won't - I'll be out of a job."

"What are you going to do?"

Beck swilled his beer and set his glass down. He spoke hesitantly.

"Well, a few of the guys have been talking already, and Killgallon's uncle has got some contacts on a site in New York. He's got me a position out there already. I can start pretty much right away."

Beck paused, knowing already that Andy was struggling to digest the news. He felt awful. He seemed to be developing a habit of bearing bad news lately.

"I gotta take it, man. I gotta leave Chicago."

Andy smiled broadly, feigning relief for his friend while a feeling of dread rippled through him. He poured himself a beer and held his glass out towards Beck.

"Of course you do, Beck. You've got to take the job. I mean, it's New York. That's awesome!"

Beck hadn't anticipated Andy's response. He smiled awkwardly and clinked his glass with Andy.

"You're not pissed?"

"Why would I be pissed?" Andy asked. "You've gotta do what's best for you. Take the job, for god's sake. It's a once in a lifetime opportunity."

"But - what about the apartment?" Beck asked, still not entirely convinced by Andy's reaction. "The rent's gonna be too much to carry on your own."

Andy brushed it aside.

"Don't worry about it, Beck. It'll work out. Something will work out."

In truth, much as Beck had suspected, Andy's heart was sinking and he was barely able to maintain the happy facade for his friend. They had shared the apartment for almost two years. It had been a comfortable arrangement for the both of them. In fact, it had been one of the rare constants when everything else was out of control. Andy had come to realize that Beck was, quite possibly, the only true friend he really had. Deep down, Beck sensed what Andy's real feelings towards his news were, but he didn't call him out on it.

"I'll stick around, man," Beck reassured him. "I don't have to leave for a week or so, so I'll keep up my end until ... you know."

"Beck, Don't worry about it. It will be all right."

"So you - uhh - talked to Samantha?" Beck asked in a rather ham-fisted attempt at changing the subject again.

"I tried," Andy responded simply. "But she's not real happy right now. You were right, man. She - uhh - well, you know."

Beck smiled triumphantly, raising his glass once more.

"I'm not a pretty face for the hell of it, Dev. Any idiot could see it," he said dryly.

"I don't know what I'm gonna do about it, Beck."

"Just tell her the truth: that you're a total whack job and far too unstable to get involved with."

Andy managed a half-hearted grin.

"Hey, I was just kidding, Dev," Beck suddenly felt awful about his joke.

"I know. I guess that it's just more complicated than I want it to be right now."

Beck nodded in understanding.

"You've gotta feel right within yourself," he said. "And when you're searching, the way you are, you won't rest until you find what you're looking for."

"Sometimes I wonder what the fuck I'm looking for, Beck," Andy replied wearily, leaning over the bar and cupping his hands together.

"Well," Beck sat up straight on his bar stool as if stretching. "I can guess at what it is. And it's not Samantha."

Beck finished off his beer and set the glass down on its side on the bar.

***

Andy lay on the sofa bed later that night unable to sleep. In the darkness of the living room, the blankets drawn up under his arms, he stared at the ceiling, unable to escape the enveloping sadness that had settled over him. He had no idea what he was going to do. Even with his regular playing at The Pub on top of his bar duties - which gave him quite a bit more in tips - he would still have to move on from this place eventually.

But where would he go?

Although he was grateful for their recent significant break-through, Andy was under no illusions about the significant gulf that remained between him and his father. The years of neglect in their relationship, the sadness and hurt, wouldn't necessarily be all patched up after a single positive conversation.

One bright spark punctuated his gloom, however. He had received a message on his cell earlier in the afternoon. It was from Sorrel Veldtman, advising him that he had been selected for an interview pursuant to his application for a place at the Melbourne International Festival for the Guitar.

He still regarded his chances of being selected as fairly slim. The selection committee was populated by the people who were determined to expel him just a few months ago, so he'd already convinced himself his fate was sealed. He considered not attending the interview at all, but he knew that would be a slap in the face to Veldtman. He owed her a lot.

The first part of the application had seemed straightforward enough. Aside from some standard form work Andy was required to write a thousand words on why this opportunity would be important for him - what inspired his passion for the guitar. And although he regarded his final submission as a somewhat rushed effort given the short lead time he'd had, Andy actually felt proud of what he'd written.

Somewhere in the earliest hours of the morning, still troubled by his thoughts and unable to sleep, Andy flipped on a nearby lamp. He reached down, feeling for a piece of paper on the coffee table beside him. He raised the photo of Denny and Sonya posing together and held it in the soft light.

He dared not allow himself to hope too much. This opportunity was his only chance to find her. Andy squeezed his eyes shut and drew the photo close to him, touching it to his forehead.

"C'mon, Denny. Give me whatever strength you can," he whispered.

He closed his eyes and drifted. He dreamed of her again, of being with her. Her presence was warm and soft. He imagined holding her hand, the way they had always done. He imagined their peace.

***

The next morning, Andy crossed the grounds of the Conservatory precinct, making his way towards the Administration Building. He was humming with nervous energy that was partially the fault of the several cups of coffee he had plied himself with after a restless night. He was still smoothing out the creases of the cream-colored shirt he had bought on the way here, having decided that none of the shirts he owned would suffice in making him look presentable for the interview. He didn't want to admit he was *really* nervous now, since he had set his expectations so low.

He passed by a window and glimpsed his reflection. Andy was taken aback by what he saw. He was healthy. He *looked* healthy. So different from the sallow youth with the black eyeliner and nail polish, the appetite for destruction. That persona was a ghost now, and Andy smiled at the irony, for it *was* a ghost who'd banished his old self.

Andy sat and waited outside the conference room where the interviews were taking place. A curious calm had come over him. Michyko, the pretty young Japanese student, sat across from him and they nodded respectfully at each other. He wanted to say something to her, but he was too nervous to think of anything.

She went in before him, summoned by Veldtman, who appeared in the doorway to the conference room fleetingly. Andy waited in silence, lost in thought for seemed like hours. He had no idea what they had thought of his written submission, or how they would react to him. He went over the little speech in his mind and started to panic, thinking that it all sounded too contrived. It was little more than a standard line, he thought, the kind of "I'd really like the opportunity to represent this school" and "the opportunity to travel overseas is a once-in-a-lifetime opportunity." There was nothing in it that sounded really impressive, really unique.

The door to the conference room opened, and Michyko emerged accompanied by Veldtman. Michyko was smiling, and the two women were chatting in a relaxed manner. They shook hands warmly. Then Veldtman turned towards Andy and extended her arm to him. Her smile did not fade; she projected her warmth towards him. Andy still felt as nervous as he did in class, when he was expecting to be pilloried by her.

"Come on through, Andrew," she greeted. "Thank you for coming."

She squeezed his elbow gently and met his eyes with hers and nodded silently, as if to offer some wordless encouragement.

Andy stepped into the conference room to find four faculty staff - two men and two women - sitting around a horseshoe table. Andrew noted that Veldtman's colleague Grantley Casper was one of the panelists. Andy's heart sank. He had run up against Casper in the past, and he knew the man disliked him intensely.

"Have a seat, Andrew," Veldtman directed as she sat down among the other panelists.

Andy nodded and sat down in the chair facing them. He suddenly felt like a prisoner sitting before a parole board.

"Andrew DeVries," one of the women panelists began. "The panel has had an opportunity to review your application and your overall student record. I must say that you have had a rather checkered history up until now."

Andy said nothing. He was unsure of what to say. He could feel fingers of tension pressing at his temples.

"Despite your academic achievement, which is sound, you have come very close to being disqualified from the program on a number of occasions. Your record indicates a pattern of nonattendance at examinations, a poor attendance at lectures and numerous warnings and penalties concerning the nonpayment of tuition fees."

Andy listened as his entire tawdry record was laid out in front of him and the panel. He cheeks flushed hotly and he squirmed uncomfortably.

"And now you are sitting before us hoping to represent this Conservatory at an international festival, among some of the finest students in the world."

"Yes, I am," Andy answered, nodding, his voice soft but firm. When he looked up, he met Casper's gaze with an intensity that caused the older man to blink.

Casper sat forward in his seat. "Why, then, do you think that we should consider you at all, Mr. DeVries?" he said.

"Because I am sitting here now," Andy said. "Because despite my record, you - this panel - saw fit to invite me here to consider me."

Veldtman and the second male panelist managed to stifle a satisfied grin at his quick fire answer, which left Casper fumbling for a follow-up question.

"I know I have not been the model student," Andy continued, feeling a sudden rush of adrenaline. "I haven't even been a good student. I haven't treated my place here with respect and I have - for the want of a better phrase - been quite happy to fly by the seat of my pants. You are right to question my suitability for this delegation."

Veldtman spoke up. "You say in your written submission that you have played the guitar since you were six years old," she said, trying to steer the conversation away from the tension she could sense in the room. "And that it was your father who inspired you to play. Can you elaborate on that for us?"

Andy relaxed back in his seat and bowed his head in thought.

His father...

Two men, father and son, sit at a kitchen table. Years of misunderstanding and regret.

The rehearsed speech Andy had prepared slowly left the center of his mind, and instead, another speech took its place.

"My father was a soldier in the U.S. Army," he began carefully, considering his words. "During the first Gulf War. He was away for a long time - I think. I was only six when he returned home."

Andy paused, looking down at his hands in his lap, then continued:

"He suffered badly from his experience. My family suffered as a result, and it wasn't long before we fell apart. I went to live with my grandmother, and while I was there, I found a guitar in her attic that my father had brought back from Iraq. That was when I first began to play. For years I learned and learned. I played and played, hoping that my father would notice me - take an interest. But he never did. I never understood why it was that he would never listen to me play or encourage me. Well… maybe I did know deep down, but I lived in the hope that one day he would notice. I gave up trying, after a long time. But recently I -"

Andy's voice caught in his throat and he looked up to find the panel completely riveted - even Casper.

Veldtman nodded at him encouragingly.

"Go on," she said.

"While my father was in the desert he met a young man - who was about my age then. He played the guitar like no one my father had ever heard. My father told me that this man played for the troops and hoped to study in Europe one day. But during a battle, the young man was caught in the crossfire and was shot and killed. It was my father's fault; he was the one who had pulled the trigger. He never forgave himself for it, and couldn't bear to listen to the sound of a guitar for years. He told me this account just a few days ago. I played, never knowing the truth of why he had shunned me for so long. Eventually I played because it became my only anchor in life. Now I play because I love it more than anything. I have learned to respect the craft, and I have learned to respect myself. It has been only recently that I have come to understand that. My father understands it now, too."

The panel sat silently as Andy finished speaking. One or two of them nodded, clearly impressed by what he had just told them. Casper appeared unmoved - not that Andy expected anything more from him - while Veldtman and the other man whispered to each other.

Finally Veldtman turned to Andy.

"Thank you for coming, Andrew. We will consider your application and advise you of the outcome."

Andy stood. His legs felt as though they might give way under him, but he quickly steadied himself and nodded respectfully to the panel before exiting the conference room.

He went straight to a nearby bathroom and splashed water on his face. He felt exhilarated and terrified all at the same time, having delivered something so unprepared. But it felt right - it felt more truthful than anything else he could have spoken. Looking into the mirror, Andy saw his eyes had changed color completely now. They were no longer the brown that he had been born with. Instead they were now a vivid, almost intense green.

Andy took off his backpack and searched inside it for the folded photograph of Denny and Sonya. He gazed at her image again.

"God, I hope it was enough," he whispered.

***

Sonya relaxed on the sofa in the living room of the beach house, glad that a long week was finally over. The doors to the balcony were open, allowing a light evening breeze to waft in off the ocean. She could hear the waves breaking gently on the shore and it soothed her. Soft jazz played in the background and she sipped a glass of Cabernet. She'd been on the go since early morning, and though she was grateful for the momentum of work, she savored the end of the day more than ever.

Sonya had showered, put on one of Denny's old business shirts - which was big enough for her that she could wear it alone - and turned off her BlackBerry. Simon lay at her feet sound asleep, grateful for Sonya's company again.

Sonya craved these moments of solitude when she could close out the world and relax in the comforting familiarity of the house. She had come to welcome the peace of her own company; indeed, she craved it, even though she suspected it was not entirely healthy. Sonya ignored her doubts, ignored the constant "helpful suggestions" from Lionel and Ruth and chose just to be. She couldn't bear the thought of exploring a new relationship. It would feel wrong, as though she were cheating on Denny. The grief counselor had told her to expect feelings like these, that they were perfectly normal, but the thought of considering another...

It made her feel awful.

She swirled the silky liquid around inside the wine glass, allowing its aroma to touch her nostrils. Denny had loved wine. He loved tasting it, pairing it with cooking, or just selecting a bottle to have with some cheeses and crackers while music played ... or he played. He wasn't at all snobbish about it, in the way some wine enthusiasts got. It was just another of those things that he genuinely loved.

He would certainly have loved to be here now, sharing this bottle, listening to the ocean and the music with her.

Familiar tendrils of grief grew inside Sonya, and she felt herself falling towards the edge once more. She pulled herself back and stifled her tears by biting the inside of her lip. She had become so accustomed to this internal emotional battle she had almost mastered "patching the wall," as she called it. The "wall" was her security blanket, within which she could wrap herself and avoid the emotions, avoid the world, avoid people, avoid attachment.

She polished off what remained in the glass and poured herself another. Her struggle gradually became diluted by the effects of the wine, and before too long, she was drifting off to sleep where she lay.

And in the spaces between her awake and asleep states, Sonya dreamed once more.

Where was she?

A beach near a city. An esplanade, a market, perhaps. There are people all about enjoying a beautiful, cosmopolitan day.

She strolls along the beach, the sand beneath her bare feet, the water lapping at her ankles. It is pretty here and she feels calm.

She feels a presence close by: a familiar presence, a familiar warmth.

Who is it? She wonders. She looks up and searches around her, then in front of her. She lifts her hand, shielding her eyes from the sun. Everything and everyone around her is blurry, out of focus. A dog barks nearby.

Simon?

Sonya tries to focus. There is someone up ahead. A man?

He stands at the water's edge, hands on hips, out of focus, out of reach.

Who is he?

His presence is familiar, it is warm. Her heart skips a beat. Is it him? Is it Denny?

This presence is different somehow.

As she approaches him, his features gradually come into view a little more but they remain frustratingly indistinct, until she sees his eyes. The only feature she can discern clearly. They are beautiful, large and worldly.

And they are green: an intense, vivid green.

Chapter 16

Andy climbed the stairs to Gideon's office and found him sitting at his desk working at his laptop. He knocked on the open door.

"Andy," Gideon greeted, looking up at him through thick coke-bottle glasses that reflected the glow of the laptop's screen. "Come on in. This new rostering system is great. I was just looking over the vacant spots I have in the performance calendar. There's a few Friday nights here, if you want to play."

Andy managed a smile as he sat down. Gideon was probably the biggest technophobe known to man, so it was amusing to see him trying to drag himself into the 21st century like this. The sight of his office, with its piles of folders stuffed with years' worth of paperwork, was enough to give an environmentalist a stroke.

"Gideon, I need to talk to you about something," Andy said.

"Oh?" Gideon said, removing his glasses and folding them up. "That sounds serious."

Andy took a folded letter out of his pocket and handed it over to Gideon.

"I, uhh - need to ask you for some time off."

Gideon's eyes went wide as he read the letter.

"Sweet Jesus," he mused. "The Melbourne International Festival of the Guitar."

"I've been selected to play in a competition, a concert series for emerging artists. There's a pretty big prize. My travel expenses are paid for, but I'll be away for a while. I don't expect you to keep my place open here."

Gideon didn't react immediately. He glanced between the letter and Andy then he handed it back. Andy suddenly felt unsure of what to expect.

After several moments, a broad smile melted Gideon's features and he held out his hand towards Andy.

"Well, bloody hell if this isn't going to punch a hole in my operation," he said with a hearty laugh. "My god, this is awesome. Have you told your father yet?"

Andy shook the offered hand.

"No. I haven't had the chance," he replied, turning the letter over in his hand. "This was just delivered to me earlier this afternoon. I haven't even started making any plans. I thought I had better to tell you first, since you'll need to find a replacement."

Gideon nodded appreciatively and stood up, went over to a corner cabinet and fetched out a bottle of scotch and a couple of glasses.

"This calls for a drink," he proclaimed.

Andy felt a wave of relief. "You're OK about this?"

"Are you kidding? Gideon glanced sarcastically at Andy. "You're not *that* indispensable."

He paused for effect before chuckling, pouring scotch into the two glasses and gesturing for Andy to take one.

"Andy, this is an opportunity of a lifetime. Not many of these come along - you'd be bonkers to pass it up."

"No, they don't." Andy said. "I can't believe I was selected."

"You have such a low expectation of yourself?" Gideon observed. "These past few months, Andy, you've completely turned your life around. You've proven you have a considerable talent. Seems a perfectly natural progression to me."

Andy's nose wrinkled up and he spluttered, as the uncharacteristically strong scotch slid down the back of his throat, burning all the way.

"Jesus, Gideon. What is this? Rocket fuel?"

Gideon grinned and knocked back his own as though it were water.

"Tell your father, Andy," he said seriously. "He'll want to know."

"Perhaps," Andy nodded, standing up from his chair and putting the unfinished glass down. "The ice is beginning to thaw a little - I think."

Andy turned away. He paused just before the doorway.

"There is one thing, though," Andy ventured. "I'll need a greater cut of the tips. I don't want to sleep on the street down in Australia.

Gideon smiled again and shook his finger at Andy theatrically.

"Don't push your luck, sunshine!"

***

Andy prepared to play a set for the packed house in the bar. He'd restrung the borrowed guitar and, even though it still fell short of his standards, it had a much better sound.

As he adjusted the microphone stand and turned towards the audience, Gideon appeared beside him and unclipped the microphone, coughing into it to get everyone's attention.

"Excuse me, folks!" he announced as the level of chatter slowly died away. "Andy DeVries here has been our house musician at The Pub for several months now and, I have to say, he has almost single handedly brought a vibrant music culture to our little corner of the city."

Gideon paused for a round of applause while Samantha, who was serving at the bar, stopped and turned her attention towards the stage. Andy saw her and he smiled wanly, but her expression remained blank.

"Well, Andy has just found out today that he has been selected to perform in a competition at an international festival for classical guitarists - in Melbourne, Australia!"

Another, more enthusiastic round of applause erupted, causing Andy to blush. Gideon looked over his shoulder at him with a "See that?" gleam in his eyes. Andy glanced over at the bar area again. Samantha had gone.

"Now, Andy has informed me that most of the expenses for this journey have been covered. However, we at The Public House feel that he should have the opportunity to travel in style, so I'd like to encourage you all - if you think he's good enough - to consider helping him gain worldwide recognition as a virtuoso performer. To kick off the fund, I'm going to put in $500."

Andy nearly choked on his beer. Gideon held up a wad of bills and turned to Andy, clutched his shoulder gently and gave it a squeeze, while another round of cheering drowned out any other noise in the bar.

Andy launched into a set that he decided to skew towards a more modern repertoire. With the help from some audience members, who were quite competent musicians and vocalists, the set became a gutsy blues and roots session that had the entire bar singing along and cheering for more. Despite the limitations of his borrowed instrument, Andy derived much pleasure and satisfaction from this raw musical performance, recognizing that the crowd in here tonight had fed into his positive vibe. It was like a drug - a far more satisfying one than any he had known before. The buzz in the room was energizing. It him happy, and it made him feel fulfilled.

Andy stepped off the stage near the end of the evening to discover that a little over $2000 had been raised towards his trip to Australia. He was speechless and humbled. As he went through into the front room, Andy found his father sitting at the bar.

Bruce stood, seeing his son approach. Andy hesitated fleetingly, then joined his father at the bar.

"That was a good performance," Bruce said. "I didn't know you could play the blues so well."

Andy smiled.

"It's not my preferred genre, but I have to admit it sounds great in a venue like this."

"That it does," Bruce agreed. He leaned down beside him and lifted a large form - a worn-looking guitar bag - onto the bar and slid it towards Andy.

"I, uhh, found this at the house. I don't know how much use it would be for you, but - I guess - if you can do something with it, then it deserves to be used again."

Andy sensed he knew what it was before he opened the zipper, but that did not lessen his reaction when he pulled out the battered but recognizable instrument.

"Oh my god," he whispered, gazing between it and his father. "Dad. This is it, isn't it?"

Bruce nodded wistfully.

Andy turned the familiar guitar over and over in his hands: the very guitar he had first played when he was young, the tragic memento brought back from the deserts of Iraq by his father.

It was Spanish-made, a grand concert model fashioned from a combination of German spruce, Madagascan and Indian rosewood. Andy recognized from the faded label inside the body that it was a Vincente Carillo guitar, a renowned manufacturer who had a 173-year history in handcrafting these rare and beautiful instruments. Its surface was scuffed in places and there was a splintered hole near where the fretboard passed over the neck. Andy guessed at what that might be as he ran his fingers over it: a reminder of a tragedy from another time.

"I know it won't replace your Taylor," Bruce said. "But I think it'll still play a decent tune."

"I don't know what to say," Andy said, very softly.

"Don't say anything," Bruce responded gruffly, shifting awkwardly on his stool. "Just clean it up as best you can. Get some decent strings for it."

Andy couldn't take his eyes off the guitar, examining it as one might examine a piece of art. He noticed a small card sticking out from inside its body. Carefully taking it out, Andy realized it was a photograph - a photograph of his father and Gideon in their battle fatigues and helmets, posing with a slight, young Iraqi man holding a guitar. *This guitar.* He wore a bright, proud smile; all of them smiled. There was a particular poetic warmth to the image.

"This is him?"

Bruce gazed down on the image in Andy's hand. His breath seemed to catch in his throat. Evidently he had been unaware of its presence there.

"That's him," he mused sadly. "The only other guitarist whose music has moved me as much as yours."

Andy gazed at it for a long moment, then he carefully placed it back inside the instrument.

"So, this festival overseas. It's a pretty big deal, huh?" Bruce ventured.

"Yeah, it is. It's kind of *the* big deal."

Bruce looked at his son and placed a hesitant hand on his shoulder.

"I want the best for you. I *always* wanted the best for you. I know that - I failed you. In the past. It's good to see you doing something that you love."

Bruce finished his drink and was preparing to stand when Andy looked up at him.

"Stay for a while, Dad."

Bruce hesitated, checking his watch. He nodded and smiled.

"I can stay for a while."

Andy smiled, then reappraised the guitar, shaking his head in awe. He determined that it was indeed still serviceable and began making mental notes of what it would require.

Bruce spied Samantha lurking nearby and summoned her over.

"That looks as though it has seen better days," she remarked hesitantly, as Bruce indicated with two fingers. She began pouring them a pair of half-pints.

Andy looked up from the guitar to find Samantha standing there. He turned his head slightly towards Bruce.

"Uh, Dad? Could you give me a minute here?" he whispered.

Bruce frowned at him quizzically before the penny dropped.

"I gotta go to the bathroom," he said.

Once they were alone, Andy set the guitar down beside him.

"It has," he admitted tapping the headstock. "But it'll do for now. I think I can give it a new life."

Samantha hesitated.

"You're really doing this, then, aren't you?"

Andy nodded. "I am, Sam." He gazed directly at her.

"Don't look at me like that, Andy. You know the effect it has on me."

She punched him lightly on the arm, and looked down at the bar with a sad half-smile.

"Sorry," Andy said. He reached out for her hand, taking it gently and squeezing it. "You deserve better, so much better than me. I have to do this. I have to..."

"No. Don't say anything more," she said, cutting him off. Though their words barely scratched the surface, both of them knew what they were really saying. She turned her hand over in his and squeezed his fingers. "This is an incredible opportunity for you, Andy. I just hope that whatever you're looking for turns out to be - you know. *It.*"

Andy leaned over the bar and kissed Samantha gently on her cheek.

She closed her eyes, feeling the warmth of his skin upon hers, and when he drew back, she gazed into his eyes once again. Then she finally knew what it was about them that was different.

Remembering the photo from his backpack she'd seen days ago, Samantha recognized the same vivid green eyes here and now as those of the stranger in the photograph. She held his gaze for a long moment, allowing herself a few moments to study the striations of his pupil that told her so much about a person. A question began to form in her mind.

But she brushed it away.

Chapter 17

The Toyota four-by-four wound its way along the highway, heading north. Jochen Zinski watched the majestic New South Wales coastline pass by as he cruised along, marveling at its unspoiled beauty and wondering why on Earth he had not taken the opportunity to explore this part of the world before now. The flight up from Melbourne had been surprisingly quick and it had allowed him some solitude, an escape from the frenzy of the Festival preparations. Grace had quickly and reliably arranged the vehicle hire in Merimbula, where Zinski had landed, as well as the taxi from the airfield to the vehicle itself. In the space of just a few hours Zinski had found himself a world away from the bustling metropolis and in a quiet coastal country side. Anja, his wife, would surely love it here.

The organizing committee had been perplexed at his sudden decision to cancel an entire day of meetings to pursue this seemingly bizarre quest but, fortunately for Zinski, his reputation had convinced most of them this was a cause worth pursuing. That he found himself now on this winding road was due in no small part to the esteem in which they held him.

A characteristic green sign loomed large up ahead and Zinski saw the name "Hambledown." Slowing to allow a large milk tanker to pass, Zinski signaled his intention, turned off the highway and continued on towards the beach.

Zinski knew he was taking a risk by turning up unannounced. But he hoped that if he came to visit Sonya Llewellyn personally, she might be more receptive towards the idea he was going to put to her. Zinski had thought much about Denny in the weeks since Sonya had delivered the sad news of his death. He had been totally unprepared for the news, guilt-ridden for not knowing that his former student, his friend, was even ill.

But he wasn't totally surprised. Zinski and Denny hadn't parted under the best of circumstances. Denny's desire to pursue architecture over music - because he needed a solid profession that would give him the kind of income he thought music couldn't guarantee - had seen them argue bitterly. Zinski believed Denny was a brilliant virtuoso, with the potential to make an indelible mark on the world stage. He never forgot Denny's unique talent. He had lamented it. But that was all so long ago now. Zinski didn't want to prolong anyone's grief by putting forward the idea he had now. Rather, he hoped it would be an opportunity to do something special in the memory of a wonderful musician and friend.

As he passed through the outskirts, he marveled at the seaside village on the shore of a curved bay that protected it from the vast Pacific Ocean beyond. He noted a pair of fishing trawlers, slowly making their way out from a small port. The beach was occupied by a gaggle of people - sunbathers, children, families; an idyllic summer scene. The road curved around to the right, and before long Zinski found himself in the main street. As he passed shops and houses he searched for a particular business: a practice. It didn't appear to jump out at him right away. He didn't see a sign or a plaque denoting a law firm, so he pulled up outside of a general store and killed the engine.

Checking a folded-up piece of paper that sat on the passenger seat, Zinski scanned the directions Grace had cobbled together for him. If they were correct - and he had no reason to think they weren't - then the practice should be right here in the main street.

Zinski decided that if anyone knew how to find somebody in a small town like this, it would surely be the proprietor of a general store. Fetching a leather satchel from the rear, he climbed out of the vehicle and stepped up onto the curb.

Inside the store, Lionel looked up to see a well-dressed stranger enter. The jacket he wore looked well tailored and expensive, and the man himself was immaculately groomed.

"Good morning," Lionel greeted. He checked his watch, noting it had just gone midday. "Actually - beg my pardon - good afternoon."

Zinski nodded his head respectfully and smiled.

"Good afternoon," the stranger said in a heavily accented voice. "I am in need of some assistance. I am searching for a Miss Sonya Llewellyn. I believe she has a legal practice here."

"She does," Lionel replied guardedly. "Are you are in a need of a lawyer?"

"Well no, not specifically." Zinski smiled. "But I am hoping to speak to her directly. "My name is Jochen Zinski. I have traveled up here from Melbourne to see her."

"That is a long way to come," Lionel said as he stepped around Zinski to pick up a crate of fresh apples and place them onto a display stand.

He was going to have to offer up more information to this man, Zinski mused. It was clear he knew Miss Llewellyn. Zinski fished a business card out of his leather satchel and held it out.

"I apologize, sir. I am the director of the upcoming International Festival of the Guitar, to be held in Melbourne. I am a friend of her late partner Dennis Banister. He was a student of mine years ago."

Lionel stopped what he was doing and looked up at Zinski apologetically.

"Oh, I see," he responded, pointing through the front window at the stone cottage across the street. "Well, then ... you did, in fact, pass by her office just down the street a little. I believe she is re-placing the sign out the front today, so it's easy to miss right now. You should find her there."

Zinski, who had followed the line of Lionel's finger out through the window, turned back and nodded.

"Thank you Mister...?"

Lionel stepped forward and offered his hand. "Lionel. Lionel Broadbent."

Zinski shook Lionel's hand more confidently this time and smiled.

"I gather you know Miss Llewellyn quite well, then?"

"Yes," Lionel answered, nodding towards Ruth behind the counter. "She is very dear to both of us. Almost like a daughter."

"I understand," Zinski acknowledged. "Well, I should call upon her, then. My time here is short."

"Yes. Yes, of course," Lionel said, scooting past him and politely opening the door.

After Zinski had crossed over to the other side of the street, Li-onel stood beside the window, watching the stranger.

"What do you suppose he wants?" Ruth asked as she stepped up beside Lionel.

"I'm not sure, but I'll wager it has something to do with those tickets Sonya received."

***

Zinski clicked open the door to the cottage and stepped into a pleasant reception area.

Immediately a woman's voice called out from another room: "Be with you in a moment!"

Zinski waited patiently, examining some framed sepia photo-graphs of Hambledown street scenes from yesteryear that hung on the freshly painted walls. The reception desk sat unattended.

Sonya appeared in the doorway and greeted the new arrival.

"Hello there," she smiled.

Zinski spun around and offered her his hand, almost too quickly.

"Good afternoon. Miss Llewellyn?"

Sonya nodded, eyeing the stranger curiously.

"Please accept my apologies for arriving unannounced," Zinski continued. "I do not wish to take up too much of your time. We spoke on the phone. I am Jochen Zinski - from Melbourne."

Sonya's polite smile faded just a little. She was clearly caught by surprise.

"Oh, ah ... well, Mr. Zinski," she stammered, gesturing for him to come into her office. "I have some time now. Why don't you have a seat?"

Zinski entered the air-conditioned office, hesitating as he noticed a dog sitting in a basket behind the desk. It growled low in its throat as he stepped in.

"Don't mind him," Sonya said, gesturing with her hand at Simon to stop. "He's a grump, but he doesn't bite."

She sat down at her desk and folded her hands.

"How can I help you?" she asked.

"Well," Zinski began slowly. "Again, my condolences to you. I had no idea that Denny was even ill, let alone gravely ill."

Sonya nodded, closing her eyes momentarily to steady herself.

"Denny was a wonderful student and a wonderful friend. I lament that he was lost to us as a musician. It - took me a long time to understand his need to grow beyond it."

"Denny did mention you once, Mr. Zinski," Sonya replied softly. "I was aware that there was some - difficulty - between you two. But he rarely spoke of it. I think there was a certain amount of regret there, on his part, as well."

Zinski cleared his throat nervously, and clutched his satchel in his lap. He looked down at it fleetingly.

"You may be surprised to know that he was actually one of the driving forces behind the original idea of an emerging talent concert series," he continued. "When he was still a student, he participated in a number of committees to facilitate its birth."

Zinski opened the leather satchel, taking out a magazine-like book and opening it for Sonya. He pointed to several images on the page. It was Denny playing his guitar on stage.

Sonya smiled wistfully at the photos of Denny that she hadn't seen before.

"This was from one of the first gatherings we staged in Melbourne, when Denny was still attending the school. There were maybe a dozen competitors back then all from schools around the country."

Sonya handed the book back to Zinski and he placed it back into the satchel.

"This year's series will host 100 competitors from all around the world. Quite a change from just a few years ago."

"So, what does all this have to do with me, Mr Zinski?" Sonya asked.

Zinski sat forward.

"I feel terrible for not keeping in touch with Denny. He was such a wonderful talent - a virtuoso of such rare and natural ability. He will be sadly missed. I would like to propose to you that this year's concert series be named in his honor. And I would like to invite you to come to Melbourne so that you may present the award to the winning finalist."

Sonya sat back in her seat. She blinked at Zinski, then down at Simon, unsure of how to respond.

"That is a very special thing to do, Mr. Zinski. I am not quite sure what to say."

"Please say you'll come and present the award," Zinski responded. "I will arrange to fly you down and take care of your accommodation. I will ensure that your experience will be a wonderful occasion - a fitting memorial to Denny."

Zinski reached into his satchel once more and took out a brochure, handing it to Sonya. She took it gingerly and examined the cover. On it was a photograph of a lovely, English-looking garden. The festival's title was printed in a flowing script at the top, and the venue - The Fitzroy Gardens - was printed near the bottom.

The Fitzroy Gardens...

An echo of a memory floated across her mind's eye...

Leaves that have fallen from a tree settle on a lush, green stretch of lawn. They blow gently across it, tumbling and turning, carried by the wind. The lawn is more green than Sonya had ever remembered. It is in a garden. Somewhere close to a city. She is captivated by the leaves and their gentle motion. She hears an echoing laughter of children nearby.

"Miss Llewellyn?"

Sonya flinched at the sound of Zinski's voice and she shook the remains of the dream away. She got up from the desk and wandered over towards the window. The curious reverie tugged at the corners of her consciousness as she looked out across the street to the ocean beyond. It teased her fragile emotions, reminding her that her grief was still raw, even though she thought the bulwark against it was strong.

"Not a day goes by when I don't think about him," she said, her gaze fixed upon a point far off in the distance. "More than anything, it was his music that defined him. It was one of the things I loved most about him."

Sonya turned back to face Zinski, who had stood and was listening respectfully. He was struck by a deep sadness in her eyes.

"Your offer is very generous and really quite wonderful," she continued. "However, I can't accept it. I have a busy practice that is still very new, and I don't have any spare time available to me right now."

Zinski sensed she was covering for a more truthful reason for not accepting his offer. He opened his mouth to speak, but then stopped himself and nodded simply.

"I understand. Again, I apologize, Miss Llewellyn," he said. "I should have contacted you before coming up here. It was unfair of me to arrive without warning."

Sonya smiled sadly and returned to her desk. "You had the very best of intentions, Mr. Zinski. I just - it's very..."

She looked down at the framed photograph on her desk and Zinski followed her gaze, seeing her together with Denny.

"It's still hard, him not being here anymore. I wake up every day hoping that it has all been a bad dream. But..."

"Miss Llewellyn," Zinski said softly. "You don't need to explain. I would still very much like to name the award in his memory, with your permission."

"Of course, Mr. Zinski," Sonya nodded holding up her hand. "I think that would be lovely."

Sonya accompanied him as they walked back up the street to the Toyota. He took a card from his pocket and handed it to her as they stopped beside the vehicle.

"Sonya, take this. If you have a change of heart at all, please call me. I will ensure the necessary arrangements will be taken care of."

Sonya took the card from him and nodded. Then Zinski climbed into the Toyota, started it up and pulled away from the curb. Sonya watched him go. She considered his card in her hand and shook her head. She crossed the street again, back towards the office, without noticing that both Lionel and Ruth were peering out from the window of the general store.

As Zinski motored away from the pretty village he turned the radio on, then flicked it off almost immediately.

"Damn," he said.

***

Sonya stood in the beach house's kitchen, dressed in an oversized T-shirt and shorts, chopping some vegetables on a wooden board. It was evening. She'd had a good first day in the local court house and was feeling satisfied that she had what it took to be a good lawyer. In the rush to get herself and the practice into the swing of things, she'd harbored doubts as to whether she could pull it off.

She peeled a carrot, smiling, remembering poor Bernard Salt who had dropped off a large box filled with a bountiful supply from his garden as promised. There was no doubting his generosity. Sonya couldn't bring herself to write up an account for him. He had single-handedly taken care of her nutritional needs for at least the next fortnight.

This was the thing about country life. It was the grace and conscientiousness of country people that attracted her to life here. Their generosity seemed boundless. It made her smile - made her feel worth something.

She tried not to think too much about the visit from Jochen Zinski. Every time she did so, she felt a knot of torment threaten to tighten inside her. His offer was lovely, wonderful in fact, but she simply had no stomach for a trip back to the city right now.

The city held too many memories.

Checking a pan on the cook top, allowing the aromatics of the curry to touch her nostrils, Sonya set the carrots aside and picked up some fresh bay leaves, rinsing them under the tap and patting them dry on a piece of paper toweling.

A breeze picked up outside and a short gust blew through the open window in front of her, picking up a couple of the bay leaves and blowing them across the counter top.

That simple action suddenly touched something off in Sonya's mind, and she frowned, flinching momentarily.

Leaves that have fallen from a tree settle on a lush, green stretch of lawn. They blow gently across it, tumbling and turning, carried by the wind. The lawn is more green than Sonya had ever remembered. It is in a garden. Somewhere close to a city. She is captivated by the leaves and their gentle motion. She hears an echoing laughter of children nearby and she looks up to see where they are.

As she does so, she sees a hand in front of her.

She shakes her head, trying to focus. She is meeting somebody, being introduced.

The young man's hand is outstretched, as if waiting to receive hers. She smiles curiously and begins to offer her own. She looks at the man's hand, his forearm, and she sees an inscription tattooed on his skin.

She focuses, trying to make it out.

Sonya shook her head abruptly and experienced a moment of disorientation, before realizing she had been daydreaming. She was still standing at the kitchen sink. The bay leaves had scattered.

Setting the knife down on the counter, Sonya gathered up the leaves from the sink and the floor and rinsed them again, before transferring them to the pan.

The dream echoed in her consciousness, lingering for a moment, then dissipated as if it had never been.

***

Andy stood on the sidewalk in the cold morning air, holding himself with his arms and hopping from bare foot to bare foot on the freezing cold sidewalk. He wore only a pair of track pants and a woolen pullover, watching as Beck hoisted two large duffle bags into the back of a pickup truck. It was still well before dawn, but Andy wanted to see Beck off personally before he left for New York. There was a heavy sadness between them. They had been through a lot together, even though they'd led extremely different lives.

When everyone else had doubted Andy or prejudged him, or even saw him as simply a means to an end, only Beck had stood apart. Only Beck had seen Andy as a person, a troubled person, but one who had the spark deep inside of him to do good. Now Beck knew that spark had been ignited.

Somehow.

Andy couldn't quite believe it had come to this.

Satisfied that his belongings were secure, Beck stood back from the vehicle and signaled for his friend in the truck to give him a moment. As he approached the curb, Andy could have sworn that he was actually a little misty-eyed.

Rubbing his gloved hands together, Beck blew frosty air into them and then smiled wanly at Andy.

"Well, I guess this is it," he said sadly. "I gotta go. If we don't get out on the highway before rush hour, we'll be fucked."

Andy nodded and offered his hand to Beck.

Beck brushed it aside gruffly and, uncharacteristically, wrapped his arms around Andy in a generous hug, holding him tightly for several seconds. Andy smiled gawkily, submitting to the embrace.

Then Beck drew back. "I don't know what happened to you, Dev," he began, "But whatever it is, man, it's magical. The way you've pulled your shit together."

Andy nodded silently, surprised by the depth of feeling Beck put into those words.

"You go down there to Australia and become legendary. I want to be first in line when that album comes out. OK?"

Again Andy nodded, fighting against becoming emotional in front of Beck.

"I will," he whispered.

Beck turned and climbed into the pickup, slamming the door shut.

He looked at Andy one more time as his companion started the engine and idled for a few moments.

"You always had it in you, Andy," Beck said, his words nearly lost in the engine's noise. "You're stronger than any of us gave you credit for."

As the pickup slowly pulled from the curb and drove away, Beck held his arm out the window and pointed admiringly towards Andy; Andy did the same.

And then Beck cupped his hand to his mouth.

"Find her, Andy!" he shouted. "If she's really out there - you gotta find her. Otherwise you'll never know if those dreams were true."

Andy watched as his friend gave one last wave and then closed the window against the cold. The truck turned at the intersection and disappeared from view.

***

The taxi pulled up to the curb and stopped for Andy to climb out. He fished his wallet out of his jacket pocket and handed the driver a bill, telling him to keep the change. He fetched his case and guitar bag from the trunk and stood back on the sidewalk as the taxi pulled away. Andy adjusted his scarf, then turned to apprise the domestic terminal of Chicago's O'Hare International Airport. He was alone.

Though it was bitterly cold, Andy didn't feel cold. The jacket, scarf and gloves he wore were suited to the Chicago winter. They were the only heavy garments he carried with him, for he knew that by the time his journey ended, he would arrive in an Australian summer. Though Andy was still trying to get his head around that concept, part of him already knew what that was like.

He smiled, thinking of those adopted memories of home.

He checked the inside pocket of his jacket, close to his chest and felt the passport that sat snug inside there. He took it out and inspected the pristine document, with a sense of disbelief. His very own passport - the first he had ever owned. He couldn't believe that he was about to embark on this long journey.

It seemed quiet, even though the terminal was already coming to life. Andy had got here in plenty of time, giving him the latitude to check his luggage in first, then buy breakfast and sit with the morning paper before the call came for his 9 a.m. flight to Los Angeles.

Andy noted curiously that he rarely read the paper. He hadn't been interested in any form of news or current affairs. But now that he was leaving the city Andy felt a strange need to read the news, to know about the things he was leaving behind. He felt an affection for this place - and a twinge of sadness - for he would miss it. Yet, at the same time, he was excited in the way one would be excited about coming home.

He knew, very much, that Denny was with him.

Things were different now.

Andy hadn't done a lot of things before. Like set an alarm clock or cook his own meals or take the neighbor's dog for a regular morning run or care about his appearance. But the change was complete now. Andy took pleasure in that early morning run with his canine companion, that first cup of coffee, that daily journey on the 'L' to the Conservatory. Though he attributed much of these habits to the influence of Denny, Andy had embraced them. They brought so much pleasure. The old life was most certainly dead.

Things were so much different now.

He sat alone in the Starbucks, every now and then looking up from the paper to observe people passing by. He wondered about their lives: what they might be like, what routines they embraced, what secret struggles they were grappling with. Were they alone? Were they like him? He saw couples seeing each other off onto flights, kissing each other tenderly. Families waving goodbye to loved ones, tears being wiped away. Smiles and laughter and sorrow.

Andy felt a familiar sadness. He was alone. No one had come to see him depart. Beck was gone now. It was too early for Samantha or even Gideon to come down - not that he expected either of them to show up, anyway. And his father was off on the road again, on another long-haul run to the West coast.

His father...

Andy put his hand down on the guitar case; his father's gift. An attempt at opening up to his son again after so long.

Andy had spent the weekend at his father's house. They drank beer, and Andy used the workshop there to work on the guitar. He had taken it apart, sanded and resealed the battered spruce and rosewood body, replaced the rusted and damaged turn screws, cleaned and oiled the worm gear and replaced the strings with a good set. The guitar had been transformed, and almost resembled its original state. The sound was perfectly balanced, with surprisingly bright trebles and deep, satisfying - yet not overpowering - basses. Andy had chosen to leave the hole in the upper surface of the guitar's body. It seemed wrong to repair it. Bruce had watched Andy work, marveled at his attention to detail, appreciated his skill and steady hand. He had lamented the years lost to their estrangement.

Andy checked his watch and considered making his way to the departure gate. He was meeting with the other delegates there.

As he stood, Andy looked up and saw his father approaching from the entrance to the terminal. He blinked in shock.

His father was here!

"Dad! I thought you were gone already."

Bruce shook his head as he stood before Andy.

"I delayed my trip. I couldn't go - not before I saw you off. Do you have time for another?" Bruce indicated towards Andy's cup.

"Yeah, sure."

Bruce ordered two, and together they sat down at the table.

"I haven't seen the inside of an airport in years," Bruce observed as he saw the ever increasing pedestrian traffic rushing to and fro. "I forgot how huge it is here."

"Hmm," Andy mused. "Did you ever think you'd see me getting on a plane like this?"

Bruce looked at his son.

"What happened to you, Andy?"

Andy considered the question as he stirred a sugar into his coffee.

"Illumination, Dad" Andy answered. "I woke up and finally saw just how shitty things had become. I began to look at life with a different set of eyes."

A different set of eyes.

Andy couldn't help but smile at the irony.

"They must be a pretty damned impressive set of eyes," Bruce remarked. "I'm proud of you."

They were words Andy had longed many times to hear. Now that his father had spoken them, he almost wished he didn't have to leave so soon.

"Your grandmother - she would've been *really* proud of you. I know she loved you very much."

The call for Andy's flight came, and both men looked up towards the overhead display screens.

"Walk with me?" Andy asked.

Together father and son walked towards the departure area. There was so much Bruce wanted to say to Andy, but he couldn't think of any one thing. He studied his son as they walked - he was different. So much so, that Bruce realized he knew his son even less now than he had before.

"Enjoy this opportunity," Bruce finally said, looking at his son earnestly. "Don't concern yourself so much with the competition. If you focus too much on that, you'll miss out on the experience."

Andy regarded his father with a lopsided smile.

"C'mon, give me a break here," Bruce protested. "It's been so long since I gave any sort of advice to you. Now when you're just getting interesting, you've gotta go and disappear across the other side of the world."

Andy shook his head and laughed softly.

"You don't have to say anything, Dad. There'll be plenty of time for that later. It's not like I'm *never* coming back."

Andy spied a small group near the security gate, recognizing them as the other students who'd been selected to attend. Michyko saw them approach, and she smiled and waved.

Andy felt awkward as she approached them, and noticed his father was studying her.

"Cute," Bruce commented from the corner of his mouth.

Andy elbowed him in the ribs. "Knock it off, Dad."

"Hi, Andy," Michyko said excitedly. "You're all set?"

Andy nodded and gestured to his father.

"Yeah. Umm, this is my father, Bruce,"

Michyko nodded respectfully, then gestured towards the others, who were beginning to line up to present their boarding passes to enter the secure departure area.

"We're all here, then. This is exciting, isn't it?"

Michyko tempered her enthusiasm as she saw that Andy wanted to say goodbye to his father. She stepped away discreetly.

They were alone again.

"Good luck," Bruce said, putting a hand on his son's shoulder. "Play - like you've always played. It was always so good to hear you like that."

A small reluctance to leave assailed him again and he looked at his father.

"Thank you, Dad. There is something..." he stopped himself then, and bowed his head. Bruce frowned.

"What is it, Andy?"

Andy shook his head and smiled. He and Bruce had just broken down a barrier that had walled so many years of their lives. Denny knew saying it would be too ridiculous a notion for Bruce right now - perhaps ever. There was no need to alienate his father again.

"Nah. It's nothing. Maybe I'll tell you another time."

Bruce held Andy's shoulders, then embraced him, a little reservedly, and Andy returned the gesture.

"Just remember what I said, OK?" Bruce said as he drew back.

"I will."

Andy picked up his guitar and stepped back as the call for boarding came from overhead. His father smiled and held up his hand. There was love in his eyes, a love that Andy had not seen for a long time.

Andy checked his boarding pass and disappeared through the security gate.

Once he had settled into his window seat on the Airbus that would take him on the first leg of the trip, Andy looked out through the window at the terminal wondering if his father was lingering somewhere inside waiting for the plane to taxi away. Andy continued to gaze until he could no longer see the terminal building at all.

Andy reached into his jacket and took out the photo of Bruce and Gideon and the young Iraqi, Nassar. He gazed at it as the Airbus taxied onto the runway, absorbing the smiles of the young men that were so full of hope. He tried to absorb the tragedy of what had been his father's unspoken burden for twenty years, as the plane waited for a few moments for its clearance from the tower. Finally, Andy smiled at having found a dialogue with his father. The jet took off, rising gracefully into the morning sky and leaving the city and Andy's old life far behind.

Changes...

Chapter 18

It was somewhere close to 7:30pm. Lionel was closing up the shop for the day when he looked across the street at the law practice's cottage and noticed a light on in the front window.

Sonya must still be there.

"What is it, hon?" Ruth inquired, noticing her husband as he lingered by the shop window.

"Oh, nothing," Lionel replied. "It looks as though Sonya is putting in another long day."

"That girl is working harder and harder," Ruth said worriedly, shaking her head as she finished counting out the day's take from the register. "It's not healthy for her."

"I know, I know," Lionel agreed wearily. "She works much too hard. But it's not our place to tell her what she should and shouldn't be doing."

He rolled his eyes out of view of Ruth. They'd had this discussion many times before.

Ruth checked the counter behind her. The two large black soup pots there were still switched on. She hadn't yet emptied them.

"Do you think you should take a meal across to her, Lionel? She'll have skipped dinner again, I am sure of it. It's not right for someone so busy as her."

Lionel baulked at her suggestion, aware of where Ruth's mind was heading.

"Look, I don't think we should go meddling. She's a very private person and fiercely independent. Sonya doesn't take kindly to any sort of interference."

Ruth had already fetched out a sealable container and was ladling piping hot pumpkin soup into it. She took a herb bread roll from a nearby basket.

"Ruth…" Lionel started, but she held up her hand defiantly.

"Lionel, I'll not have that poor child wasting away in that office all alone at this time of night without at least *something* in her belly. She may not be our daughter, but I feel an obligation to look out for her."

Ruth gathered up the items - the soup and bread, a coffee, some items of fruit - into a basket and came out from behind the counter.

"Take this over to her, darling," she pleaded. "At least encourage her to have something."

Lionel frowned and shook his head. But he took the basket from her anyway and inspected its contents.

"Well, I suppose it can't hurt to at least offer," he conceded before leveling his eyes at Ruth. "Just don't you watch me from the window. Sonya has got a sense like a bloodhound for nosy neighbors."

Lionel turned on his heel and stepped out of the shop, walking the short distance down the street towards the practice.

***

Sonya was sitting at her desk before an open laptop - a mountain of paperwork, manila folders and old invoice slips stacked messily on either side of the machine - when she heard a knock at the door.

"Hallo?" Lionel called out.

Sonya smiled at the sound of his familiar voice and glanced up from her screen.

"In here, Lionel."

Simon glanced up from his basket momentarily, then flopped back down, closing his eyes and growling pathetically in the pit of his throat. Apparently, he hadn't lost his man-hating instincts this evening.

Lionel appeared in the doorway holding the basket in both hands. Sonya tilted her head to one side.

"What have you done?"

Lionel blushed.

"We, ahhh - saw a light on from the shop. Ruth thought you might like something to eat." Lionel set the basket down on the chair and began depositing the items from the basket onto the desk. The smell of the rich homemade soup hit Sonya's nostrils and her stomach grumbled.

"Well, she must be psychic. I'm *starving*," Sonya said with a grin, as she fished her purse out from her desk drawer and began to take some notes out for Lionel.

"Oh no," Lionel said holding up his hand to stop her. "This one is on us. Consider it our treat."

Sonya hesitated, eyeing him curiously before closing the purse again and setting it down.

"You didn't have to do this."

"I know," Lionel said. "And that's why we did. We can't have you fading away on us. This town needs you too badly."

Lionel nodded at the chaos on her desk.

"That looks to be quite a - challenge?"

Sonya threw her hands up in mock exasperation, then made some room on the desk.

"I'm trying to organize all of Harry's old clients who've indicated they wanted to come back to me. I want to streamline everything into an electronic system, but I can only do it at night, after hours."

"Have you thought about getting a secretary to help you with all of this? It seems an awful lot to try to negotiate on your own."

Sonya nodded through a mouthful of soup.

"Mmm-hmm. I wish I could, Lionel, but I don't have quite enough spare cash right now to afford one. Most of the money went into getting this old dame up to scratch again."

Lionel looked around at the work Sonya had done to renovate her grandfather's cottage, changing it from a dilapidated old wreck that masqueraded as a law practice into a smart cottage with a modern office interior. He nodded admiringly.

"Well, there are people around the town who would gladly help you. You only need ask."

"Oh, I'm sure," Sonya agreed. "But this is something I have to do on my own. Besides, there is enough fodder in this disaster zone to keep the Hambledown gossip mill running for the next decade."

Lionel chuckled as he made room for himself on the chair and sat down.

"I met that fellow from Melbourne the other day," he said, venturing a change in subject. "He seemed like a decent man."

Sonya nodded noncommittally. "He was," she said.

"He mentioned he was the director of that festival," Lionel continued.

"Mmm-hmm," Sonya eyed him from behind the bowl of soup. She sensed where this was heading.

Lionel steepled his fingers together and looked down, feeling increasingly uneasy.

"Did he - enjoy his visit?"

Sonya placed the soup bowl down on the desk with an expression of mock exasperation and smiled.

"You don't do prying very well, Lionel."

His shoulders relaxed and he looked at her apologetically.

"Evidently not. I'm sorry."

"He came to ask me to present an award at the Festival. In memory of Denny. But I told him I couldn't go."

"Why ever not?" Lionel almost gasped.

Sonya hesitated, suddenly feeling as though she had to search for a reason.

"Because - I have too much to do here," her response came out much too harshly and she blinked, immediately regretting it. She continued more calmly. "I couldn't possibly leave the practice for a whole week when I've got this to contend with."

She gestured expressively at her desk for effect.

Lionel considered her predicament and tilted his brow.

"Well, I can appreciate the work you've committed yourself to in order to make all of this work. But Sonya, you haven't had any time off in over a year. Surely the practice could survive without you for a week."

Sonya rubbed her brow wearily. He had a point - not that she was prepared to admit it, however.

"I just can't, Lionel. It's just too much."

Lionel wasn't convinced. Though his conscience told him he should back away, something else overtook him.

"What about Denny?" he ventured cautiously. "This seems like a wonderful opportunity to do something, you know, special. To celebrate his life."

Sonya stiffened. She lowered her head.

"Lionel, you're going too far," she warned him. Even though she wasn't entirely serious, Sonya maintained a cautionary tone to her voice.

Lionel took the hint. He stood up out of the chair and looked at Sonya sympathetically.

"You're right. It's none of my business at all. I'm - I'm sorry I even mentioned it."

Sonya remained seated, unable to speak. Her eyes darted between him and the floor, and though she held on to the soup bowl, she'd stopped eating from it. She could feel herself shaking with the familiar sensation of threatening grief.

Lionel stood there, his features etched with concern. His inner voice told him "no more," and this time he listened.

"I should go. I'll see you tomorrow. OK?"

Sonya nodded brusquely and closed her eyes.

Lionel backed out of the office, quietly closing the front gate behind him. He glanced back at the front window of the cottage, feeling awful for having been so interrogatory. Clearly, he had upset Sonya. Ruth was right: she was like a daughter to them both, and right now he felt as though he had trampled all over her.

Lionel stepped off the curb to cross the street towards the shop.

"Why does everybody think they have a right to interfere?"

Lionel spun around to find Sonya standing at the cottage gate. Her expression was cold, her face ashen.

"No one is trying to interfere, Sonya," Lionel said evenly.

"Bullshit, Lionel!" Sonya retorted angrily, her voice shaking. "This entire bloody town wants to wrap me in cotton wool. *Everyone* thinks they have to protect me from falling apart."

Lionel shook his head sympathetically.

"That's not true," he said gently. "We just want you to be happy, Sonya. And some of us, who care about you very much, can see that you're not."

Lionel stepped toward her, proffering his hands, as though he was trying to diffuse her molten anger, but Sonya baulked. Her cheeks flushed red. She crossed her arms defiantly across her body to protect herself.

"What are you protecting yourself from, Sonya? Why do you feel you need to cocoon yourself here - working long hours, holing yourself up in that old house, not mixing with anyone?"

"I don't have to justify myself to *you!*" Sonya spat. "What I do here is my own business! I don't have to mix with anybody!"

"No. No, you don't," Lionel paused, considering his words carefully. "But if you keep yourself from living in this world, Sonya, you're going to miss out on the wonderful possibilities of it. Denny wouldn't have wanted that for you. He would have wanted you to go on. To live and to love. You have your whole life ahead of you."

"I have responsibilities!" she stammered impotently, swaying between her anger and her anguish. "My practice is too important to just step away from whenever I feel like it!"

"That's not it," Lionel challenged her, shaking his head with pity and grief. "What is it, really?"

Sonya blinked at him incredulously, wiping furiously at her eyes.

"Because *here* is where I feel safe, Lionel!" she shouted angrily, feeling herself slipping once more. "Because ... here I feel as though he never left - that he's *still with* me!"

There it was, Lionel thought sadly. The truth that she had held on to for so long.

Sonya's eyes glazed over. The tears streamed freely down over her face. Her features contorted into a mask of raw anguish and she began rocking from side to side.

"Why did he have to leave me, Lionel?" she cried. "Why?"

Lionel immediately went to her and wrapped Sonya in his arms as she went completely to pieces. Burying her head into his chest she wailed. The edge loomed before her and she could not stop herself from falling over this time. She tumbled into the abyss she had fought so long and hard to avoid.

"Why?"

Lionel closed his eyes and held her close, recognizing what was happening; his own heart was breaking.

"He couldn't hold on any longer, dear child," he whispered into her hair. "You know that. It was his time. *He* knew that. Denny wouldn't want you to hide away forever."

Sonya sobbed and sobbed, so hard she could no longer hold herself up, but Lionel held her close, supporting her, allowing her emotions to carry her. All those long months of holding herself together, of concentrating on just keeping going, of denying the ever-present grief just under the surface. All of it tumbled forth like a tidal wave now, swamping her. The wall finally crumbled and collapsed, and she was exposed.

"I don't want to go on without him, Lionel! He was my best friend, my - *best* friend. I loved him *so much.*"

Ruth appeared in the doorway across the street, her own eyes swollen with grief. Evidently she had overheard the exchange from inside.

Lionel looked over at her and nodded, mouthing, "It's all right."

Ruth crossed the street, and gingerly put a hand upon Sonya's shoulder. She dropped down onto her haunches and surrounded Sonya's small frame with her arms and held her.

"I'll make up the spare bed," Ruth said. "Sonya, you can stay with us tonight, my dear. I'll not let you go home to that empty house like this."

Sonya was too numb to protest. Lionel gathered her up in his arms, carried her into the shop and through into their house, where he gently deposited her onto the sofa in the sitting room. Ruth followed, having retrieved Simon and his blanket from the practice, and switched off its lights.

Moving a camera tripod out of the way, Ruth folded Simon's blanket into a mat of sorts at the foot of the sofa, where the dog sat down and looked up at Sonya mournfully, whimpering softly. Ruth brought in a quilt from their room and laid it over Sonya as Lionel sat on the sofa, cradling her.

"Here will be good enough," he whispered to Ruth as she pulled up a chair and sat down beside her husband. She nodded. Together they remained with Sonya until she cried herself to sleep.

***

By the time the international leg of his journey was underway - a full day and a half later - and the flight was far above the Pacific Ocean, Andy had settled in to the rhythm of the aircraft. Though they had been delayed for an extra hour in Los Angeles, time had passed by quickly, such was his excitement now. It was after midnight, and the passengers were beginning to settle in for the 15-hour journey to Australia. Some were watching in-flight entertainment, many were napping. Andy had taken out the literature for the festival from his shoulder bag and sat back, quietly reviewing it.

The festival was a week-long event that was to bring the cream of international artists to Melbourne. There would be a showcase of concerts covering a multitude of musical genres - not only classical, but culturally diverse world music, blues and roots, rock, a smattering of country and jazz. Headlining the Festival were artists and composers from all around the world whom Andy had long admired and was eager to see. This was the other dimension to being here that made him feel so privileged - the opportunity to be among real artists, exceptional practitioners of the instrument.

The program for the emerging talent concert series was laid out over the week. One hundred delegates from conservatories all across the world would compete over five days in a series of heats. Each day, two delegates would be selected from a field of twenty and they would progress to a semifinal round on the Saturday. Ten delegates would then compete for five positions in the final on Sunday. The prize was considerable: a $10,000 cheque and an invitation to record on a prestigious classical label in Australia. The resulting album would be distributed worldwide.

Andy's heat had been set down for the Tuesday afternoon just after lunch. It was as good a position as any, he reasoned. He wouldn't have to wait too long to perform, and he would be relatively fresh. It would give him an opportunity to view the other contestants and get a feel for the competition.

He had two pieces in mind for his performance: the second movement of a famed "Sonata Prima" by Fernando Sor and "The Sounds Of Rain," the piece Andy had performed that very first time in The Pub. It was the more obscure of the two, but it was no less enchanting.

Sor's second movement had an orchestral flair that lent itself well to a concert performance, and it required considerable attention to technique in order for it to be carried convincingly. Of all the great guitar composers, Andy felt a particular affinity with Sor because his works suited the solo style, with which Andy felt most comfortable.

Andy was, however, leaning towards "The Sounds Of Rain." The William Lovelady piece wasn't as long, but it was a complex arrangement with rich atmospherics and a unique flamenco feel. "The Sounds Of Rain" evoked vivid imagery that really did capture the rain in its form and movement. It was the first piece that he had mastered with the guitar. In fact, he wasn't sure now if it was himself or Denny who had happened upon it; regardless, his knowledge of the piece was intimate.

It was a risk bringing a less well-known composition with him into the competition, but he believed firmly that it would best showcase his technique. It would challenge him to find the emotional heart he had long searched for. He knew this duality was the key.

He did not want to think too much about the final, fearing he would jinx himself. But he had a piece in mind for that, as well: a concerto that would require an orchestral accompaniment. The second movement in the famed Concierto de Aranjuez by Joaquin Rodrigo was an incredibly tender and emotive piece that had taken on a life of its own in popular culture. Though Andy was wary of just how prominent the "Adagio" was, he felt that he had what it took to make the piece his own for this particular gathering.

He had recordings of the compositions on his cell phone and he listened to them over and over, memorizing their unique form and texture, their tones and harmonies. He practiced the fingerings, making mental notes of where he would need to apply his most intense concentration. He emptied his mind of almost everything else.

Almost everything.

She was never far from his thoughts. It took very little for her face to center itself in his mind's eye. He had already considered what he was going to do once the festival was finished. He would find his way north to Hambledown. Somehow, he would explain himself and convince her of the truth of his survival beyond the cancer. He was going to have to feel his way through it. There were no rules for this. For now, though, he tried to bring his thoughts back to the concert series and the immediacy of that.

Andy closed his eyes and drifted, letting his thoughts meander beyond the confines of the quiet cabin. He touched the presence of Denny within him and felt a sense of joy, of anticipation to be returning to the place where Denny had lived and where he had died. All the disparate memories and recollections of his life had become a coherent stream - a whole rather than many fractured parts. Andy opened, then closed his eyes. He could see her in his mind, Sonya as Denny had known her and loved her. It was powerful, this love. His longing to find her again was as equally potent.

***

In the dead of night, Sonya awoke with a start. She blinked in the near-darkness, looking around her anxiously and seeing only Simon sleeping curled up at her feet on the end of the sofa. Her heart thumped and she lay back, staring up at the ceiling. The dream had left her before she'd had a chance to remember what it was, but the sensation accompanying it lingered. It was warm and comforting. It was a sense of peace.

Chapter 19

The day could not have been lovelier, nor could the venue. Melbourne's Fitzroy Gardens, with its wide-open spaces, perfectly manicured lawns and long, meandering avenues lined with majestic English Elms, was the perfect place for the sounds of beautiful classical music.

It was one of the city's oldest gardens, a tranquil place, where one could be forgiven for thinking it did not belong in a metropolitan environment at all. It was serene and calm here. Its effect was magical.

Andy felt surprisingly calm as he and the others made their way into the Gardens after the taxi dropped them off. It was a beautiful summer Tuesday, not too warm. A light breeze kept the temperature even as it wafted through the trees, rustling the leaves. Andy was glad he had dressed appropriately: a linen shirt and pants and comfortable leather shoes, which he had purchased in the city the previous day, before taking in some of the festival's opening performances. He felt pleased with his appearance. He looked smart yet relaxed, a world away from the attire he would have once chosen to wear. As he walked across the manicured grounds, Andy felt the strange and powerful sense of déjà-vu about this place, the sense of familiarity that had him smiling inwardly. Numerous times since they'd touched down in Melbourne, he had found himself struck by it. The city was so familiar. He knew these gardens; he *remembered* them. Denny and Sonya spent many lazy days here, walking and talking, holding hands, lying on the grass in each other's arms, kissing. The Gardens had been one of their favorite places.

The group from the Conservatory had spent the weekend acquainting themselves with their new surroundings. They had all dealt with the inevitable jet lag quite well. Their hotel was close to the Fitzroy Gardens. They had explored the city, and dined out in cosmopolitan eateries that Andy discovered he knew well. There was a cafe called Enzo's, in Melbourne's renowned cafe strip, Lygon Street - another favorite haunt of Denny's. At the first opportunity, Andy sought it out and took the group there, where they all got to know one another better - something there had been barely enough time for since they'd left Chicago.

Among them was the shy and painfully quiet Alistair Stephens, who was a couple of years younger than Andy. Andy thought Stephens was technically superior to him as a guitarist. But he had revealed during the flight that he was prone to severe stage fright in front of large audiences. As such he had fairly low expectations for this competition.

Annaliese Ingram was a tall redhead with tight curls and an easygoing nature. Annaliese had competed internationally once before, a year ago in Tokyo, where she had come second. She had been among the top students in Andy's class and one of the first selected for the Chicago delegation.

Then there was Michyko. She and Andy were the two first-timers of the group. She was a really sweet girl, wide-eyed and enthusiastic. She had become a sort of team motivator for them all. Whenever one of them was feeling apprehensive or anxious about their upcoming performance, she was there offering encouragement and reassurance. Regardless of the outcome, they were here in this wonderful country, representing their school in an event that was truly prestigious. That alone was a significant achievement.

Today, Andy alone would be performing, and they had all come to cheer him on and provide support. There was already a steady buildup of people coming into the Gardens to see the heats. Large groups of friends and families had set themselves up on the lawns, near a historic Spanish-inspired conservatory that housed spectacular floral displays. There was a festive feel to this place. People were spread out on picnic blankets, serving food from large wicker baskets filled with lunches and bottles of wine and champagne. Children ran barefoot on the grass, playing chase or cricket or throwing a ball back and forth near the natural amphitheater, where seating had been arranged for the orchestra.

The Melbourne Symphony Orchestra had been seconded to provide the accompaniment for several of the performers throughout the week. The orchestra was regarded as one of the finest in the world, and just the thought that he might play with such an esteemed group - if he was lucky enough - made Andy feel giddy. Not even Denny had known that experience.

In this place of beauty and serenity, so far away from everything Andy had ever known, his residual apprehension fell away. He smiled at the familiar warmth he felt being in these gardens.

As Andy's mind wandered among the audience, he began drifting away from the group. He started when Michyko tapped him on the arm.

"You seem a little dazzled by all this," Michyko observed cheerily.

"Yeah, I guess I am," he replied dreamily. "Have you ever been in a more beautiful place?"

Michyko scanned around her and nodded in agreement.

"It is very pretty here. We're so lucky, don't you think?"

"Indeed," he answered simply. "I feel very fortunate."

"Are you nervous?" Michyko asked gently.

"I am. But it's not so bad. I guess I've spent a lot of time preparing myself. International flights are great for that."

Michyko laughed. The group made its way across to the registration marquee, where the performers were required to sign in and receive their performance schedule. There was also a place there for them to leave their instruments until it was their turn to perform.

With some hesitation, Andy handed over his prized guitar and watched as an attendant placed it on a rack at the back of the marquee, then returned with a ticket.

"Here you are. Now all you need to do is present that when you are ready, and we'll have your guitar waiting for you."

Andy nodded, then made his way over to a line of tables where the registration officers were handling the performers. He had completed his paperwork earlier. He took it from his pocket and handed it to a kindly man who checked it over, running a ballpoint pen down a list before him.

"Andrew DeVries," he confirmed. "Here you are. You'll be required for the first group after the luncheon interval at one o'clock."

The man handed Andy a lanyard with a photo card of himself attached to it, as well as a glossy folder containing a booklet of the week's program. Andy took a moment to check the information on his identification, and then he examined the booklet.

His eyes went wide.

There on the page was a paragraph telling him the concert series had been renamed as a memorial trophy - *the Dennis Banister Memorial Trophy*. Andy opened the program he had been given and flicked through a couple of pages until his eyes fell across a photograph of a young man.

It was as though he were looking in a mirror.

The description beside Denny's photo read:

This year's emerging talent concert series has been named the
Dennis Banister Memorial Trophy by Festival Director
Jochen Zinski, in honor of virtuoso guitarist Dennis Banister,
who lost his battle with Hodgkin's Lymphoma in October 2008.

Andy's heart thudded noisily in his head and his palms became sweaty. The color drained from his face.

The registration official looked up at Andy, concerned. "Are you alright, son? You look as though you've seen a ghost."

Andy shook his head and forced a smile. The irony wasn't lost on him.

"N-no, everything's fine," he answered, tripping over his words.

He continued to read the program as he stepped back from the registration table.

"It is hoped the award will become a lasting tribute. The trophy will be presented this year by Dennis' partner, Sonya Llewellyn."

Sonya.

Andy's mouth went dry. He felt as though the world was spinning.

Sonya's here? His mind shouted.

He began looking around him, scanning the gardens and the crowd.

Other contestants were waiting to complete their own registrations. The official gestured for Andy to step back. Looking behind him, Andy noted the lineup with a few of them eyeing him impatiently. He exited from the tent, clutching the program, bewildered. Michyko spied him standing alone and went over to him.

"Andy ... are you OK?" she said, alarmed. "You look sick."

"I'm - I'm OK. I just thought I saw - someone I knew."

Could she be here? How could this be?

Andy scanned the crowd, more discreetly this time, looking into the faces of people milling about. No one appeared familiar to him. He could not see her. How could it be possible that she would have come to this place?

Seeing that his demeanor was beginning to spook Michyko, Andy calmed himself down, stopped his paranoid scanning and turned back towards her.

"I am OK, honest."

"Your nerves haven't suddenly gotten to you, have they?" Michyko asked as they headed across to the performers' pavilion.

"A little, I guess," he answered distractedly. "I just - hope I don't mess up my performance. My piece is a pretty obscure one."

Michyko laughed sweetly.

"You love living on the edge, don't you?" she remarked. "But I guess for someone of your talent, that's where you flourish best, huh?"

Andy gave her a lopsided smile, finally feeling himself relax once more.

"What have you gone for?"

Michyko gulped. "I've chosen Paganini's Caprice in A Minor, the finale. It's been my obsession for ages. I've been practicing it ever since I applied for the competition."

"That's a beautiful piece," Andy said, his eyes still darting imperceptibly among the faces of people they passed. "I'm sure you'll do well. You'll be better practiced than me."

"Gosh, I doubt that," Michyko laughed as they entered the Pavilion.

The Pavilion was situated just beyond the amphitheater, in a fenced-off area. There were tables and chairs, an open-air bar and a dining area that provided catering to the guest performers, student delegates and invited guests of the festival. Andy, Michyko and the others ordered coffee and seated themselves at a table.

Andy kept picking up the program from the table and studying it nervously. He looked around, searching. The others seemed to take it as a sign of his nervousness about performing and didn't question him about it.

***

Not far from the Pavilion a taxi pulled up against the curb. The doors opened and Sonya stepped out, along with Denny's sister,

Joss. Sonya quickly paid the fare and the two women surveyed the Gardens and the growing crowds of people.

Joss was a vivacious young woman, a few years younger than Sonya, and exuded confidence. She was tanned, athletic and naturally beautiful. She glanced at Sonya with a radiant smile.

Sonya put on a large sun hat and her sunglasses as she appraised the Gardens nervously. Though Lionel and Ruth had finally convinced her to take the week off and fly down, she was already having reservations about the wisdom of her decision. She looked over at Joss, raising her eyebrow.

"You know, I haven't been among this many people in months," she said.

Joss smiled breezily, brushed down her dress and took off her sandals as they crossed over the lawns towards the Festival's epicenter. Sonya shook her head at Joss and smiled in spite of herself. Denny's sister had always been a free spirit. Sonya had dressed in a pair of white capri pants and a soft knee-length lace cotton coat that billowed in the breeze. She removed her own shoes, felt the soft grass underfoot, and felt suddenly lighter for it.

"Well today's the day that you're going to enjoy yourself - just for you," Joss said. "OK? It's time for you to get yourself out in the world again."

Joss took Sonya's hand, and together they headed towards the stage area.

***

Andy collected his guitar from the tent and spent a little time adjusting the strings, tuning the instrument until he achieved what he felt was its best sound. He had done a much better repair of the guitar than he'd initially thought. The sound remained exquisite through to the lower registers, and he was confident of its quality. Michyko kept him company as he walked across the lawn from the tent. He was glad for her presence, even though her enthusiasm was a little overbearing right now. He introduced himself to an official, who checked him off a list and wished him good luck. He felt a rush of adrenaline now; his nerves sang like electric wires. All those long months of struggle, both with himself and with his gift, had come down to this moment. His one opportunity to shine was here. He had never been more focused.

Michyko squeezed his hand and planted a kiss on his cheek.

"Good luck, Andy," she said sincerely. "You'll do wonderfully. You have come so far."

Andy smiled at Michyko and nodded, impressed by her observation.

"Thank you," he said quietly.

Stepping up onto the stage, Andy seated himself on the stool and adjusted the microphone in front of him. He scanned the audience, looking for her.

Was she there?

He closed his eyes as he picked up the guitar, hoping to feel her presence, but sensed nothing.

As birds chirped in the trees and the breeze picked up ever so slightly, Andy waited for the MC to finish his introduction. Andy's fingers hovered near the strings readying themselves, waiting for his cue.

The audience clapped politely - they sounded distant in his ears. He began "The Sounds Of Rain."

Touching his fingers to the strings, seeking out that perfect first note, he found it effortlessly and he launched himself - at first with an intense concentration, for he was wary of faltering on the introductory refrain. Then he settled back like a boat on the back of a wave, and he moved into the body of the piece, eliciting a sound from the weathered guitar that was all at once crisp and soulful. The music was evocative. He captured a vivid imagery of rainfall that rippled through the audience, causing them to sit up and take notice almost immediately. Every head had turned towards the stage, towards him as he disappeared into the music, feeling completely in concert with Denny as the piece flowed from their collective memory and into his fingers. He translated it with an effortless beauty.

In the audience, not far from the stage, Sonya watched utterly hypnotized by the stranger who played before them. Her heart had jumped the moment he began his performance. She knew the piece. It had been Denny's favorite - a composition he'd told her was the first he'd ever learned when he had begun playing the guitar as a boy. Denny had played it for her at the beach house, when they used to spend long weekends there. When it was raining and they were relaxing by the fire, or when they were holding one another. When they were making love.

Everything about the stranger up on the stage now, from the way he held the guitar, the way he moved with the music to the exquisite sound he produced, touched off something in Sonya so intense that she was frozen where she sat. Looking over at her, Joss, also transported, saw Sonya was transfixed. Not even a gentle hand upon her shoulder could budge her attention.

As he progressed towards the final flourishes, Andy lifted both himself and his audience towards the conclusion where he trailed it softly away, his fingers softened their touch upon the strings until the music ended.

The audience was on their feet, clapping and cheering and whistling enthusiastically. Andy relaxed back on his seat and opened his eyes, lowering the guitar with a smile. He felt a rush of exhilaration as he bowed his head respectfully to the audience then glanced down at Michyko, Annaliese and Alistair, who were all clapping proudly. Then he stood and stepped down onto the lawn where he was embraced by the others.

"Oh my god, that was brilliant, Andy!" Michyko squeaked as they moved away towards the tent.

"You definitely aced that," added Annaliese admiringly. "No doubt about it."

Andy breathed out through his cheeks and shivered.

Though his modesty prevented him from verbalizing it, the feeling he had about his performance at this moment was good.

Really good.

"I think I need a beer," he said shakily.

***

Performers, contestants, officials and invited guests gathered in the Pavilion to mingle, dine and enjoy a celebratory drink after what had been a hectic but successful day. In the warm and pleasant dusk of the Melbourne evening, where a beautiful sunset lit the city skyline, Andy was overwhelmed by all the attention he was receiving. It wasn't even the final yet, but already, all sorts of people were offering their congratulations on his performance. He had been announced as one of the day's two finalists.

He hadn't yet grasped the full realization that he was through. It was almost too much to comprehend. He had had a lovely - if a little surreal - conversation with Jochen Zinski, who had made a point of meeting both him and the other finalist from the day, a young Frenchman who had performed an interpretation of Handel's "Harmonious Blacksmith" by Mauro Giuliani. Andy felt strange in the presence of Denny's former mentor, yet they had talked easily and Zinski had been impressed by Andy's polite and gentle way. Andy wasn't sure whether Zinski had sensed anything about him.

Sonya and Joss stood at the opposite end of the Pavilion mingling with some of Zinski's colleagues as they enjoyed appetizers and champagne. Sonya was feeling relaxed, more from the effect of the expensive champagne than anything else, but at least she had gotten over her earlier nervousness in the crowd. She found she was enjoying herself.

She listened to the others in the group who were engaged in a conversation about the two finalists from the day - particularly the American, who, it seemed, had caught everyone by surprise. Sonya had been moved by his performance - not so much because of the song choice itself, but by his presence. She was afraid to admit to herself that she was intrigued by him.

Sonya scanned the crowd discreetly, hoping to see the American somewhere here. She had a name for him now: Andy DeVries, from Chicago, apparently making his first appearance at any sort of festival of note. She wanted to know more about him. She even entertained thoughts of possibly meeting him. But she felt guilty, as though she were betraying Denny. That she should even allow herself to be intrigued by any man so soon was wrong.

Sonya tried to push those feelings away as she clutched her champagne flute tighter in her hand and smiled pleasantly at Zinski's secretary Grace, the woman who had spearheaded the arrangements for Sonya to attend the festival.

"Isn't this a lovely evening?" Grace commented in an awkward tone, noticing that Sonya seemed a little uneasy. "Have you enjoyed the festival so far?"

Sonya caught herself, flushed with embarrassment for her distraction, and smiled warmly at Grace.

"I have, very much, thank you," she replied. "I have to admit, I haven't been among so many people in one place for a long time. It's a little daunting."

Grace nodded and touched her glass to Sonya's.

"I totally understand. I'm not given to large gatherings, either. However, Jochen insisted that the troops put in an appearance, at the very least to 'keep the sponsors happy.'"

They shared a light laugh together and surveyed the open-air Pavilion.

"Jochen was so glad that you decided to come. Denny was a wonderful student," Grace said.

Sonya blinked at her. She nodded, looking down at the grass.

Grace offered a sad smile.

"I'm sorry. I didn't mean to..."

"No, no - it's fine, really," Sonya said reassuringly. "It's nice to hear so many wonderful things about him. I'm really rather flattered."

Joss sidled up to Sonya, and she smiled at Grace politely.

"Well, you two have a lovely time," Grace said, excusing herself. "Remember, anything you need - just ask."

Once Grace was gone, Joss appraised Sonya.

"Are you OK?" she queried.

Sonya shook her head.

"Yeah. Everyone seems to want to talk to me about Denny. I think they're feeling guilty that they didn't know. It's like a wake all over again. But I don't mind so much."

"Do you want to get out of here?" Joss suggested. "I don't think they'll notice if we slip away quietly. They're too busy marveling at how wonderful they all are."

Sonya considered her near-empty champagne glass and quickly polished off the remainder. Then she cast her eyes around the Pavilion.

"You're hooked by him, aren't you?" Joss smiled. Sonya flinched, realizing Joss had been watching her.

"No. God, no," Sonya retorted, weakly. Her eyes darted all around, everywhere but at Joss.

"Sonya," Joss said almost chidingly, squeezing her hand gently. "It's all right, you know, to - you know."

Sonya gasped softly and pulled her hand away, recoiling at Joss's apparent insight.

"No, it's not, Joss. Don't say that."

Joss gazed at Sonya, her eyes filled with empathy.

"Sonya, when are you going to drop the whole 'I'm not on the market' thing? C'mon. It has been a year, after all."

She put an arm around Sonya and squeezed her close.

"Besides - I thought he was kinda cute."

"*What?*" Sonya glared at Joss.

"Look," Joss said, "You couldn't take your eyes of that American the whole time he was playing. And you've been scoping out the Gardens ever since, hoping to see him."

Sonya blushed and nearly shoved her glass at Joss.

"Can you just get me another drink, *please*?"

Joss laughed and sought out a nearby waiter, while Sonya surveyed the gathering in the Pavilion. She cursed herself for having been so obvious in front of Denny's sister. Joss was insufferable, but her heart was in the right place. Sonya felt too conflicted, too self-conscious to endure any more gentle nudges from anyone. She would rather have taken Joss up on her suggestion to leave this party.

She exhaled wearily, letting her eyes drift across the Pavilion. In the near distance, she saw a group of musicians, some of the performers from today's competition. All of a sudden, the air had caught in her throat and she felt unable to breathe. As she watched them, her eyes fell across him - the American.

He was here.

Andy glanced sideways in mid-conversation with one of his fellow performers and, just as he lifted his beer to his lips, his eyes fell across her, standing alone at the far end of the Pavilion. His heart felt as if it might burst from his chest. Time seemed to slow to a crawl and he froze where he stood, lowering the bottle. The dormant emotions that he had felt only as echoes of Denny's until now became his own.

It was her.

Andy's sluggish mind struggled to work. *She was here!* He didn't know what to do, but as he stood there, Andy realized Sonya hadn't looked away from him, either. She remained perfectly still. In that moment Andy could have sworn that she was looking at him with recognition.

Did she know it was Denny?

Joss handed Sonya a glass of champagne, and she took it. She tilted her head and smiled awkwardly at Andy from across the Pavilion.

Oh my god, he's looking at me!

Raising her glass slightly towards him, she mouthed, "Congratulations."

Joss followed her gaze across the outdoor room and saw the American, standing near the bar.

She smiled wickedly.

"Looks like he's noticed you," she commented.

"Will you shut up!"

"Go across and introduce yourself," Joss prodded her eagerly. Sonya frowned.

"Look, I'm Denny's sister, and I am ordering you to go over and introduce yourself. Take a chance, for god's sake."

Sonya felt flustered, unable to decide what to do. It was just an introduction. That was all. How hard could that be?"

Andy stared fixedly at her from his vantage point. He wondered what she and Joss were talking about. He shivered upon seeing Joss - his, or rather Denny's, younger sister. Theirs was unlike most sibling relationships; Denny had adored her.

Then, whispering something in Joss' ear, Sonya stepped forward and Andy realized she was making her way through the crowd towards him.

He felt as though he was going to faint.

She's coming.

Chapter 20

His breath quickened. His eyes flickered between her and the beer in his hand; his heart thumped faster in his chest. He felt as if his nerves might fray completely and get the better of him. Andy couldn't believe that she was really here - that she was coming towards him now. It was too much for him to grasp. Sonya stepped around a group of people between her and Andy. Then she was standing before him.

Her beauty, her perfume, her lustrous auburn hair. The scent of rosemary and mint was there too - that which he had always remembered. Her eyes, those shimmering jewels as vibrant and alive as in his dreams. Everything about her that Andy had remembered from the moment he had been brought back to life in the trauma room was now very real, very tangible. Sonya offered her hand to Andy and he took it, hesitantly at first, until he caught himself and grabbed onto his rational state of mind. He firmed his grip on her hand. The feeling of it in his was electric. When she spoke, her voice made his heart almost stop.

"Congratulations," Sonya repeated, smiling politely. "I just wanted to say that I thought you were superb this afternoon. That piece is a favorite of mine."

Andy nodded respectfully. He could feel his cheeks flushing.

"Thank you," he replied softly. "You know it? It was a pleasure to play, if a little scary. I haven't performed for such a large audience before."

"Well, one would never have known it. I think you managed to capture the entire audience's imagination today. Everyone is talking about you."

Sonya sipped her champagne nervously and glanced around her. She felt a powerful attraction to him that made her want to stay. She racked her brain, searching for something to drive the conversation onwards.

"How are you finding Australia?" she asked finally. "Is it your first time here?"

Andy nodded.

"It's very hospitable. I've enjoyed this city. It's different from Chicago, very warm. And I don't just mean weather-wise."

He shifted on the spot and gazed at her, almost hoping she would recognize something within him telling her he was Denny.

"You're Sonya Llewellyn?" Andy ventured hesitantly. "Jochen Zinski pointed you out to a few of the performers earlier. He told us that you were visiting to present the trophy at the end of the week."

"Oh," Sonya said, nodding. "Yes. He came and saw me personally in the town where I live to invite me here. It was his idea to name the award."

"The - guy must have been pretty special, huh?"

Sonya nodded, looking away from Andy.

"He was. Very special."

Andy noticed a glimpse of longing in her eyes as she gazed off into empty space. He sensed that she was remembering.

For her part, Sonya felt awkward. The pangs of guilt tugged at her conscience, but she tried to ignore them.

What am I doing? She thought.

Andy tried to think of something, anything to advance the conversation further.

"How long have you played the guitar?" Sonya asked finally, finding the words that he couldn't.

"Since I was six years old," Andy replied, relieved by her question. "Some would say I came to it quite late. Most of the contestants here probably started when they were still in diapers. I feel as though I'm on the back foot a little."

Sonya smiled.

"Well, if today was anything to go by, I think you'll be a definite contender. It's a wonderful event. Are you excited about the finals?"

"Terrified is perhaps more appropriate right now," Andy said. "I've never done anything like this before. I am looking forward to playing again. I think I'll be practicing every spare moment I can get in my hotel room between now and then."

Sonya nodded, lifting her brow slightly.

"Oh, that would be a shame. There's so much to see here. You wouldn't want to miss it."

Oh god, what are you saying, Sonya? She scolded herself. *Could you be any more transparent?*

She felt lightheaded, and as she lifted her glass to her lips she realized that she had already emptied the champagne from it completely.

Andy gestured towards the bar as casually as he could.

"Could I get you another drink?"

Sonya considered his offer. She wanted to say yes. She looked over her shoulder at Joss, who wore a wicked half-grin as she chatted with another group of people, every so often stealing a glance in Sonya's direction.

"I probably shouldn't," Sonya decided. "I fear if I have another, I won't be able to walk. This stuff is pretty potent."

Andy smiled warmly as she offered her hand again.

"I just wanted to say how lovely I thought your performance was," she said.

Andy nodded. "Thank you. Perhaps I'll see you again."

Sonya smiled, trying not to look too hopeful. "Perhaps you will. Don't practice too hard."

Sonya stepped back, holding his hand a moment longer, holding his gaze. Then she turned and headed back to where Joss was standing. Andy watched her go, unable to take his eyes off her until he realized he had forgotten to breathe.

Michyko appeared beside him and tugged at his arm.

"There you are! We've been looking all over for you. Have you had enough praise thrust upon you yet?"

"I think so," Andy smiled, still gazing after Sonya, who had disappeared into the crowd.

Michyko followed his gaze fleetingly.

"Well, a group of us have decided to hit a pub in the city that was recommended to us. Want to join us?"

"Yeah, that would be cool."

Michyko gave him a silly grin. "Who are you looking at?" she ribbed him conspiratorially.

Andy squirmed uncomfortably and blushed.

"Nobody," he said, a little too quickly.

Michyko studied him with mock suspicion. "Nobody - a *likely* story. Come on - we'll miss the cab."

Andy followed Michyko out of the Pavilion, looking back to where Sonya had been standing, but she was no longer there.

Sonya and Joss had hailed a cab just outside the Garden not too long after. As they rode towards the city, Joss noted a curious expression on Sonya's face and she smiled mischievously.

"If I didn't know better, Sonya, I would swear that you've gone all doe-eyed, haven't you?" she teased.

Sonya screwed up her nose at Joss.

"Oh *stop it*. You're insufferable."

But deep down, Sonya couldn't deny that Joss was right.

"Personally, I *definitely* think he's *hot,*" Joss persisted, trying to get a rise out of Sonya.

Sonya just laughed softly and watched through the window as the lights of the city passed by. She felt an old, familiar warm glow within that she hadn't felt in a long time.

***

While the others went on a tour of the city the following morning, Andy decided to slip out early and walk down to the Gardens. He had hardly slept a wink. All he could think about was Sonya, their meeting in the Pavilion and the brief conversation they'd shared. He couldn't forget the touch of her hand, or the way she had smiled at him. All of it came back, the memories of how it had been before he died. He had intended to watch the heats and take in some of the other concert events around the Gardens, but now that Andy had found her, all he wanted to do was to find her again.

His walk took no more than twenty minutes. Crossing over a wide thoroughfare separating the Fitzroy Gardens from the smaller Treasury Gardens, Andy saw that a sizable crowd was already gathering on the lawns in front of the conservatory building. Though it was not quite 10 a.m., the intense summer sun was beginning to warm the city and Andy felt beads of sweat forming on his brow. Quickly dabbing them away, he made his way into the Gardens.

Several stages had been set up throughout the Gardens that were to play host to performers from all across the world. They ranged from blues and roots artists, exponents of world music - in particular, the genres from South American and Spanish influences - and several well-known jazz outfits that were visiting from the U.K., the U.S. and Europe. There was no doubting the feast of music on offer for someone with an appetite for the kinds of musical styles that Andy had.

Andy stopped by the Pavilion and bought a coffee and a muffin - he hadn't had anything to eat this morning - then he sat down to browse through the program. He had made a mental list of a number of artists he wanted to see perform while he was here, including a namesake of his, Doug de Vries, a celebrated Australian guitarist who had caught his eye when he was still in high school. There was also Slava Grigoryan, who had immigrated to Australia with his family as a child and who had become one of Australia's most prominent classical guitarists. It was Grigoryan's interpretation of "The Sounds Of Rain" that he had first heard so long ago as a child. In the back of his mind, Andy was distracted from the festival. He kept looking up, hoping to see her, hoping that she would be here somewhere, that she would suddenly materialize. But she wasn't anywhere to be seen. It was still early, after all.

He was greeted by some of the performers from the previous day's heat and spent some time chatting with them. Their conversation was welcoming. They talked about the music on offer throughout the week, and Andy received yet more congratulations and good wishes for the semifinal. But all he wanted to do was to extricate himself and take in some of today's musical acts.

And, hopefully, bump into Sonya.

How was he going to tell her? Andy had wrestled with the question through a sleepless night. He had no idea. The notion of reincarnation was preposterous. Even he'd had trouble in coming to terms with it in the beginning. Though Sonya was a soulful person, for as long as he could remember, she had always been fairly grounded and wasn't particularly drawn to matters of faith. He couldn't just walk up to her and announce, "Hey, I'm your dead lover, come back to life in the body of a reformed drug addict."

Andy shook his head in frustration.

He had no idea how she had coped on her own once he had died. He couldn't be sure whether she was still grieving. Andy reasoned that the only way he could convince her would be to spend some time with her - get to know her in this guise, and then reveal himself. Andy felt an uncomfortable pressure building in his chest. His confidence was shaky.

How can I tell her?

He meandered up to an old stone bandstand far from the conservatory and took in a performance by a jazz quartet that had attracted a sizable audience. He sat on the grass and tried to relax. Every so often he stole an opportunity to look around in the hope that he might spot her somewhere in the audience.

But she wasn't there.

Andy eventually made his way back to the southern end of the Gardens, to the conservatory where the afternoon heats would be taking place. He bought a mineral water and made his way across the lawn to find a spot on the grass.

"Hello, Andy."

Andy spun around at the sound of her voice and found Sonya and Joss relaxing on a rug on the lawn just a few feet away. His heart skipped a beat. Sonya waved to him, and he smiled warmly as she gestured for him to come over.

"Hello again," he greeted, placing his hands in his pocket and walking over to them as casually as he could, trying desperately not to seem too eager.

Sonya was wearing a light cotton dress with a pearl-colored cardigan, and large sunglasses underneath a large sun hat. A pair of leather sandals lay near her feet. She looked radiant.

Sonya lifted the brim of her hat as he approached.

"Beautiful day, isn't it?" she said. "We've really turned it on for you, don't you agree?"

Andy nodded reservedly and lifted his hands to his eyes to shield them from the mid-morning sun.

"I'm finding Melbourne addictive. I could get used to this."

Sonya got to her feet as he stopped before their blanket, and turned towards Joss, who had also stood and was brushing down her three-quarter-length cargo trousers. She wore a multicolored top that showed off her tanned arms.

"Andrew DeVries, I'd like you to meet Jocelyn Banister, a very good friend of mine."

Andy stepped forward to take Denny's sister's hand.

"It's Andy, please," he said.

As he offered his hand to Joss, Sonya's eyes fell across his forearm. The shirt he wore was rolled part-way up and it pulled taut, sliding up as he stretched out his hand. She caught a fleeting glimpse of something there.

Sonya's eyes drifted from their exchange and across the grounds. A breeze had rustled the tree under which they sat. Three leaves were dislodged from the lower branches and fell to the ground, where they settled on the lush grass for a moment. Sonya tilted her head curiously as the echoes of the reverie played themselves out for real, here and now. She is captivated by the leaves and their gentle motion. She hears an echoing laughter of children nearby.

Her eyes refocused on Andy's arm, but he was already drawing it away.

"You can call me Joss," Denny's sister said. "Though I'm sure you've already heard this a bunch of times, I thought you were amazing yesterday. There's a real buzz for you out there already."

Andy blushed and scratched the grass nervously with his foot.

"Well, there's a long way to go until Saturday, and I'm not taking anything for granted right now. There are a lot of better performers here than me."

"Are you here to watch the heats this afternoon?" Sonya ventured hopefully, as Joss nudged her elbow with a discreet grin.

"Yeah. I thought I'd see if there was a patch of ground up near the front so I could get a good view of the performers, but somehow, I think I might be pushing my luck."

"You *could* join us - if you'd like," Sonya offered. *Oh God, could I be any more desperate?*

Andy gave the pretense of considering her offer, even though inside he was nearly bursting. He nodded and smiled again.

"Thank you. That would be nice."

They made room on the rug and then sat down to watch the afternoon heats, during which they shared a conversation that seemed very natural and very easy to sustain. Joss gently maneuvered it by asking Andy questions about himself, encouraging him to talk a little about life in Chicago: how incredibly cold it was there right now in contrast to here in Melbourne. He talked about the Conservatory and Veldtman, as well as working and playing at The Pub.

Andy's concentration drifted towards the stage for a time and he studied the performers carefully, noting how they played, listening closely to their style, looking for flaws in their technique. He was particular focused on a young German virtuoso that had scored very high in her heat the previous day and was considered to be a leading contender among the contestants and officials. Sonya found herself stealing glances at him. She watched his expressions, the way he made subtle movements of his head as he listened to the music, as though he were moving with it. There was something so familiar about him and so attractive. But she felt the troubling, distracting guilt once more. The inner voice that scolded her for these feelings, telling her it was wrong.

Andy could sense her looking at him. He did the same a few times, their eyes meeting for just the briefest of moments before both of them bashfully looked away. He had so longed to be around her again. He couldn't believe his circumstances here and now. She was so beautiful, exactly how he remembered her from his adopted memories - Denny's memories.

During an interval, Andy excused himself so he could go to the bathroom. Once he was out of view, Joss nudged Sonya in the ribs.

"What do you think?" she interrogated Sonya eagerly. "He is *definitely* interested."

Sonya flashed Joss a glare, but she couldn't maintain her facade.

"All right, all right - he is cute," Sonya grinned awkwardly. "But I didn't come here to meet anyone, Joss. I know that may have been in your plan, but I just don't need that kind of complication right now."

Joss shook her head, fishing a bottle of wine out of their picnic basket and pouring them each a glass.

"Sonya. You're a beautiful woman, but you are stubborn. Denny wouldn't have wanted you to remain alone. He would've wanted you to be happy. Why don't you allow yourself the chance for some happiness? This guy is interested in you, and you're sure as shit interested in him."

Sonya tilted her head slowly with a pained expression.

"I just can't."

Joss leveled a disapproving eye at her.

"You're stalling, Sonya. If you don't at least ask him out for a coffee, *I will*. You know you want to."

Sonya's shoulders slumped in a mock gesture of defeat and she laughed, sipping from her glass. She couldn't rail against Joss's persistence any longer.

"You are relentless."

Joss nodded triumphantly and looked over Sonya's shoulder. Andy was coming back.

"Here he comes."

Both women smiled a little too broadly at Andy as he approached, causing him to look about and check himself over.

"Do I have something on my face?"

"Not at all," Joss replied, patting the rug and gesturing towards the basket. "Can I offer you a drink?"

Before Andy could respond, she had poured him a glass and was handing it over.

He sensed right away that something was cooking between the two women.

Joss kept whispering in Sonya's ear; he could see her out of the corner of his eye.

Probably trying to engineer something, Andy mused.

Ever the social butterfly, Joss was adept at playing matchmaker when there was even the slightest whiff of potential romance. He wanted to slap his - Denny's - younger sister on the arm the way he always used to. In her presence, a whole new flood of memories sprang forth from Denny's consciousness and into Andy's: memories of his childhood, of growing up with Joss. They had been inseparable as children.

As the performances continued, Andy told the women what he was keen to study about the performers. He explained the importance of their technique, how they presented themselves on stage, how they played the pieces they had chosen. The performance wasn't merely an exercise in the technical mastery of the guitar or the music, but it was also a performance of emotions. One needed to feel the music, to know its history and its meaning, and apply those to the performance. Sonya listened to him intently, absorbed by his genuine love for the art of the guitar. She was captivated by his enthusiasm for it, how he described the stories behind the pieces themselves. It was clear he had a deep knowledge of music - a passion for it.

The concert finished towards late afternoon, and the trio remained on the rug while the crowds of people began to disperse slowly towards other parts of the Gardens. Others remained, continuing their picnics and barbecues with the clear intention of staying around long into the evening to take in a concert by the Melbourne Symphony Orchestra.

Joss looked at her watch and gestured wordlessly to Sonya that they had to think about heading off. Sonya looked disappointed, her brow furrowing at Denny's sister worriedly. Joss pointed towards Andy with her eyes and pursed her lips tightly as though she were saying, "Ask him!"

Sonya felt her pulse reverberating in her ears, felt her breath quicken as a rush of adrenaline surged through. She couldn't believe what she was about to do.

Turning to Andy, she smiled.

"We have to go," she said regretfully. "We're meeting Joss's parents for dinner on the other side of the city, and we're sort of running against the clock."

"Oh. OK," Andy replied. Inwardly his mind shouted at him: *What are you doing?*

They stood up, and Joss began packing up the picnic basket while Andy and Sonya stood to one side.

"Thank you for inviting me to join you today," Andy said warmly.

Sonya nodded, fidgeting with her hands and biting the inside of her lip. Clearly she had something more to say.

"It was nice," she said, pausing clumsily.

She closed her eyes and took a quick breath.

"Umm ... are you free at all ... tomorrow?" she asked. "I thought maybe you'd like to - you know - have a cup of coffee. If you have time."

Andy blinked, caught unprepared by the question that he himself had been building up to asking.

"I would love to," he said quietly, with a smile. "I don't have any commitments tomorrow as far as I know - so, yeah."

Joss watched the two of them gazing dumbly at one another and screwed her face up out of view. It was all she could do to stop herself from squealing with delight.

Andy checked his watch and looked up at Sonya.

"Should we meet at my hotel at, say, about 10? I'm staying at The Windsor."

Sonya nodded, unable to pull her gaze away from his, unable to wipe the smile from her face. Andy stepped forward and took her hand gently.

"Thank you," he whispered, before nodding to Joss. "Nice meeting you, too, Joss."

"Likewise. I'll look forward to seeing you on Saturday."

Andy turned away slowly, without taking his eyes off Sonya, and parted. As he crossed over a path and under a line of trees his smile broke into a broad grin and he felt a rush of endorphins course though him. He felt so giddy that he feared his legs might give way underneath him.

He could not believe his luck.

Chapter 21

Andy sat in the foyer of the Windsor Hotel the next morning, flipping through the daily newspaper. He wasn't really taking anything in, however; he was far too distracted. The only thing he had thought about since returning to the hotel last night was her. He had woken insanely early and spent several hours sitting on his bed, watching television, strumming his guitar, pacing the room. Doing anything he could think of to pass the time, wishing the minutes away until he could see Sonya again. He'd showered twice, so nervous and excited and terrified was he. It was like going on a first date all over again.

A first date.

Denny had got tickets to an indie music festival in Melbourne during the summer. It must have been three or four years ago. He and Sonya had just reconnected again at university after many years apart. It was an incredibly hot day, and they had spent most of it in and out of specially provided mist tents that had been fitted with sprinkler systems to cool down the revelers at the venue. People drank fiercely, the atmosphere was electric and the music was awesome. It was a wild and crazy day, and during it they had fallen for each other.

Denny and Sonya had been childhood friends. She was a willowy tomboy, athletic, bold and self-assured, even then. He was an awkward and shy kid, a little clumsy perhaps, but in her company he felt at ease. She exuded a calmness that rubbed off on people, especially him. They had grown up together near the Melbourne seaside. They'd attended the local primary school, played in the park, on the beach, in Denny's tree house on weekends. Their families had lived next door to each other. Sonya and Denny were practically joined at the hip, inseparable. Then, after the sixth grade, Sonya's parents moved away to Hambledown. Denny and Sonya were devastated. Though they kept in touch for a time; but time moved on and their letters petered out. Only when Sonya came back to Melbourne to attend university did they rekindle their friendship. It was as though the years they'd spent apart had never been, and before too long they had fallen deeply in love.

Andy smiled at those memories.

Every so often Andy looked towards the hotel entrance. He checked his watch, cursing himself for having readied himself so early, but he didn't know what else to do. His anticipation was too much. He put down the newspaper and looked around for the men's room. He saw it, and, as he stood to walk over to it, Andy chanced a glance at the entrance.

There she was.

Sonya was standing just inside the door, surveying her surroundings.

Their eyes met.

Andy forgot about the bathroom completely and walked towards her. She smiled at him.

"Hello," Sonya greeted. "Wow. They've put you up in some pretty nice accommodations."

Andy nodded, craning his neck to look around the foyer of the resplendent hotel. The morning sun streamed in through a large sky light far above, bathing the foyer in an ethereal light. When he looked back at her again, he was struck once again by her beauty. The sunlight danced over her auburn hair, making it seem even more lustrous than he had remembered. She wore a pretty summer dress under a light green cardigan and canvas shoes. She held the sun hat she'd worn the previous day in her hand.

"Yeah, my school did pretty well in getting us into this place. The dean might flip out, though, when he finds out how much it's costing them."

Andy smiled. "I'm glad you came. I know it must be a little awkward for you."

"Not at all," Sonya replied. "It's nice to be able enjoy a little down time while I'm here. The festival is good and all, but - it's just nice."

"So..." Andy ventured. "Do you like coffee?"

Of course she likes coffee!

Sonya nodded.

"I found this really great coffee house not far from here. It's called Enzo's," Andy suggested. "They do an awesome breakfast."

Sonya's eyes widened in surprise at the mention of hers and Denny's old haunt.

"Do you know it?" Andy asked.

Of course she knows it!

"I know it," she said slowly. "Very well."

Sonya studied him curiously as Andy gestured towards the door. "Shall we?"

He knew he was taking a risk by taking her there, and he could tell by her expression that he had touched off something in her. Andy didn't want to arouse her suspicions in a way that would put her off, but she didn't seem to mind at all. She seemed genuinely happy with the suggestion. They drove the short distance across town in Sonya's car, where they sat quietly, unsure of what to say at first. But by the time they took up a place in a booth in the cool, soft atmosphere of the Lygon Street coffee house, they had relaxed enough that they began a conversation that was easy, natural and pleasant.

Andy felt the echo of the way it had been before, when Denny and Sonya used to come to Enzo's. He remembered how they had sought refuge here, when they were studying furiously for exams on winter afternoons when it was pouring with rain outside. And he remembered how they hung out here with their circle of friends during the summer, when classes were just beginning and they were coming to grips with a seemingly insurmountable workload. Then there were the lazy weekends, when they craved just being alone together. They would come here to enjoy a cooked breakfast on a Saturday morning. They would curl up together in a booth, reading a book to each other and sipping coffee. Here was the place that felt like a second home.

Andy listened to Sonya as she talked about the practice and the beach house in Hambledown. How, in the time since Denny's death, she had fully taken the reins of her grandfather's practice, had turned it around from the wreck he had left behind and now hoped for its future. The beach house was another story. It was still dilapidated, and Sonya planned to focus her energies on renovating it once the practice was turning over a profit.

Sonya felt herself growing more at ease in Andy's company. He listened attentively. He was quiet, perhaps a little shy, but not at all what she might have expected. His presence was warm and, once again, she experienced that sense of déjà-vu - a sense of familiarity that was very potent, but also different somehow.

There was a reunion between Sonya and Enzo, who recognized her immediately. He stopped serving the other customers and embraced her warmly. Enzo had been at Denny's funeral, and had wept for him. As the elderly Italian came over to them, Andy felt a familiar rush of affection for the generous old man. He had taught Denny the art of chess, and their "tournaments" became another of the attractions of the coffee house. At Enzo's insistence, Andy and Sonya stayed for lunch. He knew about the guitar festival, and when Sonya introduced Andy and mentioned that he was competing, Enzo embraced him. His regard for musicians, particularly guitarists of the classical discipline, was legendary. Andy and Sonya stayed until mid-afternoon. Neither of them minded at all.

When they finally did leave, Andy and Sonya strolled leisurely along the sidewalk towards the city. Andy felt elated. He weighed up whether it was a good time to part company now, on such a sweet note. He would be disappointed, but he was mindful of being too hurried with her.

"I guess I should think about getting back to the hotel," he said, almost involuntarily as he began surveying the street near Sonya's car.

"Oh," Sonya said, disappointment in her voice.

Andy turned back to look at her.

"I don't have to, though. If you..."

Sonya did not want it to end now. She held his gaze, feeling a lovely warmth pass through her. It was as if Andy had cast a spell on her. The guilt had left her, now.

"Shall we go for a walk?" she suggested.

Andy's eyes brightened. "I'd like that very much."

Andy and Sonya made their way into the city. They stopped by a florist in a French-inspired arcade to pick up some lilies for Joss as a thank you for letting Sonya stay at her Williamstown apartment. Andy recognized the florist. Denny had bought flowers there before, and Andy smiled inwardly, pleased that Sonya still favored it. They walked along the banks of the Yarra River, continuing their conversation. All the while, words began to form in Andy's mind, an appeal that tugged at his conscience.

Tell her!

He tried to ignore it, pushing the irrational thoughts away. He knew if he were to reveal himself to her now, it would be too much for her to comprehend.

"Would you like to go for a drive?" she asked.

She doesn't want this day to end, Andy thought excitedly.

"Where?" he said.

"Well, I have to drop these flowers off at Joss' apartment; otherwise they'll shrivel up in this heat. It's in Williamstown. It's just over the bridge, say about half an hour from here. I can drop you back to the hotel later. If you'd like."

Williamstown! My home!

Andy managed to stifle his excitement at hearing mention of the seaside suburb by feigning a thoughtful expression, as though he were considering her proposal. He studied her with a lopsided half-grin.

"Am I correct in guessing that you're enjoying yourself?"

Sonya blushed, and eyed him suggestively.

"I *could* be," she replied coyly.

Andy wanted to take her in his arms right then and kiss her. He wanted to feel her lips against his, to hold her hands and feel their warmth, but he restrained himself.

Again, the words sounded in his head.

Tell her!

Finally, he nodded.

"That sounds like a great idea."

Picking up Sonya's VW sedan once more, they drove across the city to Williamstown, the cosmopolitan beach side suburb where Sonya and Denny had spent their childhood.

Neither of them wanted the day to end.

By the late afternoon, Andy and Sonya found themselves in Williamstown's chic restaurant district. On a balcony of a waterfront cafe that overlooked Port Philip Bay, they ordered a bottle of wine and relaxed in their seats to take in the view. A jazz quartet was playing in the background. The majestic Melbourne skyline dominated the landscape to the north, towering above groups of moored yachts that rocked gently on the swell of the Williamstown harbor, their masts swaying to and fro.

People were enjoying walks on the nearby esplanade, playing on the beach, swimming in the sea. A tall ship slowly made its way across the water, its sails billowing full in the late afternoon breeze. It all reminded Andy a little of Chicago. He took in a deep breath of the salty scent - something Lake Michigan had been missing - and exhaled, feeling a calm unlike any he'd felt before. Everything seemed so pure here, so clean. And so familiar.

It was home.

They enjoyed a lobster that was quite unlike any Andy had ever eaten. They drank a local wine and continued their conversation almost uninterrupted. The day had been wonderful.

Sonya smiled as Andy stretched and gazed out across the water.

"I can see you're enjoying yourself," she commented as a waiter cleared their plates and refreshed their wine glasses.

"I am," Andy replied. "This place is surreal. It's like something out of a dream or a picture book. Is everyone in this city so laid back?"

Sonya followed his eyes out across the waterfront.

"Hmm. It *is* tranquil here. Though Melbourne itself is like any other city. It has its fair share of problems."

"So city law doesn't appeal to you, then?"

Sonya shook her head and sipped her wine.

"Not at all. I decided that rural concerns are enough of a challenge on their own. And I prefer the people. They are far more ... real than anyone here. I would rather help them there than destroy people here. There's enough aggression in the Melbourne law fraternity. I didn't want to get sucked into it."

"That's quite noble," Andy remarked.

"It is," Sonya agreed with an earnest nod before smiling broadly, and causing Andy's heart to skip a beat.

"What about you? The guitar seems to be very much a part of you. It defines you, yes?"

Andy returned her smile with his own and swirled the wine in his glass, holding it up to the light to study it.

Sonya's breath caught in her throat then as she watched him. The way he held the glass, the way he inspected the wine.

Andy rested the glass on his crossed leg.

"It's everything to me," he said wistfully. "It's carried me through some difficult times, and I haven't always been very kind to it. But now it's the one thing that I want to do more than anything. It's pretty much been the only thing I was ever good at."

Sonya's brow creased into a frown.

"Surely you're good at more than just the guitar."

"Getting into trouble, possibly. I was exceptional at that," Andy bowed his head slightly. "Unfortunately, I think I made an art form out of calamity instead of applying myself. But there has always been the guitar. It is a gift that I've come to treasure."

"Trouble?" Sonya inquired.

"Oh, it's way too long a story," Andy deflected. "Let's just say I was lost for a long time. But I found my way back."

"Well," Sonya raised her glass, and he met hers with his. "Your gift is a beautiful thing. Music is said to be the salvation for many of us. Here's to it."

They drank, looking at each other. A sense of something electric passed between them.

"You know," Sonya began hesitantly. "I have to say this, and *please* don't think I'm crazy, but - you seem so very familiar to me. It's like - I feel like we've met before."

Andy smiled awkwardly. "That sounds like a very bad line," he said. "Even with the Australian accent."

Sonya laughed and covered her mouth, embarrassed.

"I *know*, it does, right? But it's true. Are you sure that you've never been to Australia before?"

"I haven't. Sorry," Andy said, the statement sounding like a lie to him. "Not even once."

Again, the voice tugged at the corners of his mind.

Tell her.

Andy's shifted his thoughts towards the concert series, the seemingly overwhelming nature of the final competition.

"I can't believe I'm here, that I've made it this far," he said. "I've never done anything like this before."

"It's a wonderful opportunity," Sonya agreed. "I can only imagine how nervous you must feel."

"Hmmm."

Andy looked out across the waterfront towards the beach. It was the same beach where they had frolicked as children. He gestured towards it with a nod.

"Shall we take a walk on the sand?"

Sonya nodded and smiled.

"That would be nice."

Making their way down to the water's edge, Sonya slipped off her sandals and stepped - gingerly at first - into the sea, feeling the cool water against her ankles and feet.

Andy took off his own shoes, setting them on the sand and joining Sonya as she luxuriated her feet at the water's edge.

"There is something addictive about the seaside," she mused. "I have always loved it. I've lived near the beach pretty much all my life."

I remember, he mused silently.

"Are you nervous?" Sonya asked. "About the final?"

Andy wandered a few paces along the shoreline, hands in his pockets.

"I'm petrified," he answered truthfully. "I came here with no expectations whatsoever. I mean, I was a last-minute entry. The Conservatory didn't even want me on the delegation. Now, I want it more than anything. I don't think I've ever wanted anything more."

Sonya watched him, her hand shading her eyes from the late afternoon sun.

He stands at the water's edge, his hands in his pockets, thoughtful. Yet he is neither out of focus nor out of reach. Unlike her dream.

This was the dream?

Small waves, no more than a few inches high, washed up on the shoreline now, but as they strolled slowly along, watching children playing in the shallows, a bigger wave broke unexpectedly over a ridge of sand, slapping against Sonya's ankles and causing her to lose balance. Reflexively she reached out with her hand and Andy grabbed it, pulling her close to steady her. He held her until he was sure she was safe. She looked up to thank him, and in that moment their eyes locked. Neither one could look away.

He could resist no longer.

He leaned in gently, his finger rising to touch her cheek, and their lips found each other. A soft, slow, electrifying kiss ignited a wellspring of warmth and emotion in them both so powerful that neither could pull away, nor wanted to. Sonya's hand cradled his jaw, her lips parted, and she touched her tongue to his, teasingly, exquisitely rolling around it, and then gently pulling back. Sonya sighed as Andy drew in close to her, sliding his hands around her body and holding her softly.

The moment lingered.

Time stopped.

An alarm bell suddenly rang out in Sonya's mind and she panicked, pulling herself away from Andy abruptly. She was breathless, flooded with guilt. Sonya's mind swirled and she felt as though she might fall. Her face melted into bewilderment, embarrassment, shame.

"What have I done?" she gasped.

Andy was stunned where he stood, dazed by the afterglow of the kiss and the suddenness of her pulling away. He reached out to Sonya, but she put her hand up defensively.

"I'm sorry. I'm so sorry," she said breathlessly. "I shouldn't have done that."

"No, no, Sonya please. *I* shouldn't have. I'm sorry."

Sonya felt sick as the familiar, irrational guilt assailed her. All she wanted to do was to run away from here, from him - this exquisite stranger who made her feel...

He made her feel.

"I should go, Andy," she stammered as she hurriedly put on her sandals. "I'm so sorry. I didn't mean for any of this."

Andy's heart pounded as she turned away from him. All these long months of searching, the battle within him to make sense of the additional presence that resided there. His and Denny's emotions collided together somewhere deep inside of him, melding together until they were all but indistinguishable.

This is it.

Denny's voice rang in his ears, and Andy turned to face Sonya, who was walking away from him.

"Sonya!" he called out desperately.

Something in the tone of his voice made Sonya stop, and slowly she turned around to face him.

"Please wait."

Andy stepped forward, holding his arms out.

"Sonya ... it's me. It's Denny."

Sonya's eyes went wide and she blinked.

"Sonya, I don't how to explain what happened. I was in the dark after it happened, then - *somebody* found me. In Chicago," Andy's voice quivered.

He stepped forward and Sonya flinched, clearly spooked, but he continued.

"I was lying in a trauma room in a hospital," he said. "They told me I'd overdosed - that I had died in an ambulance on the way to the hospital. But I was - revived. Something happened to me when I was revived. I woke up and I was in this - *this* - body."

Sonya's purse strap slipped from her shoulder, falling to the sand. She said nothing as Andy approached her.

"Ever since then I've been plagued - by these memories. Of this old life, of this - place. Of you. I couldn't make sense of them at first, but I realized I was remembering everything about my old life."

"I - I can't believe," Sonya whispered, her lip quivering.

"I couldn't believe it at first, either," Andy continued, his voice cracking. "But I remember everything: the hospital, our home, eve-rything we planned to do. It all came to me, gradually at first, but I *remember.* And then I found you. I found Hambledown - on the Internet. I found Denny's page on Facebook. I had these clues to go by - the things I remembered. It was all there!"

Andy stepped forward, but Sonya threw up her hand, abruptly stopping him.

"Are you *fucking* kidding me?" she hissed.

Andy shivered at the sound of her voice, and he saw anger in her eyes. He froze.

"Sonya, it's the truth. I remember it all."

"How dare you?" Sonya spat, backing away from him as tears of rage welled up. "How dare you play this game with me? How could you even *begin* to be so cruel? Who do you think you are?"

Andy felt a nauseating panic. His mouth went dry and he struggled to force his jaw to work.

"What *are* you - some kind of sick stalker?" she continued, her fury becoming white hot.

He thumped his chest firmly, interrupting her.

"Sonya, look at me. Surely you can see it. Surely you can sense something - *can't you?*" He was pleading with her now, his voice rising. "What about that kiss just then - tell me you didn't feel something! Why would I make something up like this?"

But Sonya shook her head and backed away even further as he stepped forward again, holding his hand out towards her.

"No! Don't you come near me. If you do, I *will* call the police."

She wheeled around and stumbled on the sand before running away from him. Tears were streaming down her face now, her heart and mind filled with confusion and anger. Andy stood on the beach watching her go until she had disappeared. He was too stunned to move.

"What have I done?" he whispered.

Chapter 22

When Michyko knocked on Andy's door the following morning, she knew something was wrong. A disheveled Andy peered out from behind the half-opened door, squinting against the bright light of the hallway. His eyes were bloodshot and he looked pale and sickly.

"Andy!" Michyko gasped. "What's wrong?"

"Nothing," Andy croaked, his gravelly voice barely above a whisper. "I'm just not feeling well."

Michyko appeared crestfallen, and Andy felt awful for her. It was her heat today.

"I don't think I'm going to be able to attend today, Michyko."

"Well, can I get you anything? I can get some soup or something sent up."

Andy closed his eyes and leaned his forehead against the door frame. The throbbing in his head threatened to cause him to collapse.

"No, thank you, Michyko. I'll be fine. I just want to be alone."

Andy retreated back into his room and shut the door. Stumbling into the darkness he found the bed and collapsed onto it. He caught a whiff of himself as he turned over and winced, disgusted at himself, disgusted at the stench of alcohol that oozed from his pores and his own stale breath. The curtains were drawn, preventing any light from seeping into the room, allowing him to suffer in the misery of the hangover that had him going to the bathroom frequently to throw up, until there was nothing left, and then he continued to throw up anyway.

After returning alone to the city last night, Andy had holed himself up in the downstairs bar and slowly wiped himself out with a bottle of whiskey. No one noticed him in there, save for one of the bar staff who had kindly and discreetly walked him up to his room and deposited him safely onto his bed, where he tossed and turned in a drunken haze - tormented by his catastrophic revelation on the Williamstown beach. He drifted in and out of the torment of his circumstance and several times flirted with the desire to seek out a "hit" from somewhere - *anywhere.*

That last image of Sonya, distraught and disgusted, refused to leave him. It hung there at the center of his consciousness, seared into his soul, torturing him.

How could I have been so stupid? Andy cursed himself angrily through his tears of pain.

Though he hadn't comprehended it at the time, Andy understood in the light of day why Sonya had reacted so violently. He had behaved like a crazed idiot. So eager was he to reveal himself to her that his explanation came out so mangled, and so obviously crazy that to think about it now made him want to tear his hair out. His anger with himself was only partially assuaged by the grief that assailed him. The opportunity had been comprehensively wrecked now. There was no chance of repairing the damage his actions had wrought. He knew that if he approached her now, Sonya would surely call the police on him.

As he lolled in and out of consciousness at the hands of the violent headache, Andy hated what he had become. He hated having Denny's spirit inside of him and the knowledge of that other life, the burden of that lost love. In his ruined state he dragged himself from the bed and struggled to the bathroom. As he stumbled past the mirror, Andy caught a glimpse of himself. He stopped and snarled at what he saw.

"Why did you have to choose me?" Andy hissed at his reflection. "I never asked for this! I didn't want any of this!"

Fighting against waves of nausea, Andy felt a rage deep inside of him. He looked down at his fists, balling them tightly before thumping the top of the vanity. He glared contemptuously at his arms, turning them back and forth, his breath quickening, his anger growing. Then he began clawing at his arms, scratching at them so hard that he drew blood. He saw the tattoo on the inside of his forearm - the inscription *Ancora Imparo* - and he spat at it, trying to tear the skin away from his muscle.

"This is yours!" he screamed violently, ignoring the pain of his own attempts at self-mutilation. "This belongs to you! I don't want it anymore!"

He glared at the mirror and saw his rage etched into his features, saw the tightness in his jaw and he gnashed his teeth together and spat impotently. But as he stared longer Andy was suddenly struck when he saw his eyes. He froze where he stood. His eyes were filled not with anger, but with pain and grief.

Andy stumbled backwards, horrified by his behavior, stunned at his anger. He slumped back onto the cold tiles and sobbed in the darkness, his heart swelling with grief, with an emptiness so desolate he thought he would lose himself in it. He remained there on the floor unable - unwilling - to move. He lost all track of time and drifted on the pall of his tears until finally sleep overtook him and he dreamed only of the darkness.

***

Across town, in Joss's apartment, Sonya sat on the edge of the bed similarly frozen and lost in her emotions. Her traveling case lay open on the bed and she was clutching a dress in her hands, having taken it off a hanger with the intention of putting it into the case. Sonya wanted so desperately to get out of here - to escape the city and this god forsaken festival and go back to Hambledown.

After returning to the apartment last night she'd locked herself in her room and cried herself to sleep. Joss had tried desperately to talk to her, but she had refused saying simply that the date had gone badly. Very badly.

Which it had.

She was sickened by Andy's behavior as much as she was frightened by it. Sickened, that this stranger, who had come out of nowhere, would be so cruel as to play with her emotions like that. Sickened that he would concoct a fiction so destructive and violate her privacy and security by looking her up on the Internet like some sort of stalker was disgusting and vile. Her BlackBerry sat on the nightstand, and she thought several times of calling the police and reporting him, as well as alerting the Festival organizers.

But something held her back.

She could not bring herself to pick up the phone.

Despite his insane proclamation, Sonya could not bury the fact that she *had* sensed that something about him that was extremely powerful and familiar. And she could not entirely expunge the memory of the kiss.

It had been such a soft and familiar kiss.

A kiss that she knew.

The dreams, those short reveries that had played themselves out for real, came to her mind.

Leaves falling from the tree in the Gardens…as he lifts his hand to her…

Watching the stranger on the sand who is out of focus, except for those vivid pools of green that are his eyes…

That she was even considering the possibility that the American might be telling the truth filled her with anguish. It went against everything she believed or chose not to believe. This was the real world, a world where things like this simply did not happen.

Sonya considered the case on her bed and angrily wiped a tear from her cheek.

***

The lawns in front of the Conservatory building in the Fitzroy Gardens had been transformed into a wonderful amphitheater in readiness for the grand finale of the emerging artist concert series. The lawns had been freshly manicured, the surrounding trees had been adorned with twinkling fairy lights, and the stage had been bedecked with white ribbon and flanked by planter boxes filled with lilies and tulips and roses of brilliant color. The Orchestra musicians were preparing themselves on the stage, tuning their instruments as stagehands rushed about performing a variety of tasks in readiness. The audience was already beginning to fill the available space on the lawn in anticipation of this final concert.

Andy sat in the performers' tent near the stage, quietly waiting. He had checked and rechecked his instrument, ensuring that it was ready, and now all there was to do was wait. He sat alone in a neatly pressed shirt and tie, his jacket slung over the back of his chair. Somehow he had managed to pull himself together and push the trauma of his failure away for the time being to deliver a semifinal performance skillful and convincing enough to convince everyone that Andy was still a serious contender for the grand finale.

He had performed Fernando Sor's *Sonata Prima* with an orchestral accompaniment and had scored well with the judging panel, much to his amazement. In his mind it was not a good performance and he was sure that he had failed it, such was his turmoil. He had lost that hard-won ability to invest emotionally in the piece, as he had done before, and instead had delivered a stilted attempt at the sonata. The German contestant had won the night with a rousing performance of a piece called "Pavane" - another orchestral composition that was virtually flawless. But, somehow he was here. Andy had made it through.

He had thought of nothing but Sonya.

Andy had tentatively searched the Gardens yesterday before the semifinal, and again earlier this afternoon upon his arrival here, before making his way to the tent. He wanted to see Sonya. He wanted to say something - anything - that might make up for what had happened the other night.

But what could he say?

He had wrestled with his mind for the answer, but there was nothing he could think of that would repair the damage. As it was, he hadn't glimpsed any sight of her anywhere in the Gardens and he was beginning to wonder if Sonya was even here in Melbourne anymore.

As the concert began outside, Michyko appeared in the entrance to the tent and smiled warmly upon seeing him. She made her way over and, finding a chair, she sat down quietly.

He acknowledged her silently and looked down at his hands.

"Where are the others?" he queried softly.

"They're sitting outside on the lawn. We've got a great vantage point - right near the stage."

He nodded simply and remained quiet, lost in his thoughts. He picked up his guitar again and touched his fingers to the strings, listening to the tune from them - making sure it sounded perfect. Every so often Michyko thought of something she might say to make him feel more at ease, but she kept hesitating.

"I was so glad that you came to see me play, Andy," she offered, unable to remain quiet any longer. "It meant a lot to me."

Andy looked up from his guitar and regarded her blankly for a moment before smiling wistfully.

"I'm really sorry about the other day," he replied. "It wasn't fair on you or the others. I know I wasn't very supportive of you, especially."

"Don't beat yourself up about it," Michyko said cheerily. "It didn't cross my mind at all during my heat. I was just concerned for you that - you know - something really bad was happening."

"You played beautifully, Michyko. I thought you should have gone through - most definitely. You are more deserving of this than I am."

Michyko grinned reflectively.

"No, I wasn't nearly at my best the other day. I guess the nerves got to me. Being among so many talented people was just too much. But, I'm not at all disappointed."

Andy shook his head and laughed in spite of himself.

"You really are a rare person, Michyko," he observed wryly. "Nothing ever gets you down, does it?"

"Oh, I wouldn't say that" Michyko responded. "I guess I've learned not to be too disappointed by failure - not that I think there is any failure, really - so far as all this is concerned. The experience is more important to me. I mean, I'm just still blown away by the fact that I got to be here and that I was a part of all this. I won't soon forget it."

Andy shook his head and set his guitar down, finally.

"And I'm just thrilled to be here to watch you, Andy," Michyko ventured. "Everyone is talking about you. You have such a wonderful gift - I never knew how wonderful it was until I saw you here."

Andy felt his cheeks warm with embarrassment.

"You're a little too kind, I think," he said with a smile.

"Not at all," Michyko shot back with a measured enthusiasm. "You create such a beautiful sound, Andy. It's like you can reach into yourself - into your emotions - and pour all of them into your playing."

Michyko rested her hand on his arm and leaned forward.

"You must have such beautiful memories to be able to do something like that. Or beautiful dreams."

Andy blinked. "Memories? What do you mean?"

Michyko tilted her head slightly, thinking about her response.

"My grandfather used to say that it's our memories and our dreams that are the key to nurturing our creativity. They speak to us and inspire us. They are our truth. I think that your memories and dreams must be extremely beautiful - that's part of why you play so beautifully. Don't you think?"

Memories...

Andy gazed beyond Michyko. She had touched something off in his mind - something he had not considered before. And then it fell into place.

My memories…

He realized that he had related none of his memories to Sonya - that he hadn't revealed the intimacy of them to her in that exchange on the sand.

Since Denny had returned to this mortal world in Andy's body, there were all those moments with her - all those experiences and dreams that Denny had entrusted to him that only two people could know intimately. They were as vivid and as real to Andy now as his own memories.

Denny had come to him, had rescued him from an abyss. Were it not for Denny, Andy would most likely be dead. Or worse.

Denny lived on in him, now.

And in that moment, everything became clear.

"Anyhow, I think I'd better take my place out in the audience." Michyko stood and leaned down to plant a gentle kiss on Andy's cheek.

"No matter what, Andy. You've already won."

Andy smiled and watched her go, then looked down at his guitar.

He cleared his mind of everything: every thought, every emotion, every memory, and all that remained was the music he was about to play. He could hear the orchestra preparing itself on the stage, though it sounded distant in his ears. He could hear the audience nearby, gathering on the lawn of the Gardens under a brilliant starlit night. It was warm and still out, but not at all uncomfortable.

"Andrew. It's time."

He heard the attendant's voice and nodded an acknowledgement. He stood, quickly brushed himself down, and turned towards the makeshift stairs that led up onto the stage.

He was alone.

Stepping onto the stage, Andy observed a capacity crowd before him. Every spare inch of space was taken on the lawns in front of the stage. The natural amphitheater looked beautiful before him: a place of light and peace. The orchestra was seated in a half-circle behind him, each member dressed immaculately in black and white. Andy approached his seat beside the conductor, who greeted him with a respectful bow.

This was what it had come down to now: the end of a long journey that had taken him from near-death in that hospital on the other side of the world. From a destructive existence among the trash of Chicago street crime; from the realization that he was destined for ruin if he continued in that life. Andy had dragged himself back from the edge, had grabbed onto this single gift, his passion for the guitar. He had nurtured his skill and it had delivered him here.

The orchestra musicians lifted their instruments to play. The conductor tapped the lectern before him. And the Concierto began.

The string section softly came into being, heralding the gentle beginnings of the piece, and Andy gently raised the guitar in his arms, cradling it in an upward position. He rubbed his fingers together and touched them to the fret board.

Andy disappeared into Rodrigo's signature piece, "The Adagio" and from the very first movements of his fingers across the strings, he became one with it. He looked to the young woman soloist across from him as she lifted her oboe to her lips. She gently issued forth a tender refrain that accompanied his gentle rhythm beautifully, and together they took the orchestra into the unified steps of this profoundly emotional piece. Rodrigo's second movement was said to be a prayer for the recovery of his wife, who had fallen gravely ill following the death of their child. It was a piece of haunting depth and vulnerability of a life lost, but love sustained.

A life lost.

A love sustained.

As the strings gently rose from behind him and their harmonious tone floated across the Gardens, Andy eased into the first of his solo movements, closing his eyes and finding his mark perfectly, evoking a sense of deep emotion in the audience, who were clearly entranced.

Michyko managed to steal a glance around her and saw that, already, Andy's playing had inspired deep emotions in the audience. Some were moved to tears.

And somewhere in the audience, unknown to Andy, were Joss and Sonya. Dressed in a stunning blue evening gown, her hair swept up and held in place with a glittering clip that Joss had given her for the evening, Sonya watched him play. She was moved by the beauty of his performance, but her expression betrayed nothing of her feelings. She watched with tears filling her eyes, unable to look away from his exquisite playing, the echoes of which reminded her so much of Denny. Her emotions were torn - torn by him and the things he had said to her - the things she wished she had never heard.

The things she wanted to believe so much.

She had tried to leave the city, but she couldn't bring herself to. Joss had convinced her to remain out of respect for Jochen Zinski and for Denny's memory. Whatever had happened between Sonya and the American, Joss had reminded her of the duty that she had agreed to, for Denny. Sonya hadn't dared reveal what it was that had so upset her and, fortunately, Joss made up her mind that it must have been simply too soon for Sonya to entertain any form of relationship after Denny.

The piece moved into a complex flamenco solo. Andy lifted his head slightly, his eyes remained closed and he played the performance of his life. Beads of sweat broke out on his brow and were visible in the bright spotlights that played across him from behind the stage. He negotiated the complex solo, infusing his technique with a passion and a grace that he had never before achieved. His concentration was intense, his finger dance flawless. It was breathtaking to watch.

He poured everything he had into it, digging deep into the wellspring of his memories, both recent and long past, to find the emotional core with which he could give the performance more weight.

He gave to it the memories of childhood - his own and Denny's - when they had discovered the guitar and taken their first steps on an intimate journey of music that would define both their lives. He gave to it the memories of the cancer that had afflicted Denny, the fight for his life and the moment at which that life had been lost - before he had awoken in this new life in Andy's body. He gave to it the wretchedness of Andy's existence before he had woken on the gurney. He gave to it the shame of having very nearly thrown that life away in the pursuit of drugs. He gave to it the torment of how low he had sunk and the spark of determination that had been ignited in him - Denny's spark - and he'd determined that he must find his way back to the proud person Denny had been. He gave to it the courage he had found to turn his back on that life of destruction and rebuild himself. It was Denny who had inspired that journey, who was the means to his salvation - this proud spirit, this light that refused to be extinguished from the moment he had become a part of Andy.

He had found his way to live on.

The Andy who once had been was no longer. Andy embraced this incredible gift - the spirit - and became tormented no longer.

When the orchestra erupted back into life at the climax of the Concierto, the audience were on their feet for Andy, applauding wildly - emotionally, and appreciatively. They were bearing witness to something very special. Tears streamed down Andy's cheeks as he led the orchestra into the final stanza. He let go of the conflict within him and felt the pain of his burden dissipate until all that remained was the warmth of Denny's indestructible spirit infused with his own noble being. Together, Andy and the orchestra held the audience in their exquisite hand and took them triumphantly towards the soft finale of the Concierto - the dawning of a new day.

And then it was over.

Andy slowly rose to his feet, realizing he was shaking, and he bowed to the audience. He turned to the conductor, who nodded appreciatively at him, as well as several members of the orchestra who were applauding him, and the general applause continued - enthusiastic and appreciative - for several more minutes.

Andy heard it, but it remained distant in his ears. He was too moved by the reception. He closed his eyes and lifted his head up, and held it there for a moment. Then, slowly, he bowed and opened them again, looking out across the audience. His eyes came to rest briefly on a flash of blue that stood out, far back in the audience. It was a woman wearing blue, but she turned away before he could focus directly upon her.

Was it her?

The moment passed, and the figure disappeared.

Andy walked slowly from the stage and down the stairs through the throngs of people eager to congratulate him. Overwhelmed by their praise, he acknowledged them respectfully but absently as he found his way to the performers' tent and slumped down in a chair.

He was utterly spent.

Chapter 23

Sonya stepped down on the sand and unclipped the lead from Simon's collar, letting him trot away onto the beach and sniff about as he always did on their morning walks. Kicking off her shoes, Sonya took in a deep breath of the fresh salty air and shielded her eyes as the dawning sun appeared over the horizon, beginning its slow ascent above the calm ocean. She gazed longingly toward the sun, studying the soft rays it cast across the water and the sky, tingeing everything with soft yellow hues. She felt the warmth of it on her face and drew comfort from it, closing her eyes and allowing it to soothe her. It was like an old friend she looked forward to catching up with each day. It brought her a friendship that was unconditional, a peace that was comforting.

She was relieved to be home in Hambledown, but she also felt sadness. The week in Melbourne had been too much for her - too much, too soon. And she was left with the memories of him, the American, whom she could not shake from her consciousness. His performance, which had captured the imagination of everyone present, left no one in any doubt and he had won the concert series. Without revealing anything of the circumstances on the Williamstown beach to Jochen Zinski, Sonya had engineered her presence at the ceremony such that she didn't have to present him with the award. She couldn't bear the thought of having to face him again.

Not because she didn't want to. But because she was afraid that she did.

She hadn't seen him at all in the aftermath of the concert. Andy DeVries was the toast of Melbourne now. Everyone down there was talking about this come-from-behind virtuoso who had stunned the Festival with his exquisitely beautiful performance.

Sonya did everything she could to push him from her mind.

It was quiet on the beach this morning, as it usually was. There seemed to be a greater stillness around her, however, almost as if the world was empty. The only sounds punctuating the serenity were the gentle noise of the ocean and Simon, who was yelping noisily nearby, splashing enthusiastically in the shallows, chasing a pair of sea birds that floated overhead, teasing him with their ability to be there while he remained stubbornly earthbound. They squawked at him, which served only to rev him up even more. Sonya drifted on the peaceful warmth of the sun, then opened her eyes slowly to scan for Simon, making sure he was close enough so as not to be causing trouble.

She then made her way along the beach, passing by two old local men sitting on their stools. Mugs of thermos coffee in hand, they watched over a pair of fishing rods cast out into the ocean, held in their custom-made stands on the sand, awaiting the promise of a catch. Sonya greeted them as she always did, planting a quick kiss on the old gent closest to her as she passed by. He squeezed her hand gratefully. He had recently lost his wife, and Sonya had handled their affairs with dignity and discretion - as she had always done. There was something about being around for these people. There was a quiet gratitude for everything she did for them, the kind of gratitude that you just wouldn't get elsewhere - in the city, for example. Sonya knew her place was here. There was nowhere else that she could feel she could belong.

The local boys with their surfboards sat out just beyond the sand bar, lolling on the swell, eagerly awaiting a pick up in the breeze in the hope they might catch a wave or two before breakfast and the drudgery of school. They waved to Sonya from many yards out, knowing it was she from the presence of the black-and-white dog that galloped about just ahead of her. She smiled and waved back, squinting against the growing power of the morning sun. They were good kids - never the sort to get into any real trouble, aside from being on the wrong side of their frustrated mothers, who would sooner have them dressed and ready for the school day now than welded to their surfboards. It was a never-ending soap opera she'd heard so much about from the local women in the street. And it was something Sonya had once imagined for herself.

The Tai Chi group had begun their morning exercises on the grass just above the beach. They were mainly older people, retirees who'd embraced their newfound freedom with relish and adopted the ancient martial art as a means of enjoyment in the early hours. The group smiled and waved at Sonya as she passed by, and she smiled warmly back. They limbered up while the instructor chatted with one or two of the newer participants. She noted an elderly couple among them, the Braithwaites, longtime residents of the Hambledown District who had been here longer than anyone could remember.

They had to be in their nineties now, Sonya mused.

But as she passed by she watched dear old Mr. Braithwaite, resplendent in his Tai Chi garb, help Mrs. Braithwaite with a stretch that for anyone younger would not be so demanding. For them, it was a challenge requiring significantly more attention. Satisfied that they had warmed up enough, the elderly couple embraced lovingly and then took their place in the group. Sonya's heart swelled watching them together, and an overwhelming sadness settled over her as she moved on - a sense of emptiness so powerful it threatened to consume her.

As Sonya pushed the dark emotions down deep inside her where she hoped they wouldn't rise again, she realized Simon was no longer beside her. She looked around worriedly, concerned that he had wandered off, but she found him just a few yards back, sitting on the sand, completely still.

"What's wrong with you, sweetie?" she asked.

Simon was looking forward, down along the beach to where a lone figure stood on the sand. The person was just too far away for her to see who it was. Every one of Simon's senses seemed attuned to that figure. His ears were directed forward, twitching ever so slightly, his moist nose - testing the air with equally subtle twitches, gathering the scent of whoever it was there. His head was bowed slightly in a ready position, his entire body rigid, as though ready to pounce.

Sonya studied him with concern. She placed a hand on his back, just below his neck, and slid it down gently over his coat. She realized he was quivering.

"Simon," she exclaimed. "What's the matter? You're behaving very strangely."

Simon looked up at her and whimpered, giving her a lick on the cheek before yelping at the stranger up ahead. Sonya looked up the beach to the figure on the sand. She squinted, trying to focus on it.

Suddenly, Simon launched to his feet and tore off down the beach. Sonya was almost thrown over.

"Simon!" she shouted with alarm. "Stop!"

But Simon was oblivious to everything but the figure. His sleek body seemed to blur with such a burst of speed that all Sonya could do was run after him. She raced as fast as her legs would take her, cursing herself for having got up so early and still being so tired.

And then, as Sonya drew closer to the figure Simon had scoped out from 100 yards away, she looked up and gasped, skidding to a stop in the sand. She blinked in shock.

As Simon covered the last few feet between them, Andy dropped to his haunches, smiled and steeled himself as Simon leapt into his arms, yelping excitedly and licking his face furiously. They both fell back on the sand, the dog refusing to let up, licking and nipping playfully at Andy's face as though he were being reunited with a master he hadn't seen for a very long time.

Andy eventually got back to his feet and knelt beside Simon, patting him down, scratching behind his ears lovingly, and examining him as though he hadn't seen the dog for a very long time. Andy couldn't believe how Simon had grown. The dog had been just a pup the last time he remembered him, awkward and ungainly. Now he was a proud, well cared-for adult.

Sonya dropped her shoes to the sand and she stood unable to speak, unable to think. She was utterly stunned, not only that Simon had responded to a man in that way, but that the man - Andy - was here.

Andy's smile faded as he realized that she was so close by. He rose to his feet and looked at her.

He did not speak.

Simon continued to jump playfully until Andy held out his hand, palm down, and signaled for him to sit. Simon obeyed and sat beside him, looking towards Sonya with his tongue hanging to one side, panting, his tail wagging happily.

Andy cleared his throat, considering his words one final time, the only words he had thought about at the expense of anything else on his way here. Nothing else mattered anymore.

"I remember ... getting up ... at 4:30 every morning ... before dawn," he began tentatively. "Putting on that old Melbourne Uni track suit with the tear in the sleeve and giving Simon two of those biscuit bones that Lionel got in especially for him - the beef ones, not the plain ones. He never did seem to like the plain ones."

Andy paused as he looked down at Simon, who was licking the ends of his fingers. Andy tapped the end of his nose gently, signaling him to stop.

"I remember ... leaving the house with Simon on the lead, running down here and along the beach as far south as the old jetty ruins, circling back towards the fishing port up by the Braithwaites' house and then doing two, maybe three laps of the football oval. I remember passing by the Uniting Church on the hill, then stopping by the General Store for a coffee. Simon would always get three slices of Strasburg that Lionel would cut off especially for him and have ready for when we got there."

Sonya remained silent. She watched Andy as he looked out across the ocean towards the sun, which had now cleared the horizon and continued up into the morning sky.

"Remember that day it poured here? A storm as powerful and as fierce as anyone could remember. We were forced inside from working on the balcony."

Sonya felt her breath catch in her throat as Andy looked back at her.

"Remember when I painted your toenails for the first time? How you teased me *mercilessly*, because I hadn't done it before and my hand was shaking like a leaf? You gave me such a hard time - I tickled you as payback. Remember that? Would anyone else know that?"

Andy stepped forward a little, letting the rising ocean tide lap at the bottoms of his jeans.

"Remember when I was having the chemotherapy? How you'd come with me to the clinic every week - every single week - and sit with me? You'd load up a whole heap of episodes of that podcast I liked so much - Keith and the Girl - and we'd share them while I had the treatment. Remember those dirty jokes I used to swap with the nurses? The ones you used to cringe at, but the nurses loved? Those fruit muffins you'd bake? They were so large I often wondered how you used to fit them in the basket. You'd take them into the clinic for the nurses, and we would never come home without that basket completely empty."

Sonya's eyes were already filling with tears and she was trying desperately to hold them back. Her emotions spun out of control as she listened to his words, and she felt powerless to stop them.

Andy turned towards her now and took a few cautious steps towards her, wary of not scaring her again. This time, Sonya didn't flinch or retreat.

"Remember what I said to you - in the hospice - at the end when I was close to death and all that kept me from the incredible pain was the morphine and the sleeping drugs? Remember the *last thing* I said?"

Together they uttered the sentence in unison:

"This is not over."

Through the maelstrom of her emotions, the tears that blurred her vision, Sonya gazed at Andy. She gazed into his deep green eyes, worlds within a world and in that moment...

...She knew.

They were the dreams - her dreams - the indestructible dreams that had visited her in her sleep in the days and weeks and months after Denny had gone, and they had comforted her. They were the dreams that had protected her from shattering into a million pieces, the dreams that protected her from her grief. This man standing here now recalled her memories as though they were his own. There was no possible way he could have known them without having actually lived them himself.

She hadn't noticed before now, but Andy held something in his hands that caught the breeze. As he held it out to her, Sonya looked at it. It was a posy of sorts, but not of flowers.

It was sprigs of rosemary, tied together with mint leaves.

"I came across the world to find you, Sonya," Andy said softly, his voice cracking with emotion as he handed her the memento of their past life together. As he did so, she saw the tattoo on the inside of his right forearm, those two languid words, crafted in a flowing script that had meant so much to Denny. *Ancora Imparo* - "still I am learning".

"I can't explain what happened to me, but - I didn't die then. My body did - but not my mind, my soul. All I know is - it's not my time yet."

Sonya succumbed to her tears and to the knowledge her rational mind refused to believe possible.

She embraced Andy.

She drew him close, holding him in her arms, resting her head into that familiar corner of his neck. She closed her eyes and drifted, knowing that this man spoke the truth. Andy, hesitantly at first, enfolded her in his arms. He closed his eyes.

He knew.

Sonya drew back and looked into Andy's eyes. They were the eyes that she had known for most of her life, ever since she and Denny had met as children. They were the same eyes that she had been captivated by when they had reconnected as young adults, the same eyes she had fallen in love with when she had fallen in love with Denny.

They knew.

Andy kissed Sonya tenderly, longingly as Simon jumped up, pawing at their legs, splashing them both with the cool sea water. The breeze picked up and tugged at the ocean from the north, whipping up the sea just a little - much to the delight of the surfers out on the swell.

Andy drew back from Sonya and took in her wondrous smile with his soulful green eyes.

Denny had come home.

Epilogue

A pair of gloved hands worked to pull a broken tile out from its position on the roof of the old beach house. They struggled with it momentarily, their owner grunting and groaning until the tile broke into two smaller pieces and came away easily.

Andy struggled to maintain his balance on the roof, until he put one hand back and steadied himself. He cursed, then calmed himself, forcing air out from between his teeth. Tossing the tile to one side, Andy scooted across the roof to a neat stack of replacement tiles and retrieved one. He paused for a moment, removed his cap and took in the view of the ocean before him. He smiled, feeling the warmth of the sun against his face and the cooling sea breeze against his skin.

Below him, on the ground beside the beach house, Sonya pushed a wheel barrow filled with a variety of seedlings into view and pulled it up next to a freshly prepared flower bed that lined the driveway. Setting them down in her desired positions on the bed, Sonya stepped back and appraised how the seedlings looked there, then turned around, hearing the tapping of a mallet up on the roof. Lifting the brim of her sun hat, she smiled up at Andy. He returned her smile with his own, seeing love in her eyes.

Simon barked nearby and Andy shifted on the roof to spy the dog running and jumping in the long grass down by the sand, chasing a throng of butterflies that floated above him, tantalizingly close but frustratingly just out of his reach.

The sound of a car horn issued from behind them and Andy and Sonya turned to see a burgundy hatchback pull into the driveway from the road and stop just before the house. Its doors opened, and Lionel and Ruth stepped out. Lionel waved as Ruth lifted a picnic basket from the car.

Sonya returned Lionel's wave just as the telephone rang from inside the beach house. Casting off her gardening gloves, Sonya shoved them down inside the front pocket of her apron and skipped up the steps to the porch, into the house. In the hallway, she stepped past a pair of guitars resting on their stands beside the telephone table: a pristine Simon Marty concert guitar and the Vincente Carillo guitar with the single hole in its body. Standing against the wall ahead of her, waiting to be hung, was a framed poster of Andy - the art from his debut album. Picking up the handset, Sonya smiled warmly at the voice on the other end.

Andy looked down from his vantage point on the roof as Sonya came into view. She was holding the phone out towards him.

"It's your father, Dev."

Andy set the mallet in his hand down on the roof next to the newly positioned tile and wiped his brow with his forearm.

He glanced down at her.

"Which one?" he asked wryly.

Sonya laughed softly and they shared a knowing smile.

ABOUT THE AUTHOR

Dean Mayes has been writing and dreaming for most of his adult life - in between practicing as a Pediatric ICU Nurse and raising his two children, Xavier & Lucy. Dean lives in Adelaide, Australia with his partner Emily, his children and his cross-breed cattle dog Simon.

The Hambledown Dream is his first novel.